The warriors did not ride through camp but swerved suddenly to the right and rode an entire circle around the camp, one hundred and thirty-five strong. The Crow warriors were there not for their eyes alone but for their strong arms and their battle wisdom. For a minute the officers could not react to the performance of their allies, so awestruck were they, but at last an order was shouted. The walk soldiers began to fire volley after precision volley into the air, a respectful salute to the power of the long-beaked bird. It was a moment of communication between two peoples who shared the culture of the war-soldier, and respected each other for what they shared. Each fed off the power of the other, and felt the war-spirit rise from deep in their breasts.

WARRIORS' HONOR

Michael Kosser

St. Martin's Paperbacks

WARRIORS' HONOR

ISBN: 0-312-96884-1

Printed in the United States of America

St. Martin's Paperbacks edition / February 1999

10 9 8 7 6 5 4 3 2 1

For Mom, Dad and BJ

Chapter I

Private Wayne Blount Braddock should have been a lucky man. All morning long he had sat around doing nothing because his brigade was being held in reserve. Three miles ahead Confederate units were being fed into a miserable killing machine. He knew killing when he heard it.

The Union soldiers defending the sunken road thought they had reservations for the hottest place in Hell, but it was the Confederates who called the place "Hornets' Nest" because of the swarms of buzzing bullets that cut them down as they ran across the long field in front of the road. Up ahead Braddock could hear the continuous rattle of fire, like the tearing of a bedsheet, punctuated by the crack of light artillery, pouring death into the Arkansas boys who surged forward again and again until there were not enough left for another charge.

Braddock was not an Arkansan. He was a Tennessean, born and raised on a farm barely fifty miles northwest of this battlefield. He had joined a local company of infantry at the beginning of the war but he despised his company commander and didn't care that much for his messmates. But he was a fighter, so when he decided to desert he simply headed west across the Mississippi and joined up with an Arkansas contingent full of good-natured hill folk. There was not a one of them in the entire outfit whose family owned a slave, and he was sensible enough not to reveal that his father owned three of them, and was therefore by Ozark standards a tolerably rich man. Nor did he tell them his house had glass panes. He just told them he was a Tennessee farmboy who couldn't get along with his captain so he'd run across the river to find some folks he could stand to be with.

That was good enough for them, although some did study him enough to make him uncomfortable. He knew what they were looking at. His hair was black and straight, his eyes dark as pitch, burning smokily in their sockets, his skin a deep tan, his trimmed beard as black as his head hair.

They didn't study him all that long. Indian blood was not uncommon in Tennessee or Arkansas. This boy's blanket days just seemed a little closer than their own.

They were wrong about that. He had Creek blood in him all right, from a great-grandfather who abided in Alabama and brought a quiet young dark lady back to Jackson with him when Tennessee was still so new and wild that any woman was welcome anywhere. But one-eighth Creek did not make a redskin, especially with a beard like Braddock had. Everybody knew an Indian couldn't grow a beard.

"Come on, boys, up on your feet." The command came from Captain Isaac Sharpston, storekeeper turned leader of men, short, stocky, gray-bearded, and surprisingly reliable. "Our turn to win the war, if you're ready to do the job, boys," he said with his usual dry sarcasm.

They fell in and marched off in columns—toward the guns, Braddock noticed. The Arkansans had seen some skirmish action over the last few months. It was obvious that this battle was different. It had started only twelve hours before, but they had passed any number of bodies, mostly gray-clad, sprawled bloodily in ghastly poses of death, as they marched in from the west.

They marched to the drums, toward the guns, which got louder with every step. Now they could feel branches of nearby trees begin to fall on them, cut by high stray bullets. Ahead was the edge of the woods, and a field, and the enemy. Braddock maintained his place in the formation, but he could feel his throat constrict, then go dry as he heard the command.

"At the double-quick!"

At the double-quick meant only one thing: some fool had decided that Confederate soldiers were not dying quickly enough. He could feel his heart beating a mighty tattoo through his shirt, through his jacket. He didn't want to stay. He wanted to run. But he stayed, and was rewarded by a welcome command to halt.

Ahead of them, to the left and right, sat several Confederate artillery batteries, guns hub to hub for maximum concentration. The foot soldiers stood at ease, waiting for the cannonade with growing hope.

There must have been a command to fire, though Braddock did not hear it. Suddenly the guns let loose and shells began to explode up and down the road across the open field. Gray columns of smoke bloomed like so many puffy plants all along the sunken road, until the road and the men defending it had disappeared. In a very few minutes all the small arms fire from across the field was silenced. Braddock could see only still Confederate bodies stretched out in death, but he could imagine that across the field, Union soldiers were flattened out or curled up in their little holes, their guts twisted, their breath coming in quick gasps, praying for the shelling to stop, praying that the next shell would not be the one that would blow them apart.

Minute after minute the shelling continued. He felt a poke in his right side and faced a smiling Ross Dotson. "Time them big guns are done," he said, "won't be nothin' left for us."

Braddock snickered grimly but as the shells continued to fall and still no fire emerged from the other side, he began to wonder whether the Federals had fled. He knew where the enemy was supposed to be, but their position was so obscured by the smoke of exploded artillery shells that he could not see the other end of the field. As far as he was concerned, the shelling could go on forever, but he knew that his moment was nearly at hand.

Orders were being shouted—companies called to attention, stretched into lines, ordered forward to the tree lines, then commanded to charge across the field.

The rest of the men were screaming their battle cries,

their Rebel yells. Braddock had his own, an unmilitary, unBaptist "Damn! Damn! Damn!" as his feet pounded across the beat-down grass.

The artillery had ceased firing but now Union soldiers were appearing at the other end of the field.

Where in hell did they come from? Braddock muttered to himself. Why weren't they dead? They should all be dead, damn them! The Yankees were firing and Rebels began to falter and fall. Braddock wanted to throw up; he wanted to flee from the field, but he did neither. He just ran on, in a deep crouch, sometimes toward a depression that might hide him from the murderous Yankee gunfire, sometimes a few yards directly behind one of his cohorts.

For about half a minute those around Braddock ran forward in a bunch without one of them being hit, and Braddock's confidence began to revive. Maybe the artillery had done its job after all. Maybe there were not many Federal troops left to return fire. Maybe . . . maybe . . .

Braddock saw the man in front of him lift his hands to clutch at a head that was almost half gone. Brains and blood rained down on the Tennessean in a fine red spray and gray chunks. The soldier fell right in front of him, and he had to jump over the new corpse to continue the attack. His breath was coming in agonized gasps. His side cramped up. Fear clutched at his throat. He saw his captain in front of him, now waving his sword, now falling backwards, arms spread wide.

A Lieutenant Crawford took over, a man Braddock liked, although by this time he was so terrified he was not even conscious of the change in command. Crawford was cautious. Still more than a hundred yards from the enemy, Crawford feared the enemy's fire enough to point his sword toward the left flank of the Union position. Like their new leader, his men saw no gunfire on that flank and they were desperate to go there.

The Yankee left flank included a peach orchard. Seeing the opening, the Confederates ran hard, but while still 75 yards away they saw, to their horror, a gun crew swing around a single five-pounder, load it, point it quickly at the charging Arkansans and fire.

Braddock felt a fist smack into his chest, lift him into the air and deposit him on the ground. Slowly, gracefully, he settled back into a prone position, waiting for clear vision and the onset of pain. He never felt the pain he expected.

The wind came down from the mountains and blew its breath on the long grass. The grass sighed and shivered, then stood tall as the wind died.

Young Buffalo pressed his knees against the flanks of his pony and raised himself high enough to see the tops of the tepees just over the hill. He listened for voices but heard none. There was no moon tonight; good night for stealing horses. He lowered himself into his saddle and waited, still and silent. His pony waited beneath him, without a nicker. Its tail twitched. That was all.

The young Absarokee warrior felt, rather than heard, the sound off to his right, but still he did not move. He had been waiting for the sound.

Big Chin.

And Would Not Listen.

And Blue Shirt.

Once they were all together they did not urge their ponies into a gallop, but walked them quietly away from the village. Their hearts sang like the waters of Rock Creek tumbling down from the mountains. Somehow all four young men had sneaked away from the village without the War-clubs discovering them and driving them back into their lodges.

The War-clubs knew the Sioux were not far, and they knew how a nearby Sioux village tempted their young warriors to do foolish things.

"We were once young too," Chief Running Wolf had told the young men the night before. "But we must be cautious until we are ready to strike, for the Sioux are many more than the people of the long-beaked bird."

The young men did not snicker. They respected the great chiefs and warriors who came before them. Many people worshipped the myths of long-ago heroes, men of super-human size and strength. If only they were among us today, we would be great as we were then. That was the way some people thought.

But the young men of this Absarokee village did not believe in long-ago myths. For them, *these* were the good old days. The chiefs and warriors who gave them their daily lessons in riding, shooting, and surviving were their heroes of all time. Nightly they heard stories of legendary triumphs at arms, triumphs that had to be if the Crows were to survive among their more numerous enemies, the Sioux, Cheyenne, Arapaho, and Blackfeet.

And what was the great sin of the Crows that earned them the wrath of their enemies? Only that they lived on the finest, most beautiful land on earth, a land rich in game and wild food. A land not cold and wasted like the Canadas to the north, a land not too rocky and dry like the land of the Apaches to the south, a land that was just right, always teeming with buffalo, deer, elk, and antelope, a happy place for any redman with a swift pony, a good bow, and a quiver full of iron-tipped arrows.

And so their enemies wanted that land. The Sioux especially wanted that land, not to share with the Crows, but for themselves. Perhaps, after all, the Sioux were not so different from the white men who were forever pushing them westward, closer to their short-numbered but hard-fighting foes, closer to the Crows.

Dreadful rumors swirled through the night into the councils of the Crow wise men, rumors of war, not just the hit-and-run sport that gladdened the hearts of all true men, but war to the death.

"We are coming for you," the night cried out to them. "You may ready your medicine for battle and sharpen your hatchets all you wish but we will swallow you in a giant dust cloud, and when the dust is gone, your men will all be dead, your women will live for our pleasure, and your children will be our slaves." That is what the night wind told them in the sighing of the long waving grass.

The brave warriors of the Absarokee did not quake with fear. They knew how a strong heart and a strong mind could triumph over many strong arms. They had done so before.

"We watch you carefully," said Hawk Appearing, the

legendary slayer of the people of the striped feathers, to the young, restless Crow warriors. "We see you leaning eastward. We know you long to strike our enemies, to capture a few horses and a few scalps. We love you for your courage. We need you for your courage. But you must not do this. A few horses and a few scalps cannot help us now. We must wait for the day when we can strike them so hard that they will learn to flee to the other side of the mountain at the approach of a single Absarokee warrior. That is how hard we must strike them!"

The young men listened, but they could not wait. And yet Young Buffalo smiled his smile and nodded. "I hear you, big brother," he said, and his smile brought many wrinkles up the sides of his face; unusual for such a young man, but pleasant to see, and sincere.

"It is good that you hear us," said Hawk Appearing, who was Young Buffalo's uncle and had given him his first warrior lessons. These lessons were not with the horse, or with the gun, or even with the bow. They were lessons in the art of running swiftly, of running far, of defying fatigue and defeat to triumph in a race. Other plains tribes may have scorned the man afoot for the glory and glamor of a swift pony, but the Crows knew that the strong legs and deep chest of the great runner made his thighs firm on the back of a racing pony, his arm steady as he pulled a bowstring in the midst of a buffalo hunt, his hands certain as his eye found the sights of a rifle in the midst of the battle. Running, long and swift running, was the beginning of the body and character of the great warrior.

Under the tutelage of Hawk Appearing, Young Buffalo had emerged first as a great runner, then as a fine rider, and finally as a promising handler of weapons, though he had not yet known the test of battle. On this night, in defiance of the wise men, he and his friends were determined to meet that test.

This was not pure rebellion. They knew the older men were right, but they were bred for battle as surely as a racehorse is bred to race. It was as if their flared nostrils had caught the smoke of the Sioux village forty miles to the east. They must go. They must steal horses, they must count coup, they must take scalps. They must triumph.

Should they lose their life in the attempt, that would not be so bad. Glory was glory, in death as in life.

Slowly, quietly, under a dark moon and bright stars, they rode north, away from the village, imagining that at any moment they might hear the hoofbeats of their elders. But the hoofbeats never came, and once they had crossed Antelope Creek, they turned eastward, just as their elders had feared, and headed for the Sioux village that lay but two days' distance from their own.

Each one took only his favorite pony and no spares; testimony to their belief that they would return with many Sioux ponies for themselves. Young Buffalo had dreamed three nights before that if they raided the Sioux they would be successful.

Five hours from the Sioux village they found a grove of cedars near a creek. There they ate and slept until dawn, then they arose, bathed in the frigid waters of the creek, and continued eastward. They were not much more than children—each had seen sixteen summers—but they wished to have the honors and freedom of an Absarokee man, and they were willing to risk all to earn those privileges. On they rode, singing the battle songs of their tribe, unafraid, immortal, straining to break the bonds of childhood.

Toward evening a lone elk appeared on the horizon. The four young men dashed after it, their ponies spread across the landscape in an attempt to flank and then maybe surround it. They chased it into a draw, then into a tangled thicket. As they closed in on the creature Blue Shirt drew a rusty old musket and checked the priming in its pan.

"No!" warned Young Buffalo. It was one thing to dash across the high plains like the heedless fools they were; it was another to announce their presence to any enemies that happened to be within two miles of them. Young Buffalo strung his bow, nocked an arrow, rose high on his pony, pulled back on his bow string with a steady hand and let fly with a shaft that pierced the elk just over its right front leg. The elk darted from the thicket, then its leg collapsed and down it went, into the dust. Young Buffalo was on it in an instant, knife flashing in search of a fresh kidney. Two quick incisions, one sure grasp with the left hand, a last cut with the knife, and Young Buffalo was holding the steaming, bloody kidney aloft.

They said a quick prayer of thanks to the elk for giving them its life. Would Not Listen was pointing toward a clearing among the pine forests on a hill. They made camp there, kindled a small fire, roasted a chunk of elk meat on the coals till it was charred black on the outside, then divided it among themselves and dined.

In the light of the small, flickering fire, Young Buffalo studied his three cohorts, each so different from the other, yet all of them sharing the unquenchable sense of belonging to the Crow warrior tradition. Tomorrow they would meet the Sioux. Tomorrow they would defeat the Sioux one way or another. Their fathers and uncles had drilled into them the notion that the Sioux were the mightiest of all men, except for the Absarokee, who could take the Sioux at any time, any place.

Blue Shirt, still gnawing on the charred meat, tall and lean and indomitable, was named not for any clothing he wore, but after an esteemed uncle. His uncle had been given an army shirt long ago on a scouting mission for the white men's army and had worn that shirt for many years thereafter, until it fell off his back.

Big Chin, named for the large, forward-thrusting lower jaw that gave him a look of stubbornness but who was actually the best natured of all of them, was tall and lean like Blue Shirt, but bigger boned, and already as strong as most of the older men.

And finally Would Not Listen, who laughed the quickest but who was also quick to sulk over slights real or imagined, was stout and short, but strong and tough, a relentless competitor in children's games, and a friend Young Buffalo would trust in the heat of battle. There were other young men in the village who would have loved to come, but these four wanted only each other for their first foray against the enemy.

It would have been a foolhardy quest for the inexperienced quartet, except they had Young Buffalo. Young Buffalo was special. Not quite as strong as the others, what he had was an impenetrable coolness under all trying circumstances. Boys came to him for advice. Girls came to him to defend them from the teasing of his friends. He was never too busy to help, not because he was a politician in search of future power, but because it never would have occurred to him not to help.

Medium height. Medium build. A little darker than average, with his hair long and unbraided and black as a moonless night. Calm eyes that sometimes twinkled but seldom flared up in anger. He explained to them what was to be done the following day. When he said that combat was to be avoided at all costs, they did not question him. They trusted him too much to ever question him.

Chapter 2

He had dreamed his plan of action three days before. There had been no vision quest, just a dream that came from nowhere, and the surprise of its appearance only made it seem more real.

Young Buffalo *knew* where the Sioux were. And he knew how to strike them. He did not spend time and energy creating a need to strike them. The old ones may have talked of the Lakota threat to the Absarokee way of life, but to Young Buffalo and his friends, the Sioux were the Sioux. They were the enemy. They were always the enemy. It was good to have an enemy. The enemy was a young warrior's road to glory.

Young Buffalo loved the Sioux. They were men. And they were the measure of men. To steal ponies from the Sioux, to steal the scalp from the head of a Sioux—ho! a man could be proud. A real man had good friends. And a real man had good enemies. It was so, always.

Early on the third day out, just as the dream had told him, they found the Sioux. They descended a hill, out of a pine forest, and saw the recent remains of a buffalo hunt, two dozen sets of buffalo bones and cartilage lying in the sun, flies still buzzing around what little flesh remained after the Sioux and the buzzards were through with them.

Following the travois tracks was simple. They had barely

topped the next hill before they smelled faint traces of smoke that grew stronger in their sensitive nostrils as they rode slowly across the yellowed summer grass.

Suddenly Young Buffalo raised his hand and climbed down from his pony. He handed the reins over to Blue Shirt and told his friends to wait, then he ran forward, up a long swell, and down the other side. Here was a distant view to the southwest, where faint wisps of smoke could be seen. He walked back toward his friends until he was close enough to sign to them that he wanted them to wait while he scouted out the village alone. His friends were fine fellows and great hunters but he trusted his own stealth more than he trusted theirs. If they all moved forward and any one of them were discovered then the other three were doomed. Better that he go alone.

He spotted a line of cottonwood trees that told him the Sioux were camped on a creek. Wet or dry, there would be a hollow there that might conceal him within close sight of the village. He crawled to the tree line and down the bank. The creek was a trickle, which at least meant that he could probably creep close to the village without finding a gaggle of gossiping women doing laundry, or children splashing and dunking each other.

He lay pressed against the bank and listened. There were faint sounds coming from the village, but none along the creek bed, which was still muddy. In the best tradition of the Crow wolves, or scouts, he covered himself with mud and let it dry, so he might blend in with the background as he made his reconnaissance.

He lifted his head just above the bank and the long grass. There was the village—two circles of tepees, perhaps twenty lodges in all . . . Beyond the lodges, the village's pony herd was cropping grass on the side of a hill. Many of the lodges had at least one pony tied beside it, mostly good ponies, which meant, he thought, that the warriors of the village were not out hunting on this day. The ponies tied by the tepees were the favorites of warriors who chose to keep their animals close by out of fear that they might be stolen.

Stealing ponies this night would not be easy, but, he

thought, if they waited until the entire village was asleep, they might have some success. He continued to watch the village while the sun moved a full thumb's width through the sky. It was a hot day, so the tepees all had their sides rolled up. The women were working, the men were loafing and the children were playing a wide variety of games from rolling the hoop to buffalo scout. Around the village were numerous scaffolds from which hung large thin sheets of buffalo meat, drying in the sun from yesterday's hunt.

Young Buffalo froze. In the middle of the village a single pair of eyes stared from beneath the brow of a tall, muscular young warrior. The young Crow was certain he was being watched, but he didn't dare move. Perhaps the Sioux warrior had doubts as to what he was observing through the yellow grass. If Young Buffalo moved, there would be no more doubt. Calling on his deep reserves of discipline, he kept his head still and his heart relaxed, and soon the warrior turned his head away and ducked into his tepee.

Young Buffalo lowered his head and walked along the stream bed, back to where his cohorts waited for him to return with the information they needed for their evening raid. As he walked, a plan of attack began to take shape in his brain. He had never before raided an enemy village, and yet he and his friends had made so many play raids on their own village throughout their childhood that he believed he knew what to do, and how it would feel when the raid took place. He had no doubt that The Creator would smile on their endeavor this night.

At midnight a strong wind sent clouds scudding swiftly across the face of the sky. The quarter moon hid, then appeared, then disappeared again.

"Behind those clouds will follow one great cloud," Young Buffalo told his men, confidently, and they did not doubt him. How he knew he could not say, but he knew.

The four young Crows approached along the stream bed. When they climbed the bank and stared out at the village they were pleased to see the entire village asleep, except for the prized ponies that stood silently beside their masters' tepees.

"The best ponies are there," Young Buffalo whispered, waving his arms around the village, "but the herd is there," and he pointed to the hillside on the opposite side of the village.

"Why not take them all?" asked Big Chin, and Young Buffalo was not surprised to hear his friend's bold statement.

"At least one of those ponies is tied to the wrist of the one who rides him," Young Buffalo replied. "I saw the rope." He said no more, but began to circle around the Sioux village toward the hill that held the herd.

All four of the Crow warriors carried ropes which would serve as bridles when they reached the herd. Slowly, quietly, they circled wide around the village, too wide for the dogs to sense them. Just as Young Buffalo had predicted, cloud cover had completely blacked out the moon.

The cicadas buzzed. An owl hooted. Otherwise all was quiet except for the wind hissing through the grass. The young men were careful, watchful for night herders, but no one appeared to be guarding the pony herd. These Sioux were very confident of their power; surprising since the village was not a large one. Perhaps there were other villages not far away. Or perhaps their contempt for their Absarokee cousins had grown so great that they could no longer imagine the people of the long-beaked bird daring to annoy them in any way.

They had almost completed their long half-circle around the sleeping village. Ahead they could see the dark shapes of the pony herd. A single nicker only served to punctuate the stillness of the night. If there were any young men or boys guarding the herd, they were asleep in the tall grass.

Each of the Crows chose a pony and began whispering gentle words to it as they attached their bridles. Each then mounted his animal. Blue Shirt and Would Not Listen cut about a dozen ponies away from the main herd, and drove them up and over the slope. Meanwhile, Young Buffalo and Big Chin split the night with loud whoops and began to drive the herd toward the village. Several of the creatures panicked and the rest followed at a full gallop. There were more than a hundred ponies in the herd, and when they hit the village there was pure pandemonium. In a flurry of hooves and swirling dust the animals knocked over the scaffolds of dried buffalo meat and ran down tepees as they charged through the village. People were scrambling out of the way, and those who had ponies tethered to their smoke-flap poles were mounting them and riding into the teeth of the herd, trying to drive them away from the village.

Big Chin and Young Buffalo had left the herd by this time and were riding toward the slope beyond the village. Over the crest they rode, straight ahead, for about a mile, then they stopped and listened in the black night. Behind them was the noise of village uproar. They galloped onward for another mile, then stopped again. Off to their right were the faint sounds of driven horses. They kicked at their ponies' flanks and rode at a relaxed pace until they overtook their friends.

"Swing well wide of the village, behind those hills," Young Buffalo said, pointing at a dark mass barely visible in front of them. "I will retrieve our ponies and join you at the big creek by the fording place."

"It is too dangerous," Blue Shirt replied. "Too close to the village."

"I would not leave my best war pony," said Young Buffalo. "My only war pony," he added ironically. "Besides, I think they will be chasing *you*." Young Buffalo smiled. "But I will take Big Chin with me and and the two of us should be strong enough to deal with any Lakota we meet up with."

Blue Shirt nodded. "We will meet you at the fording place."

While Blue Shirt and Would Not Listen drove the stolen ponies westward to the fording place, Big Chin and Young Buffalo rode wide around the village toward the creek bed where they had left their ponies. They approached the creek bed warily, and as quietly as the Sioux ponies they were riding would allow. Big Chin's keen eyesight spotted the ponies in the gloom while he was still a hundred yards away, but it was Young Buffalo's uncanny instincts that sensed something was not right.

He could not have described then, or later, what it was

that alerted him, but he was not surprised when a pair of Sioux on spotted ponies emerged from a clump of young pines, headed straight for the two Crows at full speed. Big Chin, reacting instantly, pulled his bow and sent a shaft into the neck of one of the Sioux ponies. The animal reared and threw its rider, weapons flying in all directions as the stunned warrior sailed through the air and crashed to earth, too stunned to move.

Now there was only one Sioux, and he was headed straight for Young Buffalo. The Sioux and the Crow pointed their rifles at each other, pulled the triggers, and in their excitement, hit neither the enemy rider nor his horse. The Sioux did not stop coming. He had a rifle in his hand, and if it no longer had a load in its chamber, it was still better than nothing as a war club.

Young Buffalo immediately understood what his enemy was preparing to do. He noticed that his captured mount was bigger than the Sioux's pony. Quickly he holstered his rifle, grabbed the reins with both hands, turned his pony to meet the charge, and when the enemy was close, he urged the pony forward. The two animals hit hard. Young Buffalo was prepared for the collision, but his enemy was not. The Sioux lurched forward, right hand on the reins, his wildly flailing left arm gripping his rifle.

Young Buffalo seized the rifle at the stock, twisted hard and jerked it out of the grip of the Sioux warrior. To take a weapon from the enemy in the heat of battle is a great war deed, but Young Buffalo was not finished. With his quirt he tapped the off-balance warrior on the shoulder. A second great Crow war deed was counting coup in battle by touching a healthy enemy with a stick, but not injuring him.

Their ponies were running in the same direction, close together. Young Buffalo could see the grim face of the Sioux, who was wearing only a breechcloth and a knife sheath. He had his hand on the sheath, groping for his knife. Clinging to his mount with his knees and thighs, Young Buffalo reached into his quiver, pulled out an arrow and jabbed it into the Sioux pony, not deep enough to maim it, but deep enough to make it rear up, and this time the Sioux warrior could not hang on. Before the Sioux hit the ground,

Young Buffalo had grabbed the reins of his enemy's pony and was leading it toward the creek bed where Big Chin was untying the Crow ponies. They drove the ponies before them for a minute or two, then changed over to their own war ponies and led their friends' mounts, plus the two they had just captured, into the black night.

Chapter 3

The journey back to the village turned out to be uneventful. Before the Sioux sent out a war party to follow, they took quick stock of the damage. Nobody had been grievously injured in the pony stampede through the camp, and the dozen missing ponies, not being among the most cherished, were not even missed until the following day, and even then no one could be sure that they hadn't just run off in the middle of the stampede.

Only the two warriors whom Young Buffalo and Big Chin had bested were able to say for certain that the enemy had actually visited them. But once they had reset the drying scaffolds for the buffalo meat, their anger had abated and their chief, Iron Leggings, was able to talk some sense into them.

"We are a small village," he said. "There are only eight warriors among us. They must all be here to defend the village if others return, and they must be here to hunt. The buffalo hunt was good but we do not have nearly enough meat for the winter."

There was a young warrior sitting in council, listening to his chief. His name was Buffalo Chest, not for the size of his torso, but for the inordinate pride with which he carried himself.

"Those thieves took my best rifle and my best pony," he whined. "I want to get them back."

"You will get them back and more," his chief assured him.

"How, if we do not find their tracks and pursue them?" asked Buffalo Chest.

"I will say no more about it at this time," Iron Leggings replied, and none of the other warriors pressed the issue. They knew that something was in the wind, but they also knew that Iron Leggings kept his own counsel until he was ready to speak.

The four young Absarokee warriors had been missed since the day they'd left, but they were not the only ones who had slipped out of the village. They were, however, the first to return from their escapade. Weary and sleep-deprived, they had camped five miles east of the village the previous night so they might get a good sleep and enter their village with proper pomp and fanfare in early daylight.

The next morning they rode in, four proud young warriors escorting fourteen stolen Lakota ponies. They didn't exactly make a formal parade out of their entrance, but they held their heads high, and tried to keep their eyes straight ahead as the people of the village gathered to watch their entrance.

Running Wolf, the village chief, was there, and all the older warriors, arms folded and stony-faced except for their eyes, bright with the memories of their own escapades and the joy of knowing that the young men still had spirit and enterprise.

The women and girls were out also, whooping and trilling and cheering the young men. Some, such as Young Buffalo's mother and sister, were smiling with the joy of having him back unhurt. Young Buffalo did what he always did when he entered the village after being gone for a few days—he looked around for new pretty faces.

This village consisted primarily of members of two clans, the Beaver and the Cougar. The only girls he liked in the village were of the Cougar, his clan, and therefore he could not be seriously interested in them. In fact it was a tribal custom for clan cousins to always joke with each other, but Young Buffalo was at an age when he wanted to care for a girl in a different way.

Such pretty girls, his cousins.

He gave a quick glance at Fleeing Deer, a girl he had known since childhood. She was the prettiest and the sweetest of the Beaver clan, all the prettier and sweeter compared to her clan sisters. He looked away quickly, lest she notice his stare and begin to hope for his favor. He never meant for her—or any other girl in the village—to hope to get him under her blanket. He knew that once a woman thought you were interested she could get downright evil if you disappointed her.

The chief and the elders of the village had their own serious thoughts, and as the young men led their captured ponies through the village, the chief gestured to Young Buffalo that he wished to speak with him as soon as possible. In a short period of time the celebration was over and the ponies had been set loose with the herd south of the village.

"Do not let these animals out of your sight!" Big Chin said sternly to one of the three boys whose job it was to guard the ponies and sound the alarm if hostile warriors were spotted skulking in the area. Young Buffalo said nothing, and made his way to where his chief sat in front of his tepee taking in the morning breezes.

"I am glad you all came back," he said without a smile. "I see that your medicine was good, and yet it was not good that you would leave the village when it was not permitted. Bad may yet come of your stubborn disobedience."

In the presence of the chief he had followed all his life, Young Buffalo lost his boldness. He stood, silently, until the chief told him to sit. Young Buffalo obeyed.

"These are the ponies of the Lakota?" the chief asked.

"These were the ponies of the Lakota," Young Buffalo replied in a final feeble show of cheekiness. He stared at the dark, pock-marked face of his chief. At his advanced age many of the warriors had big bellies and round faces. Not Running Wolf. His face still had a hungry wolf-like look, and his body was as lean as the blade of a knife.

"You must tell me, Young Buffalo, were any of the Lakota killed in this foolish raid?" he asked.

Young Buffalo gave an account of the raid, but did not mention his feat against the Sioux warrior. He did not think it was the time or place to do so, and he wanted very much to keep the respect of his chief.

"I do not believe any of the Lakota were seriously hurt," he told the chief.

"That is good," said the older man. "They would surely find us and attack us if we had killed one of their men."

Young Buffalo hated to hear his chief voice his fear and concern over the mood of the Sioux. In their history they had won many battles against the mighty Lakota.

"Big Chin has spoken much of your fight with the Lakota warrior. Did he speak truly?"

Young Buffalo thought for a moment. Warriors were supposed to be bold in proclaiming their feats of battle, but Running Wolf had done such great deeds against the Striped Arrows and the Lakota that he did not wish to speak boastfully of his first good fight. Still, it was expected of him.

"It is as Big Chin has said," he replied, looking directly into the eyes of his chief.

Running Wolf smiled. "You will soon be a pipe carrier," he said, meaning that he would have the right to lead his own raids. He chuckled deep inside himself. This young man had proved himself by leading his own raid against the wishes of his chief. And yet how could Running Wolf scold him for initiative and bravery and success in battle when Running Wolf had done almost the same thing forty years before?

"My son," he said, "the great leaders in battle must be the ones to think of the people and not take foolish chances. When warriors see a brave young leader counsel caution, they will follow him, and the village will be better for it."

"I understand," said Young Buffalo. "I will never do a thing like this again."

"You do not have to," the old chief responded. "You have proved what you are made of. The next time you do great things in battle, it will be for your people, not for yourself."

Young Buffalo thanked his chief for his words and headed back to his lodge, but on his way across the circle of tepees he saw the daughter of his uncle Hawk Appearing.

"I tried to bring you back a gift, White Doe," he said to the girl who had been a playmate when they were very young.

She flashed even, white teeth as she smiled. "Tried?" she replied. "Was it too heavy for one of your ponies to carry?"

"He would not come when I tried to take him."

"He?" she asked. "Are you telling me that you were trying to bring me a Sioux?"

"Just so," he said. He had always played games like this with her, and always loved every moment he spent with her.

"And I suppose you wanted to bring him to me, in fear of his life, so he would marry me?"

"I must find somebody—anybody—to marry you. No Absarokee warrior would marry you. For a while I thought I might find a bluecoat, his breath stinking of whiskey, who could be made to marry you before the whiskey went away and his sense returned to him, but no, I thought, a warrior from the mighty Lakota—fearing death—might be just the right man."

She giggled. "Surely some brave warrior of the long-beaked bird would have me for a third wife. Don't you think so?"

Young Buffalo thought for a moment. "Nobody I know," he answered.

Now they both laughed out loud, for both of them knew that she had turned down nearly every warrior in Running Wolf's band and others also. Every young warrior who met her fell instantly in love and her father had almost closed several excellent deals for her, but he had long ago promised that he would not marry off any of his three daughters without their consent.

Young Buffalo and White Doe had a running joke between them that White Doe was a runty, unattractive girl whom nobody wanted, and that he was an awkward, frightened little boy who was always hurting himself with his weapons and making a fool out of himself in the hunt. In truth, she was the most eligible young woman in the band,

and Young Buffalo was the most promising of the young braves.

But there was another, sadder truth. The two had adored each other almost since birth. She had turned down all of her suitors not because they would not have made good husbands but because they did not measure up to her cousin, Young Buffalo.

Young Buffalo was more resigned than White Doe to the fact that they never could be man and wife, or so he told himself. Whenever he visited another Absarokee band he always made a study of the young maidens of the village, meaning to woo the best of the lot. But none of them seemed any good to Young Buffalo. None was anything like White Doe, and White Doe was his standard of excellence.

They walked over to the nearby creek, sat on the bank, and watched the water ripple around the rocks.

"Let's run away," he said suddenly, softly, but urging her on in a serious tone of voice.

"You know I can't do that!" she answered. "You can't do that. Where would we go? To the Snakes? To the Flat-heads?"

He laughed then. "Just one time I wanted to say . . . I wanted you to know. . . ."

"But I've always known," she giggled. "And I always knew you knew. Does it matter that we cannot be man and wife, so long as we are close by each other with words and feeling?"

"Does it matter? Is that what you asked?" His eyes were wide, more with amusement than amazement. "Do you not want me in the same way that I want you?"

"I could if I let myself," she answered. "But I've always known it cannot be that way, and you have too. If it cannot be, then why torture myself thinking of how what could not be could be?"

"But it could if—"

"It could if we gave up our people."

He knew she was right. It would never occur to him to leave his people, this great people who lived in the best place on earth. "I was just having fun thinking," he said.

"Having fun?" she said. "Is this fun? Thinking about what we can never have? Men may do such things. Women do not waste their hearts on such things."

But there was something in her voice that did not ring true, and he knew that in the middle of the night, when she was alone with her thoughts, her dreams included him.

Chapter 4

Three days later, Young Buffalo decided to go hunting by himself. Although he loved the companionship of his fellow warriors, and he treasured the time he spent with White Doe, most of all he enjoyed time spent alone on the rolling plains, stalking the elk or antelope.

Every season had its hold on his senses: he welcomed the bite of the cold winter air in his lungs. Then with the spring warming there was the smell of damp earth in his nostrils, and later the touch of the warm west wind on his skin. The blue of the sky changed from season to season, and the hooves of his pony beat a different sound depending upon how long the summer sun had been drawing moisture from the grass.

The returning rhythms of the seasons warmed Young Buffalo with their predictable familiarity, and made him feel more like the master of his world. So did the long strides of his big war pony, who could move swiftly from horizon to horizon without effort.

This day the sun was nearly directly overhead and the lone track he had discovered, that of a deer, had vanished in a chokecherry thicket. He was about to return to the village when his keen eyes spotted movement over a distant hill. He rode toward the movement, then vanished in a tree line while he waited for those he had seen to approach. These days all humans were either friend or foe; there was no in-between. He must see who they were without being seen. The fate of his village could easily depend on his skills at spying and hiding.

It didn't take long for him to identify the figures as those of a village on the move, leading their pack ponies in a long, wide parade circled by flanking horsemen and wide-ranging camp dogs. A few more minutes and he could tell that the village was Absarokee, and not long thereafter he could see that it was the village of a childhood friend, Deer Tracker.

Young Buffalo was surprised to see Deer Tracker's village so far east while it was still early in the summer, but Crow camps moved often, and sometimes the movement of the game made for strange wandering patterns.

As soon as he could make out the stocky figure of his friend seated on his favorite mount, Young Buffalo nudged his pony into a full gallop, down one slope, up another, and across the face of a third. The lead riders of the moving village stopped in their tracks, but Deer Tracker recognized his friend while he was still three hundred yards away, kicked his pony's flanks, and galloped off with a whoop to meet Young Buffalo.

The two riders closed the distance between them in a matter of seconds. The old ones riding their gentle plugs watched with satisfaction. Surely there were no finer horsemen on the plains than the warriors of the Absarokee.

The ponies were soon side by side, head to tail, and the young men were on their feet, hugging each other, bursting with news. They had grown up together in the village of Running Wolf, but after Deer Tracker's father died, his mother had moved into the lodge of her sister, with the larger band headed by a powerful chief called Strong Bull. The two friends had seen each other very little over the past two years, a time of great change for both, and while neither was much of a talker, each needed to tell his stories to the other. Such was their friendship.

Strong Bull's village made their camp five miles down the creek from the village of Running Wolf, and while the women erected the tepees, Young Buffalo and Deer Tracker rode at a leisurely trot across a grassy plain to a hill high enough to see both villages. The sun was seeking its usual place below the western horizon, descending in a pink and blue display that dissolved to black. The young men watched as one by one the hearthfires turned each lodge into a cone-shaped glowing lantern. The sight of a circular Crow village glowing in the night never failed to kindle a warm feeling in these young men.

Atop their hill the young men felt the warmth of their campfire on their chests and the deep cool of the night at their backs. They pulled their blankets around them and gnawed on buffalo jerky.

"How is it with White Doe?" asked Deer Tracker. The question jolted Young Buffalo. He had forgotten all the little attentions Deer Tracker had given the young girl when they had all been together.

"She believes she will never marry if she must have a husband from her own village," Young Buffalo responded.

Deer Tracker heard the studied indifference in his friend's voice. "Ah yes, I see you still feel as you always have about her," said Deer Tracker. "But you have always known you cannot have her. Why is she still in there, gnawing at you?" he asked, tapping his heart with the fingers of his right hand.

Young Buffalo felt a brief surge of anger. He did not like being found out, even by his friend. The anger was quickly replaced by a wave of sadness, which he let out in a sigh. "I will bring you to her tomorrow, my friend. If I cannot have her, I truly hope you shall . . . someday."

The implication was that Deer Tracker had not by valor in battle earned the right to marry and start his own family, and the bright young Crow read his friend's thoughts immediately. His face creased into a smile that grew wider as he searched for the right words.

"Before long I believe I will have her, if she will have me," he said, simply.

Young Buffalo had been preparing the story he was planning to tell his friend about the last raid, but he knew that Deer Tracker had also been busy, and natural courtesy always drove Young Buffalo to listen first and speak last. "You have counted coup in battle!" he cried. "Tell me!"

Deer Tracker's smile slowly vanished. "I have done this," he conceded.

"But that is—" Young Buffalo was excited for his friend, but mystified by his friend's sudden seriousness. "—is good. Why then the cloud on your face?"

"Because in doing good for me I may have done bad for my people," said Deer Tracker.

There was silence now, but for the occasional fire crackle. Deer Tracker took a bite of pemmican and chewed it thoughtfully, in no hurry to explain. Nor did Young Buffalo want to push him. The words would come.

And they did.

"You know that the Lakota are close?"

"I have myself seen them. They gave us some fine horses," Young Buffalo replied.

Deer Tracker missed the obvious irony. "They are too close," he said. "The white men are taking their game, and now the Lakota want ours."

"But we have always allowed others to hunt on our land."

"The Lakota are too proud to hunt on the land of others. Our chiefs say that the Lakota want our land to be their land. Our chiefs tell us to stay away from the Lakota so they will not attack us until we are ready for them."

Young Buffalo laughed. "You know how careful the chiefs get as they get old. We are mightier warriors than they could ever be. Our chiefs are the same. They try to make us stay home. We did not listen. We rode to a Lakota village and came home with many fine ponies and nobody got hurt. Where are the Lakota? Have they come after us yet? We watch the horizon for the fearsome Sioux and all we see is sky."

"Listen to me, my brother."

"I am sorry. I want to hear what you have to say," said Young Buffalo.

"We rode to where the sun rises over the warmer country," Deer Tracker began. "We were looking for a village, but instead we found a Lakota war party, looking for us perhaps. They had more guns but our people had good bows and we know how to shoot a bow from the back of a pony.

Maybe the Lakota have forgotten—too much white man.

"We rushed at each other head on, seven on their side and six on ours. Bang! Bang! Bang! They shoot!" Deer Tracker was on his feet, aiming an imaginary rifle and pulling the trigger. "Their bullets all miss us and now they are running, trying to reload their guns while their ponies are running across the bumpy ground. In the meantime we are shooting our bows—like this!"

And he simulated pulling the bowstring, then pulling an arrow from his mouth and shooting again.

". . . quickly, and they see that they must flee or they will get an arrow in their rump. But there is one warrior—young, but with one of those Lakota war bonnets with many eagle feathers, a young man who has done much in few years. He slows down to reload. I can see powder spilling from his powder horn as he misses the barrel. And I take a chance. From a long distance I ride straight at him. He sees me and he stops his pony so he can load. I push my pony. Faster, faster. His powder is down the barrel. Now the wad and ball, he spits into the barrel, and tries to push home the rammer. He misses once, then gets the stick down into the barrel. I am close enough to try a shot. My arrow misses him but hits his pony. The pony bucks just as he is pulling the rammer out. The rammer breaks off.

"There is nothing for him to do but fire his gun with the rammer in the barrel. He aims his rifle. I pull my pony away and pull back on my bow. He fires. I can hear the rammer go past my ear. Now I have time. I let fly the arrow and while he is ducking, I pull my hatchet, run my pony into his and—"

Here he made a quick downswipe with his bladed hand. "My hatchet bit into the side of his neck. Blood flowed in a flood down his body all over the back of his pony. He went limp against me. I pulled my pony away and let him fall into the grass, and I yelled my cry of triumph. When the other Lakota saw the young man fall, they quit trying to fight and fled. They might not have fought well that day but they had swift ponies that carried them out of sight.

"The other men with me gave up the chase and came back to me. The Lakota warrior was dead, quickly, but I waited for the others to be with me before I took his scalp. Aho! A Lakota scalp. Not so easy to take, the scalp of a mighty Lakota warrior, hey? And I took it, and I shook it, and we sang our war songs. I took his pony too, the one you see hobbled in the grass. And his rifle, not a new rifle, but a good one. And his war bonnet, which I gave to my chief when we got home.''

At the mention of his chief the animation left his face. Once again he became thoughtful and serious. ''Ah, we went back home. My friends were singing my praises, making up songs of my conquest. When we arrived at the village, everybody celebrated. But not the wise men.''

Young Buffalo nodded. There was no more to say. To the east was the enemy. There might be war. There might not be war. Surely there would be raids. That would be all right. Absarokee warriors knew what to do with a Lakota raiding party. War? That was something else. There was nothing to do then but wait for news.

Chapter 5

Two days after Deer Tracker had killed the young Sioux with the big war bonnet, the Sioux raiding party returned to its village and touched off the beginnings of a full-scale intertribal war.

The beginnings were slow, to be sure. The dead warrior's mother slashed her hair and her arms and naturally enough was heartbroken over the loss of her son; she was a woman of unusual perseverance, and she was determined to instigate a revenge raid upon the Crows.

So every night she saddled one of her son's ponies and led it past the lodges of the village, keening her grief and speaking her mind.

"Who is there among you with the manhood to pursue a just revenge?" she asked. "You all knew my son. You saw him grow from a baby into a fine, strong brave. You were there when he joined his first warrior society. You saw him kill his first buffalo. You saw him count his first coup. You saw the eagle feathers grow on his war bonnet.

"And some of you saw him die bravely in battle. You saw him slain by our enemies, the people of the long-beaked bird. He was a young leader among you. He deserves the lives of two Crows. No! His loss could not be avenged without out the lives of five Crows, or even seven. Have the Sioux become children, or even old women, trembling in their lodges at the sound of strange horses? Who will come forward and bring grief to the Crow lodges as they have brought grief to ours?''

Although there were many men in the village who had cared for her son, they did not like being challenged in this way by a grief-stricken woman. It just didn't feel like good medicine. Month after month went by and still her ritual continued, and it was getting on people's nerves. Her relatives told her she should stop but she would not. The chiefs told her she should stop but she would not. And the longer she went on doing it, the more determined the men grew not to pick up her challenge. The result was that for nearly a year this particular Sioux village avoided raiding the Crows, though they did remain especially alert lest a Crow party come calling one night and make fools out of them.

In this village was a young warrior named Young Pine Tree. Young Pine Tree was in love with a girl his family could not stand. The girl was one of those spiteful little gossips who knows how to get under a man's skin by making nasty remarks about people she knows he dislikes but doesn't wish to think about.

Nevertheless, this girl was his first love and he was determined to marry her but none of the women in his family would heed his request to make a wedding. He decided to join the Brave Heart Society so he could die a glorious martyr's death in battle against the Sioux's favorite foes, the Crows.

The next time he saw the wailing woman walking her son's horse along the circle of tepees, it all came together for him. He took hold of the reins of the animal, the women uttered a cry of joy, the village arose and gathered around him, and there he stood, covered with glory.

This sudden development did not sit right with the chief, who wasn't at all ready to launch a war against the Crows, whom he respected as much as he disliked. So he put the young man off for a while. ''A serious undertaking like this demands long planning,'' said the chief. Young Pine Tree, who was not among the front rank of his village's warriors, did not object. His act of taking the pony's reins had constituted a commitment to lead a revenge raid. The chief's demand for delay took the risk out of the project but the glory remained, at least for a while, and his bruised ego required all the glory he could get.

The Sioux chief Iron Leggings stood up and studied the assemblage of chiefs. Beyond this council, up and down Big Goose Creek, as far as the eye could see, flickering campfires lit up the night. Not only was the entire Teton family of Sioux camped along the creek. The Striped Arrows—the Cheyennes—were here too, and even the Tattoo People—the Arapahos.

He smiled to himself. All was as it should be. The finest country he knew, land teeming with game, berries, nuts, and lodgepole pines, was occupied by the hated enemy, the Absarokee, the people of the long-beaked bird. They did not deserve such a fine place. Besides, he reasoned, his people were being pressed from the east by the white people.

"The Absarokee are friends with the white people!" he told his fellow chiefs. "If the Absarokee lose their land, let them go to their white friends for help. The white men are rich. Surely they would help their long-beaked birds." He put a twist into the way he pronounced their name that made the other chiefs laugh.

"My heart feels as big as this country to see us all camped together like this. Never have so many of the Lakota people come together in one place. When our mighty warriors ride westward we will ride over those long-beaked birds before they can see the daylight. Our ponies will be so many that they will blot out the sun!

"But we must move fast. You know how the Absarokee are always sneaking like wolves over the land. They have probably seen us by now."

There was only one more chief to speak before the council decided what they intended to do. He was Night Horse, and he was a chief of the Tattoo People.

"Many of you know me, my brothers, and you know how the northern part of the Arapahos are allied with the great Lakota people." He drew himself up to his impressive height and loosened his blanket around him.

"But you must remember that I was born an Absarokee, and you must know that I would not fight my own people.

What you are planning tonight is wrong. We have all won fame and praise on the battlefield, raiding villages, stealing horses, counting coup, taking a scalp. That is what we do, not like the white men, who make war on other people and try to kill them all. But you want to wipe out the Absarokee so you can take their land. That is a bad thing to do. It is the way of the white men. Have we lived so close to the white men that we are taking on their evil ways? I had not thought I would ever live to see this day!''

Iron Leggings could not let Night Horse's statements go unchallenged. So he arose and spoke, briefly.

''The Tattoo People are not of one mind,'' he said. ''Some ride with us. Others, to the south, prefer the friendship of the white man. You, Night Horse, your heart still rides along the Bighorn River. My heart is sad for you that you cannot understand what we understand, that friends of the white man are enemies of the Teton. It is better, then, that you do not ride with us when we go to fight the Crows.''

Night Horse did not respond, although the reply of Iron Leggings was an insult. He had a mission to save the Crow people, and he did not wish to draw further attention to himself. When the chiefs convened to make their war plans, Night Horse returned to where his Arapahos were camped, a bit apart from the long succession of Sioux villages. He entered his lodge, a large tepee that accommodated his daughter and her family as well as his younger children and his two wives. Then he summoned his two sons from their lodges, and he addressed his family.

''Tonight,'' he said, ''when all is quiet, we are leaving camp. That is all I will say for now. I want you to start packing and separating our ponies from the herd. I will talk to Big Heart; he is the only one of our village that I can trust not to betray us.''

Such was the power of Night Horse that neither of his sons questioned him, though both were grown men with families and men of stature to boot. Such was their father's power and will and strength of character that they trusted him always to make the right decision. So they returned to their lodges, told their women to make ready to leave but to tell no one, and went to sleep.

The night was still but for the scraping of travois over the prairie grass and the soft footfalls of the ponies. They would not dream of leaving their dogs behind, so there was an occasional bark. But the encampment was so large that the comings and goings of small numbers were not noticed.

Three lodges. Thirty ponies and seventeen people, including nine children. Perhaps it was unusual that they would depart in the night. Still, nobody took notice.

Somebody should have. In the light of a quarter moon Night Horse headed north along the creek, then westward through a notch in the nearby hills, pointing straight toward Crow country. When the sun rose they were seven miles west of the Sioux encampment. Night Horse was not about to stop but neither could his people travel any faster. He knew how important it was to get word to the Absarokees as quickly as possible, so he called his two sons to him, and as they rode on, he spoke to them.

"I have a risky job for you to do," he said. "You, most precious of my blood, you must go to the Absarokees and tell them the Lakota are making ready to make a big war against them. They may not believe you. They may even try to kill you, though I do not think so. Be careful, but find one of their villages and let them know, or they will all die."

He told them a bit more about the Sioux plans, and then off they rode, in the pink light of dawn, their ponies' hooves kicking up tiny dust clouds in the yellow grass as they crested a low ridge and disappeared.

Running Wolf raised his hand and the long procession that was his village slowly came to a halt. Ahead was Rotten Grass Creek, not the best of accommodations, but good enough for an evening's stay. The men untied the packs from the ponies and drove the animals to a field of good grazing hemmed in on one side by the creek and some low hills on the other. Seven young boys would guard the herd.

Lodgepole tripods were arising along the creek. Within

minutes these bare bones would be transformed into comfortable homes. Young children would be out collecting buffalo chips and by the time the night had turned the air to chill the hearthfires would cast a warm glow through the hide coverings. There would even be fresh meat, left over from yesterday's small buffalo kill.

Young Buffalo and Big Chin were completing a large circuit around the encamping village, a long scout to check for sign of hostile warriors. They found none, but just as they were about to ride into the village, Young Buffalo spotted two riders galloping through the dusk to the east.

The two men watched as the riders jogged down a long slope. These were not Crows; Young Buffalo knew that while they were still a quarter of a mile away. Other warriors joined them as they watched the strange riders draw closer.

Night Horse's two sons brought their ponies to a stop and allowed themselves to be surrounded by the Crow warriors. They signed the purpose of their visit, because neither one knew the native tongue of their father. Young Buffalo and Big Chin escorted the two men to Running Wolf's lodge, and fetched a warrior who could speak—or at least understand—the Arapaho tongue.

Eleven warriors were gathered in Running Wolf's lodge, silent as death while Night Horse's elder son passed along his father's message.

"You have heard of my father, Night Horse?" he asked, and many of them had. An Absarokee who became an Arapaho chief was quite a wonder.

"He has asked me to tell you that a great army of Sioux warriors is little more than a day away from you. He told us to tell you to move west as fast as you can and send messengers to all the other villages. The Sioux mean to kill every Crow warrior, make wives of your women, and slaves of your children."

He paused for a response from Running Wolf, but it was another, older warrior, Can't Make Fires, who spoke up.

"These men before you, these 'Absarokee' "—he put an ironic twist on the name of his people—"you see the rings tattooed on their chests. They are not Absarokee, they are

Arapaho, the allies of the Lakota. They do not speak the tongue of our people, they speak the tongue of the Arapaho, that only the Arapaho can speak!" Others nodded. The Arapaho tongue was a difficult tongue. One conversed with the Arapaho in sign or in the dialect of the Cheyenne, or one did not talk to an Arapaho at all.

"It is not that we love the Absarokee," said the elder son of Night Horse. "How can we love what we do not know? We are here because we love our father. He would be here himself but he is too old and big to travel fast by pony. We rode like the wind to get to you as fast as we could, knowing that you might not believe us, might even kill us. Would you send your sons to their death? Neither would our father. But he took the risk because he loves the people of his mother."

Sounds of approval arose from most of the older warriors but some of them were still skeptical. The younger ones did not know what to make of it. The story of Night Horse was older than they were. But they longed for war with the Sioux, and so they chose to believe the sons of Night Horse. And their most esteemed young warrior, Young Buffalo, stood up to speak.

"I look into the faces of these men, and I believe I see the truth. Why would they ride to us to spread a lie that would bring all the Absarokee together?" he asked. "If we all came together, and the Sioux did not come, we would go to find the Sioux. Nobody with sense would try to bring the Absarokee into their own villages."

Now voices were raised in loud agreement and Running Wolf knew that the time had come to act. "Young warriors," he said in a quiet voice that carried so well in the last moments of red daylight. "Do not delay. Take food and water and your fastest ponies into the night and find our villages. Have them send men from their villages to other villages. Have their best warriors come quickly to the Bighorn River, but see to it that their villages come close behind, so that we are all together if the Sioux come before we are ready. I believe there is evil in the air. I believe our people may be wiped off the face of the earth if we do not strike them before they strike us.

"But if we are ready for them, and our medicine is good, I believe we can win a great victory."

Big Chin trilled his war cry then, and the other warriors joined him. The meeting broke up in a controlled frenzy. Although night had come, the entire village was packing to move. Women prepared food, water pouches, and other necessities for the men, tore down their tepees and loaded their ponies. The young men were already scattered in about seven different directions when the old men and the women pointed their ponies toward the Bighorn River and began the long trek.

Running Wolf was satisfied, yet uneasy, as he studied the large Crow camp along the Bighorn River. There were at least four hundred lodges, which meant that most of the Absarokee nation had come together for their common defense. He was pleased that it was the warriors of his village who had brought this great union of the people. But he also knew that in numbers they were no match for their deadly enemy, and the banks of the Bighorn were no place to stage a defensive battle.

He had explained his misgivings to the other chiefs in council and they had agreed to send their Wolves out scouting all around the encampment. And now, as he gazed beyond the great encampment, he saw two riders coming hard from the east. Once they were in sight of the camp, they began riding back and forth on the parched plains. Their little riding exhibition was a signal.

Running Wolf raced for the lodge of Young Buffalo and rousted him. "Tell the chiefs the enemy has been spotted and that we must leave this place at once," he told his best young warrior. Then the chief strode around his own village, shouting to the women that it was time for them to get packed and ready to move.

Within a very short time the villages were moving out, heading westward.

There was no time to waste. Everybody rode, and everybody rode fast, across the broad plain. The scouts ranged far and wide and did not see their pursuers. Nevertheless, everybody was looking over their shoulder from the time they left the Bighorn until evening, when they arrived at winding, narrow, cedar-bordered Pryor Creek, many miles away.

Spent and weary, the women set up camp in the open air, worried that they might have to move again at any time. Fresh ponies were tethered near their fires and all the boys were out in the field taking turns watching the pony herd. The younger men roamed the plains all night, watching and listening, their senses on a hairtrigger. The older men lay hidden around the edges of the village, rifles and bows at hand in case the enemy sneaked past the scouts.

Some men dozed, others did not, and in the end it wasn't important because the Sioux did not come during the night. Before dawn Big Chin arrived, weary from living in the Lakotas' leggings over the past two days. They were coming, he told the chiefs, and to Running Wolf was delegated the authority of implementing the plans they had discussed on their fast-trot journey west from the Bighorn.

One of the young men who was to be part of their first line of defense was a warrior called Hits Himself Over The Head. Fingers of dawn were searching the night sky when he arose, slung his blanket over his shoulder, and walked off toward the herd to find his war pony. Less than a half mile from the village he topped a rise, looked to his left into a valley, and saw, half-hidden in the dust, a huge swirling mass of mounted men that could only be their dreaded Sioux enemy.

No time now to find his pony. He picked up his heels and sprinted down the hill, over two swells and down into the village. Running Wolf spotted him racing down the last hill and before the young warrior gave his warning cries the chief was himself running, in an arthritic limp, from family to family, alerting ten of the best warriors that they'd best mount up and head out. Then he gave a whoop and set about rousing everybody. In the pink and blue dawn, the Crows were about to engage a powerful enemy with their very existence at stake.

The ten chosen warriors were men of experience, but among them was one young man whose experience was both limited and recent. He was Young Buffalo, and he knew his selection was evidence of the great faith his leaders had in him. This morning's work would require toughness and nerve, and the ability to face death with indifference. He had special confidence, for he had had a dream the night before, a dream that allocated a special role for him in the coming fight. The dream had instructed him in what he was supposed to do, and although the instructions did not make perfect sense to him, he resolved to carry them out even at the risk of death.

The men were hurrying about, applying paint, stripping down to their breechcloths, and dressing up the war ponies they had been keeping in the village.all night. As they left the village they could hear the rattle of lodgepoles. The chiefs had decided to defend the village behind a palisade of stacked lodgepoles, but it would take time to complete the fortification. It was up to the ten selected warriors to buy that time, if necessary, with their lives.

Chapter 6

From behind the growing fortress the women whooped as the ten warriors headed out toward where Hits Himself Over The Head had spotted the Sioux. At a slow gallop, saving their ponies, they rode through the dawn until they arrived at a ridge from which they could look down upon the Sioux.

Steeled against fear by a lifetime of training, fierce as cornered bears, they rode over a hill of yellow grass and then down into a coulee. In single file, they then rode slowly up a steep incline, dismounted, and led their horses, saving them for the work that was soon to come. They stopped before they reached the crest of the hill, and listened. The warm summer breeze carried the noise of a mighty assemblage to their ears.

They did not hurry. For several minutes they waited for their ponies to recover their energy. The pipe carrier, or leader, of the most important mission that any Crow warrior had ever known, was a man of thirty summers called Knows His Name. The English name was an inexact translation of a Crow expression that meant he knew who he was, and that the men of the Crows and the Sioux and the Shoshones and the Cheyennes knew him by his deeds.

He wore a single eagle feather in his hair, and a shiny black pompadour. He wore the bone chest armor of his grandfather, a loincloth, and moccasins, and that was all. His rifle was secure in its scabbard and his bow hung from his quiver behind him. He intended to begin this battle with a lance, to drive it right through the body of the Sioux wearing the biggest war bonnet that he could immediately find.

He signaled silently and the men mounted up and drew ten abreast, and walked their ponies almost to the top of the hill. Below was a group of perhaps fifty Sioux warriors, waiting for the sign that would send them hurtling toward the Crow encampment. From all directions of the valley, more Sioux, many more Sioux, as far as the eye could see, were heading to join them.

Knows His Name kicked his pony forward, and the rest did the same. In the center, just to the left of Knows His Name, rode Young Buffalo, and to the left of Young Buffalo, moccasin to moccasin, rode Big Chin. Down the hill they swept, without a war whoop, without a gunshot. They knew that the Sioux were full of themselves and their power, and that if they rode hard they could be among the enemy before they were even noticed.

Suddenly they were in the midst of the Sioux. Knows His Name did not find the biggest war bonnet but he found an enemy chest, and drove his lance directly into it. The first sign of attack to the Sioux was an explosion of blood from the chest and back of their comrade. Three of them barely had time to notice before their time had come, dispatched by the rifles and arrows of the attackers.

The ten Crows rode right through the Sioux, leaving four unmounted ponies and three more with warriors clinging desperately to their backs, warm blood pouring down their sides.

Young Buffalo had killed his man with a single arrow that had buried itself almost to the feathers in the chest of a warrior. As they had planned, they rode completely through the Sioux forces; two hundred yards farther, they turned to survey their results. From the surrounding hills nearly a thousand Sioux warriors were pouring into the valley, quirting their ponies with fury, so determined to tear to pieces the arrogant enemy that they scarcely knew what they were doing.

The ten Crows had not a scratch among them, so complete and stunning was their attack. Now they had to test the speed and stamina of their ponies against what seemed like the entire Sioux nation. But they had a head start along the creek that led to the Crow village, and so numerous and insanely passionate were the Sioux pursuers that they were getting in each other's way.

In the Crow encampment, behind their just-completed wall of lodgepoles and buffalo hides, lay hundreds of Crow warriors, most of them armed with well-maintained, if not brand-new, rifles. They had learned early on that the secret of good marksmanship was plenty of ammunition with which to practice, and in their trading with white men they did not spend their wealth on whiskey but on bullets and powder. They were about to hand the Sioux a deadly surprise.

The Sioux charged headlong down the valley, intent on overtaking the cheeky ambushers, then destroying the encampment and killing every Crow strong enough to pull a bowstring. On the hills overlooking the valley appeared crowds of Sioux women, children, and old men intent on witnessing the great victory, and a victory it would be, of that they had no doubt. The mighty Sioux nation had been kind to allow the Crows their beautiful hunting grounds for so long. Old chiefs who remembered asking permission to hunt in the Bighorn valley rocked back and forth in their blankets and waited for their young men to finally win justice from the barrel of a gun.

The hooves of the Sioux ponies roared like thunder as they approached the Crow encampment, protected by a flimsy wall of stacked lodgepoles. The ten Crow raiders had disappeared through a gap in the center, which was being closed quickly by men piling pole upon pole. The Sioux galloped across the creek and split into two groups to flank the wall on each side, and as they did, Running Wolf gave a war cry and from behind the wall the Crows fired their rifles in a single deadly volley. Lakota warriors tumbled from their ponies. Whoever did not have a rifle to fire bent a bow. A shower of arrows flew from the top of the wall, and more of the flower of the Sioux fell into the dust. The Sioux retreated beyond the creek, with more gunfire from atop the wall to help speed their retreat.

The attackers did not stop to converse. They had discovered the strength of the Crows' position, now all that was necessary was to make another charge, firing from their mounts, and not stop until they had overwhelmed the Crows. The Crows had drawn blood. The Sioux would now exact a terrible revenge.

Again they splashed across the shallow creek and headed for the ends of the wall, firing with their rifles as they approached. Again Crow rifles barked, and Crow bows sang, and more, many more, Sioux warriors slid from the backs of their ponies and fed their blood to the earth.

While the attackers were milling around beyond the creek, trying to figure their next move, a veteran chief who had been riding in the ranks as an ordinary warrior announced that he intended to lead the next charge. He was no fool. He could see the courage of his young men wavering and he was certain that if they feinted toward the center and then attacked the right flank they could sweep over the wall and stampede the dismounted Crows into a panic.

The old chief, who held the modest name of Old Prairie Dog, was one of those grizzled warriors long past his glory-seeking days but reliable when the action was hot and the outcome uncertain.

"The Raven People cannot touch me with their rifles," he shouted. "Follow me this once and never again, and this great land will be ours!"

He did not wait to see if he would be followed. He popped his pony's flank with his quirt and off he went, across the creek, with a thousand warriors streaming behind him. Shrieking their war cries, quirting their ponies, firing their weapons, they closed in on the makeshift wall, dead center. Fifty yards from the wall, just as Old Prairie Dog veered suddenly right, a Crow volley roared death, echoing across the valley.

Old Prairie Dog never heard the echo. At least five bullets hit him at once and a black curtain came down on his life. Cries of dismay and anguish came from the hills as women saw their men once again yanked from their saddles by the invisible force of the Crow rifles. Before Old Prairie Dog's body had touched the golden grass, the Sioux had turned their ponies and headed back across the creek.

As the hoofbeats and war cries faded, the Crows waited calmly behind their wall, knowing that the Sioux were not through with them. The mounted warriors had retreated far beyond the creek, and no doubt were busy planning their next move. Young Buffalo chose this moment to act.

The center of the wall opened up and out he rode, straight as an arrow in the wake of the retreating Sioux. By this time they were safely out of range, and when they spotted the solitary horseman they stopped and turned, and waited to see if the lone Crow warrior was brave enough to ride among them. If he was, it would be his last ride.

Shiny black hair with the Crow pompadour, one red feather, white lightning streaks down his face and on his chest, he sat ramrod-straight on the back of his pony and crossed the creek, then stopped by a big spruce tree. He began to sign to the Sioux, who rode slowly forward toward the Crow village until they could make out the details of his hand signs.

"My brothers," he signed. "You have come from far away. There are so many of you that you must have come to take something from the people of the long-beaked bird. You think there are so many of you, and so few of us, that you must win."

He had their attention because his signs read their thoughts so well.

"We will give you more fight than you ever thought. We have stopped you cold although we are only one warrior to your ten. But we have sent for the others of the Absarokee. They are coming from the mountains. They are coming from the rivers. We are fine warriors, the men of the Absarokee. We will ride over you, and you shall never have our land!"

Although Young Buffalo was still obeying the commands of his dream, he did not truly believe that help was on the way. What he had done was pitch a gigantic bluff. His elders, who understood what he was doing, marveled at his poise, and prayed that the Sioux would be fooled.

But the Sioux were no fools, and were not about to be tricked. Not until a woman on the crest of the hill to their right pointed back over the hill and let out a cry. "They are coming!" she shouted.

She had seen a large dust cloud blowing up from the floor of the next valley. The kind of cloud that could be stirred up by an approaching column of friendly warriors—or elk.

The woman was not young anymore. She could not see the riders on the backs of the ponies but her fears made her want to see something bad.

And on the hill across the way a young boy squinted in the pale sunlight, peered into the distance and spotted another, larger cloud of dust.

"There they are!" he shouted, pointing at a larger cloud of dust that could only be another savage band of Crows. In fact it was a small herd of buffalo.

Young Buffalo wanted to say more, but he knew that too much talk would make his enemies believe him less. So he dismounted, placed his rifle carefully on the ground in front of him, folded his arms, spread his feet, and stood straight as an arrow, facing the Sioux, who were little more than a hundred yards away.

Again there was shouting from a hilltop, followed by an urgent messenger informing the braves in the valley that another large dust cloud was arriving from the west. Young Buffalo stood quietly, arms still folded. Why weren't they coming? Why was he still alive? Why are they turning away? The Sioux warriors had pulled farther back and were holding a fevered conference well beyond the creek.

"Come back here, Young Buffalo," came the voice of Running Wolf from behind the barricade. "In a moment they will attack! They are many, we are few. We need you and your gun."

The voice of Running Wolf broke the spell. Slowly, deliberately, he picked up his rifle and checked it for dirt. Then he turned his back on the agitated conferring Sioux and slowly, deliberately, led his pony back toward the wall of lodgepoles and hides. Several of the Sioux warriors had glanced back at the Crow position while the conference was going on. They saw the young Crow and his slow, quiet movements. To them it seemed that he was deliberately provoking them by being arrogant and presumptuous.

The Sioux often laid traps for their enemies by stationing a handful of warriors close to the opposition to lure them forward into an ambush. Some of them thought that Young Buffalo must be doing the same thing with his brazen behavior, so they waited indecisively, while messages from the hills above warned them of nearby dust clouds being stirred up by—something.

The Sioux chiefs finally assumed that the approaching clouds of dust must be reinforcements for the Crows, and only then did they decide to attack quickly, before the new bands arrived. When the chiefs sounded their whooping call to battle, their warriors wasted no time mounting up. They quirted their ponies hard toward Young Buffalo, toward the wooden barricade.

"Watch behind you!" shouted a warrior from behind the wall. Young Buffalo heard the hoofbeats, well away from him but closing fast. He cocked his rifle but he turned slowly. He had time, plenty of time.

There were two of them leading the charge, not chiefs but young bucks thirsty for glory, hungry to take coup in full view of their elders. Young Buffalo turned and dropped to one knee, as he had seen the soldiers do outside the fort. The two were in a race to ride him down, and fortunately for the Crows, one giant with a chest as wide as that of his horse had a fifty-yard lead over the other.

"Ayayayaii!!" The lead Sioux warrior whooped as he cocked the hammer of his rifle and hoped that the weapon would fire. It was a good weapon—when it worked.

The lead Sioux was now fifty yards away, his companion ten yards behind him. Young Buffalo would have preferred a closer shot but he had two men to take care of, not one. So he squeezed the trigger and was pleased to see the first one fling his rifle into the air and topple backwards over his pony's tail and into the dust. There was no time to reload. He pulled his hatchet from where it was tucked into his loincloth and flung it at the second rider charging hard on a dappled gray pony, then reached quickly for his knife.

The hatchet struck the pony on its snout. It did not stick, but the pony shied and reared. Its rider somehow stayed on, but in doing so his rifle fired and he no longer had momentum toward Young Buffalo. Also he noticed that he was alone and closer to the barricade than he wished to be. He turned to seek cover, then realized that several hundred of his brothers were in full gallop across the creek, almost close enough to ride over him, so he gained control of his mount and got out of their path.

From behind the wall came whoops and cheers of encouragement and admiration for Young Buffalo, but the latter saw the Sioux charge and knew that he was not going to hold off all the bands of the Tetons by himself. He turned and dashed for the tiny opening in the center of the barricade, flung himself over the lower lodgepoles and helped Would Not Listen replace the other poles. He loaded his weapon by feel as he peered over the barricade and watched the Sioux approach at a headlong run.

At a hundred yards they divided, meaning to flank the barricade on both sides. They had seen white men fight behind a wall, but never had they fought Indians like this, and they were sure that if they pushed the attack they could spook the Crows out of their position. Men on horseback can easily annihilate a force fleeing on foot.

Only the Crows did not flee. As the Sioux divided, their charging ponies brought them closer to the barricade than they would have wished. Running Wolf gave the command to fire, the barricade seemed to explode, and too many good men fell from their horses or clung desperately to their frightened mounts while blood flowed from their wounds.

The damaged Sioux army pulled back but continued to blaze away at the barricade. The Crows fired back. Both sides had ample ammunition and soon the valley was filled with gray smoke. Sioux warriors bravely rode forward to reach down, grab an arm or a leg, and drag their dead or wounded comrades away from the killing zone to save them from the this-world torments of torture—or the frightening prospect of the other-world without scalp or fingers or other body parts. Both sides continued to blaze away at each other without much further loss of life, and then, as men from both sides watched through eyes smarting from the acrid smoke, they saw something almost beyond their ability to believe.

A single warrior charged down the hills to the right of the Sioux position, wearing the briefest of loincloths, his long, unbraided, unfeathered hair bouncing in the wind behind him. His pony was midnight black, with white flashes on both flanks, and his face and shoulders were painted such a bright red they could have assumed the rider was covered in blood. The pony must have been fresh; he came down from the hills like the wind.

The rider carried a great, three-pointed lance. He galloped in among the startled Sioux and jabbed swiftly at the closest warrior. The warrior cried out and reached for the shaft but the red-covered rider was too quick for him. The lance was out and into the next Sioux warrior before the rest could react.

Two Sioux braves were reeling on their horses from the deep wounds they had suffered, and then fifty Sioux reacted, closing in on the lone, blood-red rider. Cleverly, he kept himself in the midst of his enemies so they could not fire for fear of hitting one of their own, yet he stayed out of knife or lance range. As they attempted to close in on him, he galloped back within range of the Crows behind the barricades. The Crows fired and once again, brave Sioux warriors were crying out and falling from their horses. They turned and retreated, and when they did, the red-painted stranger followed and sent two more Sioux into the dust with deep wounds in their sides. Desperately, several Sioux fired at him, and succeeded only in wounding one of their own. The red Crow warrior remained unscathed.

Once Running Wolf understood the full extent of the confusion of his enemies, he wasted no time, but ordered his men to mount and finish the job. His younger warriors did not need to be told twice, and the older, more cautious men were swept along by their passion.

In a mighty, brightly colored tide they swept around the ends of the barricade and through the middle, their fresh horses overwhelming the jaded mounts of the Sioux. Big Chin galloped out leading Young Buffalo's best war pony. He dropped the reins for his friend but did not wait for him to mount. Big Chin was out to kill Sioux, the more the better. Young Buffalo would have to catch up as best he could. Blue Shirt and Deer Tracker were there too, along with Hawk Appearing and a legendary, tough old fighter named Two Rivers.

The Crow warriors were crying, "Kokohay!" "Kokohay!" over and over; a cry that would echo in the ears of the Sioux for years to come. More warriors were sliding lifelessly from the backs of their ponies, and nearly all of them were Sioux. The mightiest of the plains tribes had had enough on this day. They turned and fled over the creek and up the valley as fast as their mounts could run. There would be other, better days, but on this day they were beaten. In another place, another time, the Crows might have stopped then and there and left the Sioux to contemplate the folly of fighting their Crow cousins, but the Crows were furious that the Sioux had attacked them not for glory, but to obliterate them on their own land. Remorselessly they rode down the stragglers and killed them. In years to come the Crows would refer to the route into the hills as "The Trail of the Dead Sioux," and they would tell of the red-painted mystery warrior with the three-pronged lance, knocking one Sioux after another from his pony. They would also tell of Two Rivers, a man past his prime, a man who had not been well in many moons, suddenly showing the form that had long ago made him the most feared man of his village.

The Crows chased the Sioux to the top of the rim, then abruptly, Running Wolf halted them with a long, shrill blast on his eagle bone whistle.

The huge crowd of Sioux noncombatants had vanished from the hills above the valley. The thousand or so Sioux warriors, their numbers notably diminished, ran from their less numerous enemy like a child from a grizzly bear. They rode through their camp at the end of the next valley and never gave a thought to stopping and gathering their belongings. The Crows followed soon thereafter, just to make sure the Sioux would continue running, and such was their discipline that day that none left the pursuit to gather loot.

On and on they rode, out of the valley and onto the open plains. The hunters and the prey had switched roles so quickly that the hunters were stunned. Onward they rode across broad stretches of high rolling plains until they were certain the Crows had ceased their pursuit. Even then, they did not stop, though many of their ponies were so worn that they could no longer run. Some of the braves dismounted and led their ponies, while others allowed their horses to slow to a shambling walk. There were many wounded among them, and their cohorts had to slow their retreat to see to it that the wounded got home alive. Their camp was only a few more miles, at Big Piney Creek, and when their tall tepees finally rose above the last grassy swell, they breathed a sigh of relief and settled down to lick their wounds.

Iron Leggings was one of the last to arrive, just before dark, with his younger brother draped over his saddle. He led his pony to his tepee, carried the young man in through the flap, left him with his wife, then ducked out and calmly walked among his men.

"We got licked today," he said, simply. "Now, you'd better grab another pony and scout out the nearby hills. If they come we must be ready to fight them." Some of the younger men looked at him as if he were crazy, but the older ones had regained their composure. Stolidly they released their lathered war ponies, exchanged them for fresh ones, and slowly headed out for nearby vantage points. Most of them rode in the direction from which they had come, not because it was the most likely direction for a Crow attack—it wasn't—but because they were anxious for some of their friends who had not yet returned.

By now, the last of the stragglers had returned to the camp. As the night wore on, they doused their campfires and waited in the dark, longing for sleep but not daring to close their eyes. Many of the men stood guard, and others sat in their lodges beside their door flaps, weapons in hand, listening to the night sounds. The hours dragged by. The wind rustled the hides of the tepees as it blew past in no hurry.

Finally, worn by the fighting and the flight, and the sadness over the loss of so many good men, their heads began to nod. Their scouts, who had seen no sign of the enemy, made their way back to camp and lay down beside their lodges, the long leads of their ponies wrapped around their wrists. By dawn silence had taken possession of the Sioux camp.

A moment after dawn, the Crows attacked.

Chapter 7

With a certainty born of vast experience, the Crows knew that they had beaten and demoralized their assailants. They had sent out a few scouts of their own, to take no chances, and while the Sioux wounded were pouring their blood into the parched grassland on the long flight south, the Crows rested.

Their women began to rejoice, but Running Wolf quickly put a lid on the celebration.

"There is much more to be done," he told them. "Feed your men and let them rest. The battle is not yet over and they must be fresh if we are to teach the Lakota a lesson they will not soon forget."

So while there was still daylight the men lay down, and many slept.

Deep in the dark, Young Buffalo felt a touch on his shoulder. He arose without a word, picked up his rifle and his knife, and walked out into the night. Along with many other warriors, he ran to the pony herd, caught his number two war pony, prepared it for battle, and swung onto its back.

There was no hurry. Their scouts had found the Sioux camp, not close but not far either. The leader of this raid would not be Running Wolf but a chief named Hillside, from a neighboring village; a young man known for his daring horse-stealing expeditions among the Sioux's Cheyenne and Arapaho allies.

Young Buffalo's friend Would Not Listen had been watching the Sioux throughout the night. He had returned to the Crow camp to lead his people across the stretch of plains that lay between the triumphant and the defeated. Now he and Young Buffalo rode side by side in the light of a bright quarter moon. There was no talking among the raiders as their ponies ate up the distance in a steady, rolling gallop.

There was dew on the plains that night. Young Buffalo could smell the damp grass. It was a good smell, a smell of life. There would be more death soon. Young Buffalo welcomed it. Seldom did one tribe make war on another as the Sioux had made war on the Crow this day. War was for revenge and honor. Enemies treasured each other enough that they did not concentrate their forces and try to wipe each other out. But the Sioux had done exactly that, and the Absarokee warriors had made the Sioux pay the price. They were about to make this night even more expensive for the Sioux.

Hillside raised his hand and the warriors came to a halt. Although the Sioux campfires had burned low, Young Buffalo and his cohorts still caught the odor of wood smoke lingering in the night air. The warriors walked their ponies up one last slope and looked across a long field. In the middle were several circles of tepees, silhouetted against the bright night sky.

The Crow warriors fanned across the field and waited while Hillside moved into the center. He raised his hand and held it high until he felt he had everyone's attention. Then he made a downward motion and the warriors screeched their hideous war cries and galloped into the Sioux camp, just as opaque clouds sailed across the face of the moon.

Now the night was pitch black. The warriors could see nothing as they rode hard into the valley, toward the circle of tepees. Young Buffalo felt a strange exhilaration as if he were flying through a black sky, trusting to his pony and his medicine to preserve him in the total darkness. For the moment he had no idea what might happen next. Only the thunder of hooves and the war cries were real. They swept down the invisible hill, closer and closer to the invisible village. They heard the sporadic crackle of guns, and saw the orange streaks of fire from the barrels of the rifles, orange streaks that told them that the guns were not pointed directly at them. Down they swept, down down and then, suddenly, there they were, terrified Sioux fleeing from the paths of horses' hooves.

The Crows rode past the tepees, cut the rawhide ropes and pulled them down on top of their inhabitants. They slashed at the flatfooted warriors wakened quickly by the need to protect their village from annihilation. Many rifles were fired blindly on both sides, but it was the people on foot who went down, sometimes bowled over by Crow ponies, sometimes the unfortunate victims of stray lead fired by friend or foe.

The Crows spotted individual ponies in the village, tied to the lodgepoles. They cut the lines and led them away. The Sioux warriors raced through the dark for their pony herd, falling into gullies in the pitch dark, rising up and running again, some of them turning to fire pistols at their pursuers, others thinking only of putting horseflesh between their knees and resisting the ghost riders.

One fallen tepee was ablaze, probably from the glowing coals of an almost-doused hearthfire. Men could now see each other in the flickering light. Some Sioux men were coming in hard on their ponies, while a few were fleeing, terrified by the sudden attack.

Young Buffalo could see a number of Sioux bodies lying still in the grass. The survivors were forming for a stiff fight. Hillside cried out an order. The Crows did not press the attack; they simply stormed through the village, leveled it, killed a few resisters, and then hurried off into the night.

Young Buffalo loved hunting alone. Alone he could do as he wished and nobody could ask him why. He had his own way of stalking a deer or an elk. And he was not fond of killing buffalo. In his short career he had lost two of his best ponies in buffalo hunts. He was not afraid for himself, but the pain of losing a good pony was like the pain of losing a friend.

So he often went hunting by himself, leading a single packhorse to carry the meat he expected to kill. He was two days west of his band now. He had trailed a deer most of the day before only to lose the trail in a hard-packed coulee toward evening. Losing the deer track did not discourage him. His people were not short of meat and he was hoping for a longer journey anyway, so he pointed his pony toward the early sunset and rode on.

It was nearly winter. There had already been a snowfall, but an unseasonably warm spell had melted all the snow, save for the thin covering in the mountains; snow that gleamed pink in the setting sun. The yellow buffalo grass stood unmoving in the cool afternoon stillness as he walked his ponies up a long swell to the top of a grass ridge.

He knew this land well. It was the most beautiful place on earth, a place touched specially by the Great Spirit. On the other side of this ridge would be a long, grassy valley, with a creek running through the center toward the Greasy Grass River—nearly a day's journey away.

Just before he reached the ridge, his nose twitched and wrinkled, and he brought his ponies to an abrupt halt.

Smoke.

He hated to find smoke in a place where he had thought himself alone. He felt insulted, as if someone had dared to trespass upon his life without first asking permission. Who could it be? Sioux? Big Bellies? Cheyenne? He dismounted and walked to the ridgeline. He scanned the vast grassland below, and quickly spotted the glint of a single small fire far down the valley. By the fire sat a single lone figure, so small, so far away that even his acute eyesight could not identify what kind of human was camped by the fire.

It didn't matter. He knew by the nature of the fire that the figure had to be a white man. A hundred feet away from the fire stood a lone dark horse, its neck stretched downward as it nibbled the grass.

Young Buffalo thought for a few moments. He could wait until the man was asleep, then he could come in and steal the horse. That might be a good thing to do. He did not consider killing the white man. From the time he was old enough to understand, he had been told that the people of the long-beaked bird did not kill white men, because the whites were their friends. Very well, if they were his friends, he could come into camp and eat with the man at the fire.

Slowly he made his way down a rocky slope into the grassy bowl. Good. He had never before met a lone white man out on the plains. But he would be very careful. His chiefs had explained that although the Absarokees and the whites were friends, white men were not easy to understand. Some of them did bad things and it was usually best to steer clear of them if one could. Young Buffalo had scoffed irreverently when he had received that piece of advice. Some friends, that they should be steered clear of. "Maybe not such good friends!" he had quipped to Running Wolf.

"Maybe better friends than the Lakota!" the chief had responded.

Wayne Braddock leaned forward and tossed a large piece of deadwood on the fire. Let the damned Indians find him, he didn't care, he just didn't want to spend another night chilled to the bone. He pulled his blanket tight around him and leaned back against his saddle. What in hell was he doing out here? he asked himself for the hundredth time.

Where else would he be? He had fought at Shiloh, fought hard at Shiloh, caught a bullet in his shoulder and gone back to his family near Jackson, Tennessee, only to find that suddenly there was no family anymore. The neighbors had told him that the Federals had come through, that a general named Grant had chosen his father's house for headquarters, but when Grant's aides had approached the little farmhouse they had found angry rifle muzzles pointed out the windows at them.

"Reckon you're gonna have to take this house from me!" his father had cried from the window over the front porch.

"Don't be a fool!" a captain on a big bay horse had shouted back.

Braddock's father had chosen to be a fool. He drew a bead on the captain and when the smoke had drifted away the old man had been satisfied to see the captain writhing in the fescue with a bullet in his gut.

Unfortunately the captain had brought an infantry escort with him. These men quickly surrounded the house, found cover, and peppered the house with some rifle fire of their own. Braddock's father and his two younger brothers responded in kind, and things could have gone on into the night, had not one brave corporal kindled a firebrand and hurled it onto the front porch.

The dry wood caught quickly enough, the neighbors told him. Soon flames were snaking their way up the sides of the house. The father and his two young sons were trapped. There was nothing to do but surrender. But Luke Braddock would not surrender, and neither did the boys. Mercifully, the smoke had rendered all three Braddocks unconscious before the fire consumed first the house and then them.

All that was left were charred beams and the remains of a basement where his mother had once kept rows and rows of canned beans and corn. His mother was nuts about beans and corn. Her grandmother had grown it, she had said.

Her grandmother—his great-grandmother—had been a full-blooded Creek Indian.

His mother had died only a week before word of secession had reached west Tennessee. Now, with the rest of his family dead, and a shoulder that felt as if a bobcat had made a home inside it, he did not feel that there was any reason he should continue fighting. His father had lost his three slaves to his creditors, and the land was about to follow. Why was it that the big landholders never lost their slaves and land to the banks, no matter how much they owed?

He was twenty-five years old, too old to fight just for the sake of the fight. One fight like Shiloh was enough to make a man doubt the whole business, anyway. Thousands of fine soldiers killed by their own brave generals, who would fight to the last ounce of their men's blood. The war was still young, most of the soldiers had received little or no training, and yet they had hung in the battle until they were dead, wounded, or out of enemy soldiers to kill. Braddock was not afraid of a fight, but Shiloh was enough fighting in this war for him.

With tears in his eyes he had turned his horse away from the pathetic cotton patch the creditors had not taken, and headed out toward Denver. There, he had heard, gold could be had for the picking, or plucking, or panning, or whatever it was one did to pry gold out of the ground.

Once he had got there, however, he found that there were too many others there first, ready to defend their claims with Colts and Bowies, or take his away from him with the same, should he stake a claim himself. More importantly, he quickly realized that most "strikes" were a few paltry flecks panned off the bottom of a creek bed. Gold mining, it seemed, was one percent gold and ninety-nine percent hope. Hope was what he had very little of. He left Denver so heartsick that he hoped for a snowstorm to swallow him up and put him to sleep.

And that was almost what had happened, exactly ten months ago. On the South Platte River, in snowdrifts so deep that his horse could no longer move forward, he scooped out a pocket, lined it with pine boughs, covered it up with more pine boughs, and hunkered down under five old CSA blankets with a sackful of crackers. The wind blew so hard that the snow did not pile up and crush the pine boughs. He ate snow and crackers for three days and decided he did not want to die.

But neither did he know how he wanted to live. He spent the spring and summer working on a lonely farm, with his Navy Colt under his pillow because the skinny, ugly wife of the farmer was always trying to flirt with him and the brawny, angry husband was always catching her doing it. He couldn't decide which of the two scared him more.

Once the crops were in he'd been kicked out and he couldn't decide whether to cross the Rockies or head back to Denver for the winter. Well, he really knew he couldn't very well cross the Rockies in the winter, but he didn't very much want to go back to Denver either. On this night, he was sitting in the middle of an open plain, his campfire summoning hosts of hostile warriors who would enjoy taking a lone white man and making their night warm by roasting him for the pleasure of hearing him scream.

He had killed a bird that afternoon, not a very big bird,

but any fresh meat would do in a pinch. He didn't even know what kind of bird it was, or whether it made a decent barbecue, but he plucked it, spitted it and roasted it. It was pretty well charred and now he was nibbling on it, working hard with his teeth to strip meat from its tiny bones.

Against the sound of a fire that smoked and crackled from too much live wood, he heard a human voice. He wasn't sure what the voice said, but he knew the speaker had wanted to be heard, so he didn't go for his gun, he just turned slowly and saw, ten feet away from him, a tall, lean Indian with a rifle in his hands that was not pointed at him.

"Heidy you, there," he said, half holding his hand up in greeting, half holding it out for a handshake.

Young Buffalo nodded, stepped toward the ex-soldier, and held out his hand. "Good, good," he said.

Braddock pointed to a rock by the fire, the seat of honor. Young Buffalo walked to the rock but did not sit on it. Rather, he picked a grassy spot five feet away and sat down, half facing the fire, half facing the white man, who did sit down on the rock.

Young Buffalo studied the white man, who wore a full, long mustache, but only the stubble of a beard. Braddock was accustomed to shaving his chin maybe once a week.

The Absarokee warrior reached out his hand and offered Braddock a strip of dried pemmican. Curious, Braddock took it, sank his teeth into it, and pulled off a small piece. He began to chew and instantly regretted it. The taste was nasty, even nastier than the small, charred bird he had been trying to eat.

Young Buffalo nodded again. "Good, good," he said, and Braddock knew he had better finish the pemmican if he didn't want to offend his guest.

He chewed the greasy mixture of deer meat and dried berries and tried to get his mind thinking about other things. But all he could think of was his family or the war, and either depressed him. Good then, he thought, I'll chew this meat and I'll have to think so hard about not throwing up that I won't be thinking the bad things. He took three huge gulps from his canteen, washed the whole sorry mess into his stomach, and smiled. "Good," he said, and quickly patted his stomach to show that he was full, before Young Buffalo could offer him another piece.

"What brings you out on a night like this?" asked the Tennessean. Young Buffalo nodded, said "good" again, and Braddock realized that the Indian had no idea of the limitations of the word.

What brought Young Buffalo into the camp was curiosity. His entire life he had heard from the chiefs that the whites were to be treated as friends, yet not to be trusted. Whites were mostly good people, he had been told, or at least better people than the Lakota. And yet he had rarely met a white man.

What were they like, these curious-looking non-redmen? And so he sat chewing slowly on pemmican, staring at the white man, hoping the man could sign a little. But all he did was make strange sounds. White man sounds.

Knowing that the Indian would understand nothing of what he said made Braddock want to talk. He had been alone for so long that he had begun to talk to himself. Maybe it would be nice, he thought, to at least talk at a human, even if the human could not understand.

Chapter 8

"Name's Braddock," said the ex-soldier, pointing to himself.

"Braddock," repeated the Indian. "Young Buffaro," he said, speaking the only two other English words he knew. Running Wolf had told his warriors that white men seldom tried to learn the Crow language, and it would be useless to try to teach them. One time he brought an army interpreter into camp to teach them all their names in English, plus a few other useful expressions. It would be useless, Running Wolf had explained, to try to make white men learn their names in the Absarokee dialect. Most white men simply could not do it.

Over the next few years Running Wolf's band stayed so far away from places where white men went that Young Buffalo, and most of his friends, forgot the few words of English that they had learned. He did manage to retain his name, and the word "good." Having used these up, he and Braddock now stared at each other. Young Buffalo chewed his pemmican, and Braddock pretended to chew, though he had swallowed his foul-tasting gift long before.

The silence grated on Braddock. It could still turn into hostility.

"I'm still new out here," he said. "I don't hate Injuns and I hope you won't take my hair."

"Good," said Young Buffalo, who was too polite to insult a host by failing to understand his language.

"I come out here from Tennessee. You know Tennessee?"

Young Buffalo stared fixedly at the second button on Braddock's ragged coat.

"Didn't think so," Braddock continued. "Lots of folks out this way don't seem to know Tennessee."

He paused, and the two men listened to an owl hoot.

"I was fightin' a war—scare the paint off you, I'll bet. Damned artillery. Artillery. I believe we could've whipped them bluebellies if they didn't have all that artillery. I hear Injuns don't much care for artillery neither and I gotta tell you, y'all are pretty sensible. Takes a damned fool to go runnin' into the mouth of a cannon. That's a fact. Now me, I ain't afraid of no Union boy with a musket and a bayonet. I'll stand up to a hundred of them, I will, but I ain't about to get blown up by no cannon."

Young Buffalo took a drink of water and offered his water bag to Braddock, who raised his canteen and politely declined.

"Got my own here, you see," said Braddock, "and if your water don't taste no better than your food, then I'd as soon decline. Anyway, I don't want you to think I run, 'cause I didn't, but I took my fingernails and I started diggin' in the ground and I stayed so close to the earth I thought they were gonna have to dig me out. Turns out we almost won the battle, but I guess we didn't 'cause we were the ones that had to leave.

"I got shot in the shoulder, here," he continued, flexing his arm a little stiffly. "And when the battle was over we had so many wounded they let us go home to get better. I only lived maybe fifty miles from the battle, you see.

"End of my fourth day coming home," Braddock said, "and I get to the road that runs by my house—well, it don't exactly *run* by my house, it kind of snakes by it, you know. And everybody else's house looks just fine, you see, then I come over a hill and instead of a house all I see is a big black hole, you know."

He paused to choke back the emotion, and when he resumed he was raising his voice.

"The Federals come by and burned us out!" he shouted in a voice filled with emotion. Young Buffalo leaned back and watched Braddock's hands. His own hand was on the handle of a pistol he kept hidden under his vest. He had no idea what he could have done to get the white man mad at him, but he was prepared to defend himself if necessary.

"I go to old man Omohundro, our neighbor down the road, and he tells me the soldiers had a fight with my pa and my two brothers and killed them in the house while it burned. Says I shouldn't feel bad because they shot at least three bluebellies themselves. Then I ask him where Robert and Johnny and their families go after the soldiers left and you wouldn't believe what they tell me."

His voice had calmed down, and now he leaned over toward Young Buffalo, as if the next part of the story were an intimate detail meant only for a few trustworthy ears. Again Young Buffalo leaned back.

"Well, says my neighbor. The slaves done got sold to Clyde Hillis in Jackson a month before. I tell him that's gotta be a lie cause my pa loved them folks too much to sell 'em. The old man gets kinda snippity on me then, says it ain't no lie, the slaves are gone and so is all my best land, to the bank in Jackson that loaned him seed money last year and never got paid back."

Braddock took out a short-stemmed pipe and began to pack it with tobacco. Young Buffalo took some interest in that, but he did not get out his own pipe, and he was too proud to ask the white man for tobacco—he knew white men were stingy. Braddock was so into his story by now that he did not offer any tobacco to the young Crow warrior, although his manners were usually better than that.

"Can you believe that while I was fightin' the biggest battle of the war, some damn banker was taking my Daddy's land away? Can you believe that? I'll tell you this, my friend. Most of the folks at home are all for the Confederacy, but I wanna tell you I got no use for it."

Abruptly Braddock realized he had run out of conversation. For five long minutes both men stared into the flames and watched sparks rise with the smoke toward the heavens. Young Buffalo then stood up with a suddenness that startled

Braddock and almost made him go for his gun. The Crow stuck out his hand and shook Braddock's hand vigorously, with a grip of iron. As quickly as he had arrived, Young Buffalo was gone, leaving Braddock without even his name; for in his nighttime campfire stupor, Braddock had forgotten even that.

Young Buffalo walked to his pony, his ears attuned for any noises behind him. His late grandfather, Walks In The Pine Woods, used to tell him about white men. "They are not our enemy," he would say, "so we must be nice to them. But they are not our friend, so you must not trust them. You may meet a white man of the spirit, and he will pray for your soul and give you food and show you kindness. So you will think that all white men are kind. But it is not so. Many white men are crazy. You must not turn your back on them. They think that Absarokee or Lakota or Shoshone are like the ones without fires."

"Ones without fires" was an Absarokee description of the animals that were not like men, believing that though these creatures did not have the ability to make a fire, the Creator had given them other powers that He had not given to the people—powers that the people could not understand.

Walks In The Pine Woods had paused in his soliloquy because Young Buffalo wore a look of astonishment on his face. "You have a question, little one?" he said.

"They believe that we are the same as Lakota or Shoshone?" Young Buffalo asked.

"Most cannot tell the difference."

"It is as if I could not tell the difference between a rock and a tree," said the young boy. "And they believe that we are the same as the ones without fires?"

"That is the way they treat us, only you must understand that they do not think of the ones without fires as we do. They would not thank the spirit of the buffalo for giving us its life, because they believe the buffalo has no spirit."

"Surely the whites are wicked people," Young Buffalo had replied.

"Many are, but many others are simply ignorant," his grandfather replied. "I have heard they live in huge villages where the grass does not grow, that they have killed off all the ones without fires except *ichilay* the horse."

Had it not been his grandfather talking, Young Buffalo might not have believed what he was hearing.

"I am afraid of the white people," he said to his grandfather.

"It is good to not be around white people," the old man admitted, though he would not have conceded fear of anyone. "They know so little, and yet they know things that we do not understand," and Young Buffalo knew his grandfather was thinking about guns, and the strange thing they are made of, and their noise and how it kills with a bullet one cannot see.

"I have heard," the old man continued, "that when white men walk among the people, sometimes the people begin to die just by looking upon them."

The following year, when Young Buffalo saw his first fort, he had been afraid to go inside. But Running Wolf wanted to trade there and Young Buffalo's mother wanted to see some of the white men's things, so she took him in with her and for the next few days thereafter he waited to die. He did not understand why nobody died from going into the fort, because his grandfather always told the truth, but he could not ask, because the old man had died scarcely two moons after this conversation.

The result was that while Young Buffalo was very cautious when it came to whites, he was also very curious. Curiosity had brought him to Braddock's camp. Curiosity had made him drink in the white man's long speech, searching for words he may have heard before, hoping that the Great Power might help him understand, hoping that maybe the white man might begin to speak with his hands. None of this had happened, and yet, as he mounted his pony and raised his hand in farewell to the white man, he sensed that this one, at least, would not kill him either with a gun or a look.

Braddock stood up and walked toward the Indian as he mounted his pony. The ex-soldier raised his hand in response to Young Buffalo. Tired, lost, eternally low-spirited, he wondered if he needed to snuff out his fire and move, so the Indian would not come back and kill him. He thought it over. The Indian could steal his horse without taking the trouble to kill him. The Indian had not seen his weapons or any other tempting things to steal. The Indian knew where he was now and could watch him easily enough in the dark if he tried to move—he had heard Indians could see in the dark as well as a cat.

No, he would trust his instincts. That Indian meant him no harm. Still, he would sleep with his Navy Colt in his hand under his blanket. While he was ignorant of life on the plains, Braddock was not totally foolish or careless. And anyway, if the Indian took his life as he slept, maybe that would not be a bad way to go.

Young Buffalo kicked his pony into a stout trot. The moon had risen and it was as bright as the sun to a young Crow warrior with places to go. Young Buffalo had owl medicine. The night held no terrors for him. At night, alone on the northern plains he felt as safe as if he were home in his mother's lodge in Running Wolf's village. He would sleep later. The night here, alone in the silence, save for the soft clopping of his pony's hooves on the winter grass, was a good time to think.

He had more than proved himself in battle, which meant that he could take a wife. He wanted very much to have a wife but as yet he had seen none that pleased him. He saw how many men were with their wives: "Do this! Do that!" and the woman, quietly, because she had little choice, would obey. He wanted a woman who would do for him because she wanted to.

His mother had told him that that kind of woman wants a kind man more than she wants a great hero. "Never mind," he had said. "I have already enough ponies that a father would give me his daughter no matter what she thinks."

His mother had laughed. "The woman you want is one who has a kind father and such a father would not merely give his daughter to the highest bidder."

One other thing, he thought, as he slowed his pony down and rode carefully over uneven ground. He had seen too many squabbles in homes where there was more than one wife. It's all right, he guessed, for an old warrior to get a young wife later on when the first wife is worn down from too much work and too much child-bearing. An old wife can use a little help around the lodge. But when the wives don't like each other then the man has no peace. He'd met one man who stayed away from his village all the time because his wives gave him no peace.

He would not let that happen to him.

Chapter 9

Sometimes two villages would camp together, and that was a special time for the village of Running Wolf. Running Wolf's band was not a very large group, and folks just got tired of seeing the same faces day after day. They all had friends and family living with other bands, but for most of them, their favorites lived in the village of Gray Coyote.

Crow villages often moved every ten days or so, especially in the summer when the smell of decaying garbage got very strong very fast. There were only so many good rivers and creeks along which to camp so they were bound to run into each other from time to time. Young Buffalo had been thinking about Gray Coyote's village since they had last crossed paths at the end of winter and he had become aware of a particular young girl.

Her face was pretty, and her body trim and athletic, but what grabbed his heart in a fist was the look of earnest contentment he saw on her face as she performed the arduous task of working a piece of buffalo hide into pliant leather. So on this late spring day he waited for Gray Coyote's people to erect their tepees and settle into their camp routine, then he put on his best leggings and moccasins, fixed his hair in the best Crow fashion, fetched his best hunting weapons, mounted his best hunting pony, and rode through Gray Coyote's village on the way out to his favorite hunting route.

At first he didn't see her, and he found himself tense with worry that perhaps she had died, or her family had moved to another village. He slowed his pony's patient walk almost to a crawl, watching from a distance as he passed by their arc of lodges. In front of the last tepee were a half dozen girls, seated in a circle, playing a game with sticks, laughing, singing the chant that went along with the game. He drew his pony a little closer, brought it to a halt, and looked carefully at each one of the girls—as if he were just passing by and had stopped just to see what was going on.

She was there, with a happy smile on her face, young, but almost a woman by Crow standards, enjoying the company of her friends, engrossed in the game. Although all the girls were chanting, he imagined that he could make out her voice, and it was a sweet voice, not too high and shrill, but not husky either. He was still shy with girls he did not know, but he was so interested in watching her that he did not notice his pony slowly edging over toward the girls, until one who had her back to him sensed his presence and turned around.

A little flick of his heels and the pony broke into a slow trot away from the girls. He did not yet know her name, and was not even ready to talk to his friends in Gray Coyote's village to find out about her. The possibility of learning that she was already pledged was so grim that he decided not to commit to an interest, not now, not yet. Seated tall and straight and proud, he urged his pony into a leisurely rocking gallop that took him down to the Little Bighorn Valley.

He found a familiar deer trail that led up a steep, grassy slope away from the river and he followed it away from the villages. There were fresh hoofprints along Lodge Grass Creek, and he knew they were from a hunting party in his village that had been out since morning. His friends Big Chin and Blue Shirt were among that party. He wanted to find them and ride with them so he would not be thinking about the girl.

He rode his pony to the crest of the hill and looked across the valley. He thought he might see them far off in the distance, returning home with a couple of kills. He was surprised to see them coming in on a run, much closer than he had thought they would be. He rode back down the hill and crossed the creek and rode directly toward them.

Big Chin spotted Young Buffalo as he emerged from a coulee, and shouted to him.

"Big camp of Big Bellies down where the big cliffs bend!" he shouted.

Big Bellies! Gros Ventres, their enemies from the north. If they were down here on the Greasy Grass, it could only be for the purpose of attacking the Crows. The hunting party galloped down the valley, past the camp of Gray Coyote, into Running Wolf's village. Young Buffalo peeled off from the party, rode directly to the lodge of Gray Coyote, and told him the news. The chief and several of his important warriors wasted no time but mounted up and rode down the valley to an area outside Running Wolf's tepee where already the important men of the village were assembling.

"Many warriors," Hawk Appearing was explaining. "Too many to fight." But others in the hunting party were not so sure.

"Only Big Bellies," said Big Chin. The chiefs sat quietly and listened to the young men argue for a few moments, then Gray Coyote raised a hand for silence.

"I will send out His Medicine Is The Wolf to see for himself. He is our best scout and he does not let his heart get in the way of his head." He nodded and a tall, quiet warrior wearing only a breechclout slipped silently from among them. He and his pony were gone within a few seconds, and then the young warriors started to argue again.

"No more talk," Running Wolf interrupted. "Get fresh horses. See to your weapons. Whether we fight or we run, we must be ready." The men scattered to their lodges.

Young Buffalo went back to his mother's tepee. "There may be a fight," he told her. "Start packing, if we decide to leave instead of fight."

"Lakota?" she asked, calmly.

"Big Bellies."

She nodded, and began to fold up blankets and pack them in large leather bags. All around the camp there was plenty of hustle but no panic. Everybody past the age of six knew what they were supposed to do. The older boys were out getting the pony herd together while the women and old men were packing. But the tepees stayed up, while the people waited for the word to come from His Medicine Is The Wolf. As the time dragged by, some of the people began to get nervous and one fainthearted family actually began to pull the hide down off their lodgepoles.

Young Buffalo brought out his rifle, a percussion cap muzzle loader that was one of a dozen Running Wolf had bought from a white arms trader the year before. It had cost the little village not their best horses, but their biggest. Half the rifles had proved to be poor specimens but Young Buffalo prized his weapon and kept it clean and oiled, unlike that of most of his cohorts. Big Chin had hefted his own rifle one day and sneered, "Why do you treat your rifle as if it were a baby? Feel how strong it is. Nothing can break it, this new rifle. Look!"

And with that he threw it into the dust and jumped up and down on it. Then he loaded the gun, pulled back the hammer, aimed at a tree fifty yards away and pulled the trigger. The rifle bucked and both braves could hear the wood splinter as the bullet split the bark.

"You see?" asked Big Chin, turning and walking away like a man who had proved his point and had nothing else to say. But Young Buffalo knew better. He had talked to a warrior named Pointed Head, the best shot in the village, and Pointed Head explained that a rifle could take a lot of abuse for a while, but it would wear out before long if it were not treated right. So now, even as he waited for the return of His Medicine Is The Wolf, he rubbed the weapon down with a rag and checked the action.

He heard several shouts, followed by the rapid sound of galloping hooves, and the heavy breathing of an Indian pony. His Medicine Is The Wolf leaped from his pony while it was still in motion and let it continue on until one of the boys of the village grabbed the lead and brought it to a halt. Young Buffalo joined a dozen others in front of Running Wolf's tepee.

"There are many of them," the scout conceded. "More

men than in our two villages together. But . . ." He smiled. "The leader is Hairy Nostrils."

A great laugh arose among his listeners. How the Big Bellies could follow such a man was beyond their comprehension. Hairy Nostrils wore a mustache, like a white man, and his battle tactics were just as funny.

"Let's send the women out after him," said Blue Shirt. Other warriors laughed their agreement.

Running Wolf stood up and motioned for silence.

"The Big Bellies are great warriors," he said. "You know that brave men can make a war chief great no matter how foolhardy the chief may seem to be. Still, it would be good to take that blowhard and scalp his upper lip."

Another round of laughter split the afternoon.

"Let us go out and make them sorry they came," said Running Wolf. "I will carry the pipe."

Gray Coyote rode back to his village. Meanwhile Young Buffalo and his cohorts stripped almost naked and prepared for battle. In less than five minutes, Running Wolf was leading his contingent onto the plain, where they met up with Gray Coyote's warriors, and on they rode.

Across the valley they could see a windblown cloud of dust—a bigger cloud of dust than the one they were making. As usual, they would be outnumbered.

Running Wolf made his decision and communicated it to his warriors: We must not retreat in the face of a superior force or we will be wiped out.

"Attack strong!" he cried. "Ride into them, and kill!"

They had the advantage of the downward slope. On a ridge they sat their ponies and watched the enemy as it topped a swell and headed into view, a larger force, but not so large as to intimidate them. As the wind swept feathery clouds across the blue sky and made the grass shiver, Running Wolf raised his right arm, then brought it down, and the men swept down the grassy slope. Hairy Nostrils spotted the Crows in plenty of time, pointed them out to his warriors, and urged that they meet the Crows on a dead run.

There was nothing fancy here, no flanking movements, no retreat toward a better position, no pause to dismount and fire. The two groups simply charged each other from opposite sides of the valley letting out fearsome demonic screeches and whoops.

Hairy Nostrils had planned to halt and fire a volley into the Crows just before the two armies came together. He did not expect the headlong recklessness of his adversaries which carried their ponies into his before he could give the command to fire. Some of them fired their weapons anyway, without effect, and then their ponies absorbed the impact of Running Wolf's horsemen.

The Crows rode headlong into the horses of their enemy. Hairy Nostrils' ponies staggered and some were even knocked off their feet by the stalwart Crow ponies, but most of the warriors rode past one another, and though several men were injured, there were no mortal wounds. For a while, the opposing warriors were so mixed up among each other that all was dusty confusion, but before long Running Wolf managed to get his men back together and they rode around the Gros Ventre warriors to put themselves between the attackers and the Crow villages.

Now the Gros Ventres had to reorganize before they charged, and while they did, the Crows pulled back up the slope to give themselves the best position. The two sides fired at one another but they were more than a hundred yards apart now and the bullets and arrows did little damage. The Gros Ventres moved forward and the Crows backed farther up the hill. There were so many of the enemy, and Running Wolf's warriors had no cover, only the upward slope. They must stay between their villages and their assailants. The Gros Ventres were fighting well. If the Crows lost their nerve and fled, their women and children could be slaughtered. Running Wolf knew his young men would not lose their nerve, but the enemy was too many.

They were on the ridge now. They could retreat no farther, or the enemy would have the high ground. They stood their ponies in a long line, their shields shining in the noon sun, sweat glistening on their bodies, the wind fluttering the feathers on their heads and shields and lances.

Hairy Nostrils was no joke now. Two strides ahead of his men, he led them forward to the foot of the slope, then upward, walking slowly, preserving their ponies. For one time in his life, Running Wolf could not come up with a logical choice for his men. He felt no fear for his own safety, but he felt great trepidation for the people of his village, and that trepidation was paralyzing his powers of judgment. The Gros Ventre line was so long that it flanked the Crows on both ends, and there were more warriors mounted behind the first line.

The Gros Ventre line continued to move forward, slowly but confidently. At any moment they would charge.

It was the reckless, foolish Big Chin who broke the spell.

The young man left his position on the left flank and moved to a place in the center and thirty feet ahead of the Crow line. He leaned left and dropped his shield and lance to the ground. Curious, the Gros Ventres halted their advance and watched.

Big Chin pulled his rifle from its scabbard, leaned left again, much lower, and let his rifle fall gently to earth. He pulled his pistol from his waistband and dropped it into the grass. He did the same with his ammunition bag, then his knife.

The Crows were as curious as the Gros Ventres. What was their crazy, headstrong young warrior up to? Especially curious was Running Wolf. His moment of paralysis was over. His mind was going a mile a minute.

Having rid himself of his weapons, Big Chin now began to sing his battle song, then drew his feathered coup stick and raised it over his head. So that's what he was up to. Unarmed, he intended to win honors by riding to the enemy and touching as many as he could with his stick. Counting coup on an uninjured enemy was the ultimate test of bravery in battle.

The Gros Ventres saw what he was doing and they were enraged. Big Chin had his blanket tied around his waist. Now he untied it and grasped it firmly in his left hand. He held his reins in his teeth and somehow continued singing. With his heels and knees he urged his pony forward, first into a trot, then into a dead run down the hill. His fellow warriors screamed their war cries in support of their courageous brother.

Down the hill he dashed, toward the enemy, his blanket

in one hand, his coup stick in the other. As he approached the enemy, they began to shoot but they could not seem to hit him. As he closed in he began to wave the blanket over his head, then in front of him. Some of the nearby horses shied, spoiling the aim of their riders. Other warriors held their fire for fear of wounding or killing their cohorts. He was among them now, riding in and out, touching first one then another with his coup stick. He worked his way past several, including one who swung a tomahawk only to lose his seat when his blanket-wary pony bucked him off. It seemed impossible that Big Chin should survive such a foolish charge. Either his medicine was irresistible or the enemy was so incredulous that they simply could not concentrate on killing him. He, on the other hand, had a big, fast, agile pony that shied away from every movement of the nearby warriors. The whole thing was happening so fast that without the immediate threat of death none of the enemy could make the moves necessary to end the charade.

When he had worked his way close to Hairy Nostrils, he swung his coup stick and smacked the chief hard across the face. The chief howled and fired his pistol, but not only did he miss Big Chin, he wounded one of his own men. The blood shot up from the man's leg and he was suddenly dizzy, reeling in his saddle, falling.

Hairy Nostrils let out a bellow of rage. The men closest to Big Chin rushed him and it was then that Running Wolf gave the order to charge. With a mighty ululating screech the Crows flew down the hill toward their distracted enemy and suddenly there was not a battle, there was a chase, with thirty Crow warriors chasing nearly fifty Gros Ventres across the valley. There was some shooting and two or three men fell, but mostly the raiders ran for the hills on the opposite side of the valley.

Young Buffalo, in the center of the line, charged with his brothers until he saw the Gros Ventres scattered along a half dozen hilltops, with Crow warriors still harassing them. He turned his pony around and raced for the spot where Big Chin lay in the grass, the long lead of his pony still firmly grasped in his teeth.

Running Wolf had split the enemy into several scattered

forces, any one of which he could handle with the men he led. He chose a group on a hill to his left. His men galloped up the slope and the warriors they challenged disappeared. If there was one main skirmish it was on the center hill, and there the redoubtable old Two Rivers was causing havoc with his lance.

It was a day when Gros Ventre bullets and arrows would not go straight. All around the sounds of battle were giving way to the sound of the summer wind hissing in the grass like a thousand snakes. Young Buffalo knelt in the grass beside the limp form of Big Chin, who was wearing a colorful array of bruises and bumps, but other than a few abrasions, he showed no wounds. He was breathing freely, lying on his back. Young Buffalo took the lead of Big Chin's pony, reached up and grabbed hold of the waterskin, and bathed his friend's face.

Stupid, stubborn, rash Big Chin! Had he conceived his foolish one-man charge as the distraction that might change the tide of battle? Had he striven for an act of legendary valor? Or had he just decided to show off for his friends, believing with all the faith of a fool that he could ride through the enemy and emerge unscathed to the cheers of his cohorts? Young Buffalo knew with all his soul that without the one-man charge of Big Chin, the Gros Ventres would have destroyed the Crow force, then stormed the villages and killed or captured the women and children.

Big Chin opened his eyes just as most of the Crow warriors began to abandon their pursuit. The Big Bellies had all ridden back to their camp. Running Wolf had dispatched His Medicine Is The Wolf and three others to keep an eye on the enemy. He was not at all certain that, once reunited, feeling the strength of their numbers and their anger at being routed by a much smaller force, the Big Bellies might not try another attack.

Running Wolf would not be caught by surprise.

Chapter 10

His Medicine Is The Wolf did not return to the village until the following morning. As soon as the scouting party appeared, Running Wolf called a council for all the men of the village. He sensed from the leisurely trot of the scouts that the Big Bellies had left, and he wanted everybody to get the news. He dispatched a messenger to Gray Coyote's village and by the time the scouts had tied up their ponies, the men from that village had also assembled in the large space in front of Running Wolf's tepee.

Running Wolf stood back and let his scout report. His Medicine Is The Wolf at first stood in silence, the faintest of smiles playing around his usually impassive face. Tall, painfully thin, pockmarked and painted and leathery, he was the man every boy in his village strove to emulate, and the men respected him no less.

"The Big Bellies have packed up and started for the north country," he said.

Nobody said anything. They knew there was more.

"We let them go home to their north country," he said, and his listeners laughed.

"But before they went away, Hairy Nostrils called the men together."

"To mourn for those they lost?" asked Blue Shirt. The Crows could not guess at the losses of their enemy, because the Big Bellies had retrieved those who had fallen, and taken them away.

His Medicine Is The Wolf made a puzzled face. "They had a victory dance," he said.

Running Wolf ran his tongue around the inside of his cheeks. "My brother, let me understand. We chased Hairy Nostrils half way back to the cold country and they called it a victory?"

"I do not think their hearts were in it," said the scout. "Either that or the Big Bellies are not very good dancers. It was like our scalp dance, only they had no scalp."

The wise chief trusted His Medicine Is The Wolf, but the scout had been out all day and was very tired, so Running Wolf sent Big Chin and Young Buffalo west to see if the Big Bellies were really gone. The two young warriors galloped out past the camp of Gray Coyote, across the valley where the battle had taken place, and on to the site of the big village the scout had reported.

When they arrived, the found that the Gros Ventres had left in a hurry. Quite a few lodgepoles were strewn across the campground, and in several cases the poles were still in place. Several packs had been left and, unbelievably, two ponies were grazing along a creek bottom.

In the center of the campground they found a single wooden framework that might have been used for a ceremony. Hanging from the framework, blowing in the breeze, was a small dark object. Young Buffalo dropped down from his pony, walked over to the frame, and examined the object.

"It's a scalp," he said. Big Chin's eyebrows arched quizzically. The Crows had lost no warriors in the battle.

"A very old scalp," Young Buffalo added, and his friend understood. The two young Crows tethered the Gros Ventre ponies and headed out following the tracks of their enemies toward a difficult mountain pass.

"They must be in a big hurry to get away from Absarokee country," Big Chin said with satisfaction as they rode easily over the wide trail made by the fleeing Gros Ventres.

"It seems that way to me," Young Buffalo agreed. "But if you are right, then why did they hold their dance before they went?'' The two thought in silence for several minutes as they rode on with a warm breeze drying the perspiration on their necks.

"Maybe Hairy Nostrils thought it was good medicine,'' Young Buffalo suggested. "Or maybe he wanted to lift the spirits of his people. They would have been very sad.''

Big Chin made a sour face. "Or maybe,'' he said, "Hairy Nostrils is just crazy. Why do all these people—Big Bellies, Lakota, Cheyenne—why do they all say, 'Crow small people, we can go and take their horses, and their women, and their country, and they will be too few to fight us'? How many times must we drive them away before they understand? Why are they so foolish?''

"Because after all this they still do not know us.''

All this conversation had been carried on with a light heart. They were proud of their victory, proud that they had been selected to confirm the flight of their adversaries, proud to be young Crows who had counted coup, killed the enemy, and stolen their ponies. It was a beautiful summer day and the grass in this valley smelled fresh and sweet. On days like this life seemed sweet and endless.

"I must tell you this, my brother,'' said Young Buffalo, suddenly serious. "Do you see this sky?'' he asked.

"As blue as any summer sky could be,'' his friend smiled. "Our chiefs have always said that our country is the best country there is, and that is why the others want to take it away from us.''

"Look to the country of the morning sun, Big Chin,'' said Young Buffalo.

Big Chin halted his pony and turned eastward. "What am I looking for?'' he asked, annoyed. He hated when Young Buffalo gave him a riddle. Big Chin did not have much imagination. He hated riddles.

"Do not look with your eyes, but with your heart. If you look with your heart, you will see a little dark cloud that gets bigger and bigger, and some day will storm all over us.''

Big Chin's face wrinkled up the way it always did when he was trying to think. He kicked his pony into motion and they rode on for perhaps a minute before the wrinkles vanished. "Ah, I know," he said. "You are talking about the white man."

"I am not talking about the white man," Young Buffalo replied. "I am talking about the Lakota, with all their tribes, and so many people that they are like the grass in the valley. My uncle is very wise and he told me it is the Lakota who will come into our country and try to take the land away from us."

Big Chin laughed. "They tried to do that once, don't you remember? You gained great honor that night. We beat the Lakota, so badly that they left some of their dead behind. We have taught them a lesson. They will not be back."

Young Buffalo shook his head. "You and I, we know so little," he said. "We defeated one Lakota band, or one tribe, or one something, but my uncle says that if the Lakota ever united to drive us out, we had better be on our fastest ponies or we will be roasting over the fires of the Tetons."

They traveled north until noon the next day and never did catch up with the fleeing band of Gros Ventres.

"Ho!" said Big Chin, weary from the long ride, and still feeling his bruises from the battle. "I do not think they will stop until they are in the cold country, what do you think?"

"I think they believe the entire Absarokee people are on their trail. We have found pack straps, lodgepoles and even a pony along the way, and they never stopped to get them. It is sad when an entire people loses its spirit."

Big Chin brightened. "Why don't we follow them until nightfall, then steal their ponies?—I mean the whole herd. They must be so sad and tired that it would be hard for them to fight back. Think of how our people would feel if we returned to the Greasy Grass driving an entire herd of Big Belly ponies."

Young Buffalo thought for a moment. "My brother," he said. "If they caught us they would kill us. What glory is there meeting death at the hands of those we have just driven out of our country? If we are successful, we will have done a bad thing. Right now they are going home saying that their chiefs made a mistake, that they should not have attacked great fighters like the Crows. If we steal their horses they will say, 'Those cowards the Crows stole our ponies when we were defeated.' They will feel disgraced. They will rally their brothers and they will come back twice as big as yesterday.''

"Then we will kill twice as many," laughed Big Chin, warming to the subject.

"Yes, and many of our warriors will die too."

Big Chin thought about that for a moment. "But my brother," he said. "It is no tragedy for a warrior to die in battle against the enemy."

"That is so, but let me remind you one more time that our great enemy is the Lakota. The Big Bellies might not come down again for years, but the Sioux—the Sioux will always be sneaking through the coulees, thundering over the plains, trying to destroy us so they can take our land."

"We have beaten them too."

"They have many warriors," said Young Buffalo. "They can lose many battles and still come back and fight again, but let the Absarokees lose one great battle and there will be no more Absarokees. Can't you understand this?"

"Our warriors fight too good to lose a battle," Big Chin insisted.

Young Buffalo sighed and reined up. "Let's turn for home," he said. "We'll claim our ponies on the way, and look a little closer at their camp. Maybe they left more behind than we think."

Young Buffalo did not really think so, but Big Chin was a simple, gullible man and it didn't take much to tempt him.

Chapter II

Young Buffalo was a big young man in the eyes of his village. Still very young, he had already led a successful war party, counted coup, and taken a weapon away from an enemy in the heat of battle. He had been initiated into one of the greatest of the Crow warrior societies, the Lumpwoods.

But he was still living in the lodge of his mother, and he was lonely for a young woman to be with. There were girls in his village who were interested in him, not only because he was a rising star with many ponies, but because he was known to be kind and good-natured. But none of these girls excited his interest. The only girl who had touched his heart, and that only from a distance, was the young girl in the village of Chief Gray Coyote.

He went to his friend Big Chin and discussed his problem. Big Chin was not half the warrior Young Buffalo was, but he considered himself to be twice the lover. He had all the answers.

So a week later they went riding out, with hunting on their minds, or so they said.

"We did not tell them what we were hunting," Big Chin said as the village disappeared behind them.

They followed the Little Bighorn for many miles until they came to a creek they called, simply, Mud Creek. They turned northward on the creek and found the village of Gray Coyote an hour later.

"I have come to see my cousin White Hot Smoke," said Big Chin to the first familiar face, which happened to be the chief himself. Gray Coyote was adjusting the saddle on a strong black pony, a pony with long legs and a deep chest that promised both speed and endurance; a pony for a chief.

"I see you bring a friend, also for White Hot Smoke?" asked the chief, who had many strong memories of his youth and therefore was suspicious of all young warriors.

"We were hunting together, pursuing the deer westward but finding none."

"No matter," said Gray Coyote, who was as smart and cunning as the animal for whom he was named. "Young Buffalo honors us with his presence. Our village is bigger, our young girls many." In a blur he was up on his pony and trotting away from the tepee circle.

"Do not anger the jealous young men of our village," he said, then kicked his pony, which splashed across the creek and up a slope on the west side of the camp.

The two young men dismounted and led their ponies through the village until they came to the lodge of his cousin. They tied their ponies in front of the lodge and peeked through the open flap.

They could not see Big Chin's cousin in the dim light of the small fire, only her wrinkled old grandmother and two camp dogs who took in the warmth of the hearthfire.

"Bearface!" The sound came from deep within the lodge. Young Buffalo saw his friend smile.

"I cannot see you," said Big Chin. "Have you finally become so ugly that the eye can no longer look upon you, my lizard-lipped cousin?"

Young Buffalo heard a giggle from within the darkness of the tepee, and then, abruptly, a thin, agile, mischievous figure leaped through the opening. She collided with Young Buffalo, hard, but his solid body did not flinch. She bounced off him and found herself seated unceremoniously at his feet.

"Oooh!" she exclaimed, as if in exaggerated appreciation of the young warrior's firm body. "What do you have here," she asked, "a rock wall on feet?"

"He is my friend, Young Buffalo," said Big Chin.

"Not *that* Young Buffalo," she said, again with a peculiar, humorous exaggeration in her voice.

"Maybe another Young Buffalo," he replied.

"Some kind of buffalo, I think," she said, and the way she looked him up and down as she said it tickled him. There was no bridle on her tongue; she said what she wanted to say and didn't care who did or did not approve, or so Big Chin had told him on their long ride to the village. Her face was very thin, which made her clear dark eyes look like huge pools into which he could plunge, if only he had the nerve. Her neck was long and thin, her breasts small, her feet small, and yet her shoulders were wide enough to promise stamina on the long journeys. A smile constantly played around her mouth, yet never actually happened.

He had come to the village to get to know another girl, and yet he felt instantly drawn to this one.

Big Chin could be stubborn; he could be dense and willful and self-absorbed, but even he could see instantly that his friend was taken with his cousin. What he could also see was that the feeling was mutual. He was delighted for reasons of his own.

"My friend here came to meet a girl whose name we do not know," said Big Chin. Young Buffalo thought he saw the almost-smile leave the face of White Hot Smoke, but he wasn't sure.

"What does she look like?" she asked.

Young Buffalo and Big Chin both tried to describe her but they made little progress until Young Buffalo spotted her on the other side of the camp, carrying a load of firewood from the creek. He pointed her out.

"Ah, that is Wild Berry," said White Hot Smoke. "She is very pretty, don't you think?" she asked.

"Let me walk over to her and bring her to meet my great friend," said Big Chin. But as soon as he left, White Hot Smoke took Young Buffalo by the arm and led him toward the creek.

Young Buffalo looked back at his friend as he let White Hot Smoke lead him away from the camp. White Hot Smoke saw the look and gave his arm a yank that knocked him off balance.

"I am so so sorry," she said in a tone that indicated she wasn't sorry at all. "I need to talk to you about something."

Her relaxed, informal way caught his full attention. The truth was, he had very little intimate experience with females, and he wanted some, very badly. Her warm hand on his arm gave him a good feeling. She was female and she was pretty and she was forward, which meant that he would not have to guess whether she was interested. He positively hated girls who made him guess.

They climbed down the creek bank. She kicked off her moccasins and he did the same. It was an unusually warm spring day. The water felt good and cool on their feet as they walked along the creek bed. She kicked water on him, then ran away, down the creek, away from the camp. He followed her, without any sense of hurry. He thought he knew what she was doing. If he was right, then good things would happen before the end of the day. If he was wrong, well, he was good-natured and didn't mind being teased. As for the girl he had come for in the first place—he thought he might like this one better.

The area was not unfamiliar to him. His village had camped along this creek in the past. He knew where a thick stand of pines lay about a mile upstream, and he thought she might be leading him there.

But when he reached that place he was still alone. There was a series of small rapids ahead. He climbed the rocks, carefully, then saw the path which led upwards alongside the creek before disappearing among a rock formation. He knew she had taken the path even before he spotted the footprints.

He left the creek and walked along the path, between two walls of rock, up to the top of a hill and then across a ridge that led down into a wooded area layered with soft pine needles.

"Here!" came a voice from a small clearing in the pines. She was sitting on a rock in the clearing, watching him, the corners of her mouth almost—but not quite—smiling.

This is foolish, he thought suddenly, chasing a girl he had never met before through the hills into a forest—for what? Still, he walked over to her. Her hands were out-stretched, and took his.

"My cousin Bearface—I am the only one who calls him that—when we are together he talks about you. I have heard so much of you. He said that next time he came visiting he would bring you. I have been waiting."

Young Buffalo laughed. "My brother brought me to meet you, did he not?"

"He loves me very much. He would like me to have the best."

Now the almost-smile faded to blank seriousness. "When I saw you, I was surprised. He had told me about Young Buffalo in the hunt, Young Buffalo in battle. He did not tell me how handsome you are."

He regarded her statement as an invitation. He put his arms around her and was surprised to feel her head against his chest.

"Oh, you do feel good," she said, her playfulness gone.

Gently he picked her up from the rock, and lowered her to the floor of pine needles. He knelt beside her, held her and began to kiss her, expecting her at any moment to stop him and say, "Let's go back to the village and get to know each other better before we . . ." but she did not stop him. She hugged back. She petted back. She responded to all his touches with touches of her own. He had killed deer. He had killed a buffalo. He had stolen ponies and defeated men in battle at such a young age. But he had never done this. Many lesser young men had already done this and he had ended the winter filled with a fierce desire to love a woman.

Now, as they felt each other's skin warm and close, he knew there would be no stopping until they both had what they wanted. This was no time to think. This was a time to feel.

Chapter 12

Big Chin got what he wanted too, in another hillside pine grove, and when he and Wild Berry had finished they strolled back into the village hand-in-hand and headed for her mother's lodge. For Young Buffalo and White Hot Smoke, the ending was different.

As they walked back to the village, her eyes stared sadly at the face of Young Buffalo. For a while he did not notice, so alone was he with his thoughts—thoughts of sweetness and gentleness, and passion, and release, and joy. He could scarcely believe that he had found a girl he could love. Young as he was, he had wondered if such a time would ever come, and when it did, would he know it? Why, of course. What could be simpler? Then, somehow, her gaze pierced his thoughts.

He stared back, walking more slowly, wondering if her look was one of sadness or just serious thoughts of her future—perhaps thinking of her future with him, perhaps worried that he would just ride out and never see her again.

"Why do your eyes frown so?" he asked. The two of them stopped and faced each other.

"I have wanted you for so long," she said. "You are surprised, but I am not surprised that my cousin could keep such a secret. I know he makes a big noise about himself, but he would never hurt me by telling another my secret thoughts. He has known for long. Once I did not want him to tell you because I was too shy. But now there is a secret I could not even tell him.''

"Will you tell me?" he asked.

She nodded. ''I must. The last . . .'' her voice quavered and he saw a path of tears down either side of her nose. He took both of her hands in his but she freed them, gently, from his grasp. ''The last full moon Lone Eagle came to my father to ask for me.''

"Lone Eagle?" This was serious. Lone Eagle was a great warrior with many coups and many horses.

''He offered more ponies than any man in the village had, for as far back as anyone could remember. My father does not need the ponies, he has so many himself, but he was so honored he could not refuse.''

"Did you tell your father you did not wish to have Lone Eagle?"

''I started to, but when I did, he said that it would be a great thing to marry Lone Eagle, that he is a great man, that any woman would be honored to have him.''

"But—" he began.

''But you were only a dream then,'' she said. ''How could I know you would come to me? How could I know that you—'' she interrupted her speech and almost smiled ''—how could I know that you would be so . . . that loving you could be so sweet? You were only a dream.'' And at that she began crying and walked away from him.

Such was Young Buffalo's character that he did not spend time mourning his loss. He watched her walk away, his heart weighed down with sadness. But before she was out of sight his sadness gave way to hope. She and Lone Eagle were not man and wife. How could he get her away from him? It would be difficult. A bold man could maybe bully a timid man into giving up his claim on a woman, but Lone Eagle was afraid of nothing save possibly going into battle without first unbraiding his hair.

Still there had to be a way. He would talk to Big Chin, then Blue Shirt, then his mother, maybe even Running Wolf, for advice. He laughed a laugh that had no pleasure in it. They would tell him that to cross Lone Eagle could be deadly.

The next day, as they rode, Big Chin saw that his friend would be bad company all the way home. Before they had left, White Hot Smoke had told her cousin about the impending marriage.

"Ah," he had said, angrily. "So you give yourself to Young Buffalo and tell him nothing until it is too late? You are like the otter, full of play and mischief. Do you want him to fight your tomorrow husband?"

"No. *No*. I would kill myself if he suffered on my account. But I had to be with him. I had to. I've been thinking about him for so long that it seemed impossible, with him so close, not to be with him. Even now, it is not my being with him that seems unreal, it is the thought that I should have to be without him!"

She had wanted to say more but she knew that Young Buffalo would be back from getting his pony ready for traveling, and she did not want to see him. Not then. Maybe not ever.

It was a hot summer afternoon on the Rosebud River. On this day four Absarokee bands were camped side by side along the river. They had come together only three days before and spirits were high, because the people were doing one of their favorite things—riding up and down the river visiting friends and relatives they had not seen in many moons.

The river was white with children splashing and swimming. On a flat stretch an eighth of a mile from the creek, boys were racing horses and carrying on mock battles, trying to touch each other with sticks without being touched. Observing from a discreet distance were some of the old men, keen to discover future mighty warriors among the playful youngsters. The villages were all camped on the east side of the Rosebud but there were a few young men of the Lumpwood Warrior Society scouting to the west. They were not looking for buffalo or other game. The summer buffalo hunts would begin a week or two later, when the last of the bands joined them. These scouts were on the watch for the enemy.

Red enemy.

"I still do not understand why Sits In The Middle Of The Land has us roaming up and down the river like ghosts looking for a place of peace," Big Chin was telling Young Buffalo.

"I have told you more than once and still you do not understand," said Young Buffalo, on the edge of his patience. "I believe you are so anxious to be home with your wife that you do not want to be a warrior."

This was a gently cruel joke on Young Buffalo's part. Having lured his friend away from Wild Berry, Big Chin had had a clear path to marry her, only to discover that her sweet face hid a temper. Neither his village nor Wild Berry's village enjoyed having them, so noisy were their battles. Young Buffalo naturally did not resent the fact that his friend was the one stuck with a sharp-tongued woman. On the other hand, Big Chin did not complain about Wild Berry. He was a fighter, he said, and she loved him, and sooner or later he was bound to tame her down.

"You are truly not angry with me, my brother?" he had asked Young Buffalo a year after he had been married.

Young Buffalo smiled. "I feel as if you have taken a bullet meant for me," he replied.

Big Chin did not smile. "That is because you do not know her the way I know her," he said.

Time had passed. The tongue of Wild Berry got even sharper. Big Chin spent much of his time away from his lodge, but when he was home he was happy, even when Wild Berry was giving him grief. On this day he was curious, but not complaining, about his long scout up and down the Rosebud.

"You still do not speak much, my brother," said Big Chin. "You used to laugh often, but since White Hot Smoke married, it is as if the sun went out of your life."

Young Buffalo nodded. "It was hard for me to find a woman I cared for," he said. "Wild Berry is very pretty, but I believe that had I met her the day we came to her village, I would have learned of her temper before I asked for her."

"But see how fast you wanted my cousin," said Big Chin.

"I would not have been mistaken about her," Young Buffalo responded. "And I know she felt—now—"

His eyes were squinting to shut out the sunlight as he peered southward. "Do you see?" he asked.

"You mean the dust?"

"Down below that rock shelf there," he said, nudging his pony into a quick trot.

The trot became a paced gallop as the two young men approached the dust cloud. Before they were close it was clear that they were about to encounter a party of about a half dozen warriors. Sioux warriors.

"They are not painted," Young Buffalo observed. "They are not trying to hide. They wish to be seen."

"Why do you suppose they have come?"

Young Buffalo shook his head. "I do not trust them," he said. "They come in peace, to find out if we are many and how we are camped. Maybe there are a thousand warriors hidden behind that hill. They eat our food, then ride out beyond that hill to tell their chiefs where we are and how to attack us. Bad people, the Sioux."

Still, when men came in peace, it was the way of the Absarokees to present them with hospitality. Not trusting them, Young Buffalo waited until the six Lakota men wearing many-feathered war bonnets were close to the first of the Crow villages camped along the Rosebud. He and Big Chin had been following them along a ridge above them. Now they rode down the dusty slope at an easy gallop. Halfway down he saw that they had been spotted. The six Sioux turned to face him and Big Chin, and one of them raised an open, empty hand as a sign of peace. Young Buffalo's keen eyesight missed nothing. Rifles were holstered. Bows were nowhere in sight. Only the leader with the upraised hand carried a lance, and it was pointed skyward.

Young Buffalo slowed his pony to a walk, raised his right hand, and across the yellow-green grass, beneath the endless deep-blue summer sky he approached the six Sioux with stolid dignity. Below, the people of the nearest Crow village had spotted the approaching Sioux, and now many of them stood in bunches, silently, watching the courageous young warrior as he approached his enemy, alone. He had told Big

Chin to hang back, that at the first sign of suspicious movement he was to turn his pony down toward the Rosebud and bring an army with him to avenge Sioux treachery.

This time there was no treachery. The Sioux ignored the activity they noticed below, ignored the scurrying as chiefs and warriors scrambled for their ponies. At this moment it was the young Crow warrior taking the risk, but in a few more moments the risk would be theirs.

"We come in peace, Brother of the Long-beaked Bird," said the oldest, a wiry man with a hard, seamed face, seated upon a beautiful bay pony.

Young Buffalo knew that he did not have sufficient rank to bandy insults or challenges with the honored Sioux, the tail of whose war bonnet trailed far down his back.

"I will take you down to our villages," he said calmly.

As he led them down to the Rosebud, he could see activity below; swift riders heading to the nearby villages to alert them of the approach of their deadly enemy. Soon the most important men of the villages would be arriving in the village of Sits In The Middle Of The Land. In his village a council would be held that Young Buffalo could not attend, because the scouts were trusted with guarding the villages. It would be just like the Sioux to lull the Crows with noble visitors, then attack them in the middle of a council.

But on his way down he could see Crow warriors swarming the hills around the great encampment, searching for the enemy. There would be no surprise attack on this day. Three Crow warriors approached the six Sioux from behind. They kept a discreet distance, but Young Buffalo knew they were there to protect him.

The six Sioux rode like cavalry, in columns of two, and showed complete disdain for the warriors scouring their flanks and watching them from the rear.

Young Buffalo entered the village first, to the open admiration of the people who lined the main path. But his eyes were not on the people of the village, they were on the distant hills, the treeless hills of buffalo grass. They were empty, but he kept expecting to see long lines of Sioux warriors appearing suddenly at the top, ready to swoop down upon his people. The Sioux chiefs would point to the hills and say, "There are the men of the mightiest people on earth. They will wipe you out if you do not hear our voices. Do not think to use us as hostages, for we would gladly die for the sake of our people."

What would Sits In The Middle Of The Land and the other chiefs do then? he wondered.

Not far from the lodge of that Crow chief was a grassy clearing. The Crow chiefs were waiting there, standing quietly, wrapped in blanketed dignity like Roman senators in their togas. Young Crow warriors seized the bridles of the Sioux chiefs and helped them off their ponies. Two of them were old, their bodies stiff from the long ride. Young Buffalo's fears subsided. There were at least a dozen Lumpwood scouts riding the hills. They would have sensed any large Lakota force even before they could see them. Still, he saw Running Wolf tap Blue Shirt on the shoulder and point to the east. Blue Shirt in turn pointed to several scouts who followed him to where their ponies were tethered, and soon they were riding a dusty trail away from the Rosebud.

He saw Running Wolf whisper something to Sits In The Middle Of The Land. That chief nodded, and Running Wolf signaled to Young Buffalo to join them in council. Ceremonial pipes were being unwrapped with loving care. Food and drink were being hurriedly readied, not for a joyous banquet, but for the grim hospitality that would precede the discussions that were about to take place. For all the wisdom of the village chiefs and the medicine men, nobody in the village knew why the Sioux had come. So numerous were their bands and tribes, so multitudinous the numbers of their warriors—even when a fraction of them came together—that they normally behaved with pride and arrogance in the presence of their Absarokee cousins. Yet here were six men of great honor, risking their lives in the midst of their aggrieved enemy, for what purpose?

Chapter 13

The eastern horizon was dark and three stars shined in the heavens by the time the rituals were through and the time for talk had come. The council fire flickered on the faces of the six Sioux and fourteen Crows seated close to the fire, but behind them, dark and shadowy, were many people of all the villages, straining to hear what might be said.

The cautious Crow chiefs had called in the Lumpwoods, who had been out all day, and replaced them with Foxes, men of a rival warrior society. The tired Lumpwoods ate quickly and did not linger to listen, but returned to their lodges and slept, knowing that their services might be needed later and wanting to be at their best. Only several leaders of that society remained, and Young Buffalo, the one young warrior whose youth only multiplied his prestige.

Sits In The Middle Of The Land stood up and welcomed the Sioux chiefs. "For many moons we have longed for peace with our mighty Lakota neighbors," he said. "We care only to hunt, and raise our families, and enjoy the land. When others come and ask our permission, we always say, come, share our buffalo, our elk, our deer, but when you are done hunting, return to your own lands and feed your people there. We hope the great chiefs of the Teton people have come to share our desire for peace as you have in the past shared our buffalo."

The speech was short, dignified, both humble and proud;

but softly, beneath the humility, came the warning: you may share the bounty of our land, but the land itself is ours.

The Sioux chief was an astute man who understood the Crow language well, its nuances as well as its broad meanings. In another day he might have been annoyed by what he considered the impudence of a tribe so small that his people could rise up and step on them if they chose, but on this day he had to be realistic. The Crows were not only fiercely proud. They were fierce warriors who would make important allies in a fight against a common enemy.

Slowly he rose to his feet, defying the painful arthritis in his knees. He was not yet a very old man, but his body suffered from the effects of too many battles, too many buffalo hunts, too many hard winters. Still, he concealed his pain and stood straight up, his lined, handsome face impressive in the unsteady glow of the council fire.

"Brothers of the long-beaked bird," he began. "Our stories tell us that once, in another land, at another time, we were one people. Then we went different ways and our tongues changed. Tonight, as I speak, you must watch my hands so you can understand what I am saying. Yet if you close your eyes for a moment, and listen to me, you will find that you almost understand what I am saying. That is the sadness that has come between our two peoples. We 'almost' understand each other.

"In better days 'almost' was enough. Your young men would raid our villages to steal a pony or two, and ours would do the same, but we would not stay mad. But a bad thing has happened that has changed everything. That bad thing is the white man, so now, 'almost' is not enough. We must understand each other now, or we will all perish at the hand of the white man."

Ah, so that was it. The important men of the Crow people gathered around the fire all knew why the Sioux were here. But as the Sioux chief had said, they almost understood. What they were about to hear was not quite what they expected.

The Sioux chief looked around the fire at the Crow chiefs and warriors. For several moments he was silent, as if he expected an argument. Young Buffalo had a strong feeling the Sioux chief felt uncomfortable seated among the Crow lodges. The young Crow warrior resented the discomfort, which he knew stemmed from the chief's innate feeling that the Sioux were a superior people. Others must have felt the same as Young Buffalo, because there was no attempt at polite ceremonial dialogue. They wanted the chief to say his piece and go home.

Whether or not the Sioux sensed the feelings of his audience, he did not wait long in silence before he opened his heart to his cousins.

"You know of the many bands of Lakota that cover the land like the long grass of the river valleys," he said. "We are divided and we do not always get along so well. But our chiefs are together now. Brule, Oglalla, Miniconjou, Blackfoot, Hunkpapa, Sans Arcs, Ooh-hen-on-pa—all of our people have tired of giving our land to the *Wasichus*. Our brothers of the striped arrows have joined with us, as well as the good hearts."

The Crows understood his signs, knew that the *Wasichus* were the whites, the striped arrow people were the Northern Cheyenne, and the good hearts were the Arapahos. They were not surprised. All three had been hostile to the Crows for many years.

The Sioux chief again fell silent, as if he had words to say but could not bring himself to say them. Finally Running Wolf spoke up.

"I understand," he said. "You are going to war with the whites. All the bands of the Sioux and all your friends. This is what you come to tell us?"

The edges of the Sioux chief's lips curled downward as if he had a mouthful of underripe persimmons. His audience was not making it any easier for him. He sighed and unconsciously put his right hand on the hilt of his knife, which was stuck in the broad sash tied around his waist. Young Buffalo almost laughed aloud.

"I have come to you because I know that you are close to the *Wasichus*," the chief blurted out, the words fairly fleeing from his mouth as he signed. "I am here to tell you that we know your warriors scout for the *Wasichus*, you and the filthy Arikara. I am here to tell you that we will wipe out the *Wasichus* and if we find you with them, helping them look for us, we will wipe you out too. Then we will go to your villages and wipe out all your women and children too—all of them. We will pluck the feathers of the long-beaked bird until no one will ever remember that you once rode your fine ponies across our plains.''

The Crow chiefs showed no emotion, not because they feared the Sioux chief, but because they did not wish to give away their feelings to the arrogant man who dared to ride into their villages and threaten them like this. Young Buffalo exercised no such restraint. He made a rude noise with his mouth. The Crow chiefs did not chastise him, aloud or with a disapproving look. They may have been above such demonstrations, but he was free to express himself as he wished.

And he did.

He stood up, walked over to the Sioux chief, and kicked dust on his moccasins. He was standing within three feet of the man, his blazing eyes unflinching as they burned their way into the Sioux chief's brain.

''Who is this pup?'' the Sioux chief asked. ''That he might be the first to surrender his blood to The People?''

''This pup has already poured Teton blood into the native soil of the Absarokee,'' snarled Young Buffalo. ''This pup has stolen Sioux horses without taking a quick breath. This pup has taken a rifle away from one of your warriors and smashed his head with it. This pup has counted coup, taken scalp, killed too quickly for your warriors to begin his death song, and caused wives of the Teton to gash themselves in mourning. There are empty lodges in your villages because of this pup.''

The Sioux chief was losing his composure, not because someone was berating him, but because the Crow chiefs were allowing such a young man to humiliate him before their assembly.

''You will regret this!'' he growled directly at Sits In The Middle Of The Land.

The young Crow leader stood up and took a step forward, not toward the Sioux chief, but into the light of the fire, where everybody could see him.

''You came here today to make an alliance with us,'' he

said. "I know that was your intention. Yet such is your hatred of us, such is your contempt, that your request for alliance jumped from your mouth as a threat. Let me ask you this, Chief Of The Many Snakes. Suppose we stood by and did not help the whites, and you did win a victory over them? Would you then come to our villages and thank us and embrace us as brothers? No, you would try again as you have before to take our land away from us. Why are we friends to the white man? Because to us you are just like they are, only you are crueler than they. Every few years we must go out and whip you just to remind you to let us alone. We hate having to do that. We would rather just steal your horses from time to time, not that your horses are much good."

The Sioux chief breasted the torrent of insults in silence, but he remembered each one, and stored them away for future reference.

"I will tell you this," Sits In The Middle Of The Land said calmly. "We sat with you and smoked with you, and prepared to hear what you had to say as if you were our brother. We thank you for letting us know what was truly in your heart instead of trying to fool us." He put such a hostile twist on the end of his last sentence that the Sioux chief felt constrained to threaten one more time.

"If you are thinking of killing us here, now, I would counsel against it," he said. "If I die, before the sun is completely gone my warriors will be black against the sky—" he waved his arm around the horizon as if to summon his legions. "And they will burn your villages to the ground."

Running Wolf spoke up at last.

"Big words from such a little man," he said, though the Sioux chief was taller than he. "My wolves have been watching you since long before you knew you were being watched. They have been watching all the valleys. If your great bands of warriors are riding today they must be riding in the clouds. Do not be afraid. We do not kill those we have just fed in our village. We are not treacherous. The treacherous always seem to be the ones who most fear treachery. Do not fear. Go from us in peace." He shot a look of withering fury at the Sioux chief. "But I would counsel you to go quickly. I would be ashamed for my people if you took so long to depart that one of our foolish young warriors might forget that when you came to us you were our guest."

Running Wolf smiled unpleasantly. "I have a gift for you," he said, reaching out to him. "This is a very good quirt. After you mount your pony, use this quirt. Use it plenty. Make your pony hurry from our valley, for its own sake." At that, Sits In The Middle Of The Land kicked at the fire, scattering the logs. The meeting was over.

Chapter 14

With such a large gathering they could not remain in one spot for more than a few days. There was too much garbage fermenting along the creek banks. So the various villages scattered once again and, except for the intensive scouting activities of the warrior societies, there was no evidence that the people were overly concerned by the Sioux threats.

"Threats are how a lazy man tries to get his way," said Running Wolf. "Men who intend to act do not warn their enemy by threatening him first." Still, he was responsible for the safety of his village, and to that end he kept the Lumpwoods and Foxes on the hills and ridges of their domain, and the chiefs were in almost daily communications with each other via courier. Frankly, they warmed to the challenge and had no doubts that they could lick the Sioux wherever they found them.

Not that they always licked the Sioux. Once in a while the Sioux licked them, but the children of the long-beaked bird were eternal optimists, and as such, their memory of victories was considerably more vivid than any recollection of their defeats. And considering the numerical superiority of the omnipresent Sioux, the Crow had performed great work over the years.

As the Sioux threat receded from his daily pile of concerns, Young Buffalo's thoughts again turned toward all the girls he had known. Mostly he thought of White Hot Smoke, now married to a Fox Society warrior in Gray Coyote's village.

He hated himself for thinking about somebody else's wife. Long ago his grandfather had told him that many villages had been divided because one man could not keep his hands off another man's wife. In his desire to be the perfect embodiment of the Crow warrior he had been determined never to desire another man's woman.

But this was different. She had not wanted to be the wife of that man. She had been bought years before, by a man who had awed her father by the size of his gift. Now that Young Buffalo had the luxury to think of something other than the Sioux hordes, he thought about her, night after sleepless night, until he felt certain that he would go out of his mind. He could not see a way out for himself, so white hot did his flame burn. He decided to make a clean breast of it with his grandfather. Perhaps the old man might say something so damning that he might break the spell, at least.

Instead, his grandfather galvanized him with new dreams and hopes.

"Let me tell you about the customs of our people, my son," said the old man to Young Buffalo as they looked at each other across a small fire in the lodge of Young Buffalo's mother. "Some customs are part of a people's heart, and some are just excuses for making other people do as they're told. I would have never made your mother marry a man she did not want to marry. If you love your child, why would you do such a thing to her?"

Young Buffalo shifted his eyes thoughtfully from the face of his grandfather to the dancing flames, then back.

"Is it so then, that the girl liked you, and that she did not like the man she was pledged to marry?"

"I am certain that this is so. She told me." He looked down at the fire. "I felt so sad for her when she told me."

"And this husband of hers, is he a dangerous man?"

Young Buffalo tilted his head indifferently. "Dangerous enough to stand up to me, not dangerous enough to whip me, I believe." Young Buffalo looked straight into his grandfather's dark eyes. "Grandfather, surely you are not advising me to steal another man's wife, are you?'' He put his hand over his mouth in amazement.

His grandfather smiled. ''I am a believer in customs,'' said the old man, ''especially customs suitable to the moment. Tell me carefully, because I must be certain of the truth. Did you not say that her husband was a member of the Fox Society?''

''I know that to be true,'' Young Buffalo said.

''And I am honored that you are a Lumpwood. Do you not know that after new leaders of the societies have been elected, you can go to another village and kidnap the wife of a man from the Fox Society—if you have been close to her before?''

There had been many rituals and customs to learn after he had joined the Lumpwoods and he was ashamed to admit that he and Big Chin had not always been attentive during the teachings. He blinked his eyes, not believing the words he was hearing from his grandfather. Surely this must be a dream.

''Is this true?'' he asked.

''I am old but I am not yet foolish,'' the old man replied. ''This is an old custom between the two societies.''

''But grandfather, if I were to do such a thing, would it not cause bad blood? Would he not come to our village to steal her back? We have enough trouble with the Sioux on our hands, without us being at each other's throats,'' said Young Buffalo.

''It is like you to think of your people even when you are in love. But do not fear. You would be taking a risk by going to Gray Coyote's village and taking the girl, but if you succeed, he must let her go, or he and those with him will be disgraced. Such a thing happened once while I was young and the warrior who lost his wife was warned by his chief against doing anything to get his wife back.''

His eyes were shining as he met the young warrior's gaze with his own. ''Young Buffalo!'' he exclaimed. ''If you want this girl, go to the village of Gray Coyote and get her. Otherwise I do not want to hear anything more about her.''

There were just the two of them on this raid, a raid on their own people. It was perhaps as dangerous as when they went to the Sioux village. Brave as Young Buffalo could be in the face of the enemy, he was more daunted by the idea of facing an angry husband than a village full of Teton warriors. He had explained his project to Big Chin and his reckless friend was so delighted that he volunteered to go with him before Young Buffalo could even ask. Big Chin's heart was as big as the sky. Young Buffalo could not love White Hot Smoke any more than he loved his friend Big Chin.

At this time the two villages were not camped close together, and Young Buffalo was glad. They started from the Bighorn River valley on a bright early summer's day and headed eastward toward the valley of the Rosebud River. They could tell they were close when they emerged from a coulee and spotted a pair of young Crow scouts walk-trotting their ponies across a ridge about a mile distant.

"Let's lead those boys a chase!" Big Chin suggested.

Young Buffalo shook his head. "We don't want anybody knowing we're here," he insisted. "My brother, for today you must not think that we are playing a game. That is your cousin sitting in her lodge crying because she must lie every night with an ugly man she dislikes." Chastened, Big Chin fell in behind Young Buffalo and the two young warriors followed the scouts, and that's how they learned the exact location of Gray Coyote's village. But as soon as they spotted the smoke rising up from the valley, they peeled away and made camp in a thick grove of willows along a creek that drained into the Rosebud. They tethered their ponies in a small field of grass, and stretched out to wait for nightfall.

Shortly before dawn they crept into the village on foot. Big Chin pointed out the tepee his uncle had given White Hot Smoke on the occasion of her marriage. Noiselessly they crept over to the tepee flap, opened it, and peeked in. In the dim light of glowing coals Big Chin could see his cousin sleeping away from the fire, close to two of her little cousins. There were perhaps seven people asleep in the tepee, including her husband, who was sleeping closest to the fire on his back, snoring loudly, a huge buffalo robe wrapped around his body.

Young Buffalo studied the scene quickly but carefully, and pointed toward the Fox warrior's wrist. He had a rope tied at one end to his wrist and at the other to the wrist of his young wife, the way some warriors protected their ponies from midnight thievery. Neither of the young men had ever seen a man do that to his own wife. So, he was a jealous man already.

Big Chin smiled and carefully cut the rope. Then Young Buffalo crawled over to where White Hot Smoke was sleeping, gently laid a hand over her mouth, and when he saw her eyes open wide, signaled for her silence.

As if she had been prepared for her abduction, White Hot Smoke grabbed a bundle and preceded her two kidnappers out of the tepee. Young Buffalo followed her, then came Big Chin, holding the end of the rope, which proved to be about twenty feet long. They paused in the pre-dawn stillness. White Hot Smoke whispered that her bridled pony was tethered just outside the tepee circle, along with a pony that belonged to her husband. She mounted one, Young Buffalo mounted the other, and they waited for Big Chin.

Big Chin was nothing if not sporting. Not for him a quiet retreat into the night. The two lovers watched as he stood up and tied the end of the rope to one of the smoke-flap poles. The other end was still tied to the wrist of White Hot Smoke's husband. Big Chin took a firm hold of the rope and gave it a stiff yank. A ferocious roar arose from within the tepee. Young Buffalo swept Big Chin up behind him and the two ponies galloped through the tepee circle and across the shallow creek while the village came awake like a swarm of nocturnal hornets.

The initial reaction was confusion, then a scramble for ponies, then a milling around as the villagers tried to understand what, if anything, had happened. In his fury White Hot Smoke's husband jerked so hard on the rope that he pulled down the smoke-flap pole and the interior of the tepee began to fill with smoke. Blinded and choking, he had to locate his rifle and find his way through the door flap, then remember to untie the rope from his wrist. By the time he and the other warriors had established some direction and momentum, the kidnappers had ridden to where they had hidden their own ponies. They set loose the pony of White Hot Smoke's husband, mounted their own animals, and headed for the ridge that led out of the valley. Far behind them they heard several pointless gunshots. All three quirted their ponies and up they went, over the ridge and down into the adjoining valley, along the Rosebud.

They had left their pursuers far behind but they knew they were not out of danger yet. They intended to cross the river, ride east for several miles attempting to hide their trail, then execute a wide circle west for the long ride home. Ahead they could see a thin ribbon of pink on the horizon, the first blush of dawn.

Something was not right. The horizon should have been a fairly even line of hillside against sky, but it was uneven.

And moving.

A dozen Sioux were almost upon them by the time they understood what was happening. Big Chin pointed southward—he wanted them to make a quick escape into a cedar grove along the river.

"We have to go back and warn the others!" Young Buffalo cried.

"No, no!" Big Chin insisted, but the other two had already turned and he had no choice but to follow, with the sounds of war whoops ringing two hundred yards behind. They rode back toward the village, back toward the murderous intentions of White Hot Smoke's husband.

Ahead they could see their Crow pursuers. Young Buffalo motioned to his two friends to turn southward abruptly while he rode into the teeth of Gray Coyote's band, at the head of which loomed White Hot Smoke's husband. When he was within a hundred yards of them he rode back and forth in front of them to indicate that he had sighted the enemy. He received a volley of gunfire for his troubles. He continued to ride back and forth between the two charging contingents. When he saw, before and behind him, both contingents reining up in a cloud of dust, only then did he sheer off and head southward for the Rosebud.

Still, he could not just run off and leave his tribesmen in a dubious contest with their hated enemy. No sooner was he out of the way than he brought his pony to a halt, drew his rifle, and waited to see what would happen next.

So startled were the two groups that both turned and rode

off into the gloom, the Crows back to the creek line, which they could easily defend, and the Sioux back to their home village, knowing that there would be no surprise pony raid on this night. Young Buffalo kicked at his pony, crossed the Rosebud, and found his friends on a slow trot exactly where they thought they'd be.

For a moment they dismounted. White Hot Smoke threw her arms around Young Buffalo. Her scent was sweet to his nostrils and the feel of her body against his galvanized him. "What have you done?" she asked. "There will be war between our villages."

"If your husband wishes to avoid disgrace not only will there be no war, there will not be a sound out of him once he understands what has happened."

The three had remounted and were riding at an easy gallop across a long stretch of flat plain. All around them was silence. The pre-dawn dark covered them like a blanket. Young Buffalo pointed to a low rocky bluff ahead, then waved his arm to show that beyond the bluff they should swing westward.

"Does this mean we can be together now?" she asked with wonder, and his heart leaped at the joy in her voice. For the first time in his life he heard a girl he longed for voice her longing for him. Accomplished warrior that he had been, only now, with her acquiescence, did he feel the final bonds of adolescence slip from his shoulders.

"You are mine now and forever," he said, simply, as the hooves of their ponies clattered over the rocky ground and began their wide arc toward their home village.

Chapter 15

When they made it back to the village of Running Wolf they paused only long enough to collect Wild Berry, one old lodge skin and a set of old lodgepoles, and then headed westward for a short hunting trip which would double as a honeymoon for Young Buffalo and White Hot Smoke.

Young Buffalo's family advised against the journey. The Sioux were on the warpath against the whites. That meant that any whites might be capricious and angry enough to take out their wrath on any Indians they might encounter, Sioux or not. Likewise, ambitious Sioux bands looking for white scalps would be just as happy to kill a few Crows foolish enough to allow themselves to be overwhelmed by superior force.

But Young Buffalo and Big Chin felt invulnerable. There were isolated mountain fastnesses where game was abundant and people were not. Places difficult to get to, but not for very young, very strong people like Young Buffalo, Big Chin, and their women.

The four young people spent a week there together, the sweetest time of Young Buffalo's life. By day he and Big Chin stalked elk and deer and birds. Often they did not have to stalk for long. A few hours of pursuit, a killing shot, and they were back in their camp with hides to be staked down and dried, and meat to be cooked and dried. They were young and filled with love and energy. When they came back they did not loaf while their women did the hard work. They helped the women with the butchering, and kept their knives sharp, and when the work was done, they splashed in the cool mountain creek like children and then each couple found a cool bit of mountain shade where they spent the afternoon.

During this time they did not see another human soul. Life was better than any of them had ever dreamed. They had intended to spend several more days in this most beautiful of all places, but on the tenth day they found a small buffalo herd. The two men killed a young female, did some field butchering, dragged the pieces home on an old bull hide, and realized that although they had brought four extra ponies, they had killed all the meat they could carry. That night they feasted on buffalo tongue and haunch, and lay out under the stars, listening to the night sounds and feeling the mountain breezes rushing over them like soft, very light, mountain water.

"I wish we could stay here forever," White Hot Smoke whispered to Young Buffalo. "Why can't we stay here forever?"

"Our village needs us," said her new husband. He thought for a moment. "We need our village."

"I need only you," said White Hot Smoke, so softly and lovingly that Young Buffalo briefly could have considered another way. He put two fingers to her lips, two fingers that told her to say no more, that he was weak from feelings and did not wish to make a bad decision out of weakness. And then, slowly, sweetly, perfectly, they conceived their first child.

The following morning the four of them made ready to leave for their home village. While they were loading meat on the spare ponies, Young Buffalo suddenly put a finger to his mouth and all four froze. There was a breeze blowing from the east and Young Buffalo thought it had carried a man-sound with it. Like deer frozen in a clearing, they listened for the sound to be repeated, and when it was, Young Buffalo knew its nature immediately—the clanking of a canteen against a saddle.

The two young men rushed to a hill overlooking a nearby

trail. Perhaps a hundred yards away they saw a lone figure on a mule, trailing another mule behind him. On the back of the second mule they could see mining equipment. The clanking thing had not been a canteen, but a large mining pan.

Now what could they do? They knew that white men could be mean when they were afraid. All it took to scare some white men was the sight of an Indian. They lay and watched the miner, a stubby, short-legged fellow wearing a huge floppy-brimmed hat that cast a shadow over his shoulders. He also wore a new pair of overalls and a well-worn pair of high-topped boots. His right cheek bulged with chewing tobacco and every time his mule's gait rocked him forward he spat a tiny quantity of juice forward over the mule's head. Chzzt! Chzzt! Chzzt! Sometimes the spit didn't quite clear the mule but landed between its ears, and then the animal would toss its head, stop and look back at its rider, who would curse and give the mule a light kick. Chzzt! Chzzt! Both of the young warriors found white men to be strange and wonderful characters, to be observed from afar but not to be approached unless absolutely necessary. They watched and waited until they were certain the prospector would continue down on the lower trail.

"What is he doing up here?" Young Buffalo wondered aloud.

"Looking for yellow metal," said Big Chin, who had heard many stories about the extreme things white men would do to possess gold.

"Yes, but why here? I have never seen such things here. Do they just go anywhere hoping to find it?"

"Maybe he is on his way to somewhere else," Big Chin suggested.

"Then he is lost," Young Buffalo replied. "You know the trail ends beyond the next ridge."

They had their little caravan moving east—the four ponies they were riding, four carrying heavy loads of meat, and one dragging lodgepoles and carrying the heavy buffalo-hide lodge cover. There were no travois. Crows did not use travois like the other plains tribes. In the world of the Absarokee everybody rode on the backs of their ponies.

The going would be slow but they were in no hurry. It was a beautiful summer day with a sky as deep-blue as the turquoise that upon occasion showed up on the bodies of dead Utes.

Slowly, quietly, they made their way along a ridge line, down into a valley, up across a saddle and then into the next valley. They traveled mostly across open grassland, sometimes across bare rock or meager piney forest. What thoughts they may have had they were not communicating. Words were not necessary. Among the four was a sweet bond that would be tested through the years. Suffering always tested bonds, and in between the good times there would always be suffering. It was the lot of their race, or of their time. For the men it was the freedom, the occasional glory, and the constant striving that made the suffering bearable. For the women, it was simply their need and obligation to keep it all together—the village, the families, the children. Let the men play at power. Let the men have their glory. The women would cheer them but they knew that life was more important than glorious death, and life would go on because of them.

Early in the afternoon some wispy cirrus clouds sailed across their sky and as the afternoon wore on, other clouds followed from the west, thicker, lower, and finally, darker. Although there was still plenty of daylight left, they camped in a valley that sheltered them from the winds that were already hissing through the grass. The women put up the tepee and built the fire while the men unloaded the ponies and tethered them. They lugged all the food into the tepee and covered it with the big inner tepee liner that was not needed during much of the summer. They cut a large piece of venison and let the women roast it while they stood outside and stared anxiously at the sky. This might be more than an ordinary summer shower. They certainly did not want to be high up on some ridge with the lightning exploding from all directions. Still, a valley held its own perils.

They had tethered the ponies where the grazing was good but now they moved the animals closer to the tepee, though the grass was not as lush there. They made certain the ropes were staked tight to the ground, and then they stood by, speaking softly to the animals, who were growing restive in the hissing wind and the distant roll of thunder.

The men and their women ate silently, listening as the first barrage of hail began to pelt the tepee. The hail gave way to rain—rain that came hard at first, leveled off for a time, and then came much harder, blown horizontal into the west side of the tepee so loud that they would have had to shout to make themselves heard.

Night had come, but now was no time for sleep. To the roar of the rain was added the crack of nearby thunder, thunder high on the ridges, and lightning so bright it penetrated the hide and lit up the interior of the tepee. There was no wide-eyed fear on the faces of the four. Survival was a business and fear was a luxury they could not afford.

They were listening.

The wind let up and the rain pelted straight down. They had long ago extinguished the fire; now they closed the smoke flap.

And they sat still, listening.

And finally it came, first a gurgle, then quickly a roaring watercourse. A dry, dusty creek become a stream, then a swift-flowing river that threatened to fill up the valley. There was no choice. Quickly the men were outside, first pulling up stakes, then leading the ponies one at a time up the side of the valley, as close to the top of the hill as they dared. They tied the ponies' leads as securely as they could, then went back for more. The women struck the tepee, dragged the liner up the hill, and went back down for their bundles. There was no time for the lodgepoles. The bundles were thrust beneath the tepee liner. The women then crawled underneath, and the men sat beneath the edge of the liner, as close to the frightened ponies as they dared, trying to keep dry, but the ponies were in such a panic they had to come out and calm them down.

Beneath them the flood roared through the spot their tepee had occupied, sweeping their lodgepoles away like so many matchsticks. Above them the lightning continued to crash and the rain poured down, first in a vertical torrent, then in windblown sheets that sometimes hit the men so hard they could barely keep their feet on the slope of the hillside. But keep their feet they must, lest they tumble into the raging river below, to be swept into oblivion like their lodgepoles.

It was a long, varied nightmare, inky blackness broken by crashing flashes of lightning outlining panicked, plunging, gape-mouthed ponies, eyes wide with terror, trying to rip out the tether pegs so they could go screaming down the hill to their deaths. But Big Chin and Young Buffalo would not let them die. They exhausted themselves tugging on the leads of the animals, somehow trying to soothe them as they shouted over the horrifying sounds of the rain and thunder. And then it seemed like the rain was less than it had been, and the thunder was receding into the distance, and for one foolish, unreasoning moment, Young Buffalo wondered if the lone miner he had spotted on the trail the morning before had survived the night.

With the first grim blue light of dawn they wondered at the river that surged through the valley below. The lodgepoles, of course, were gone. Their arms ached from a night of holding their ponies. They had worked hard, but they knew that they were under the protection of the Great Spirit to have not lost a single one of their ponies.

They kept to the dry ridges and hilltops to avoid the surging creeks and the mucky flood plains. To do this they had to alter their route considerably southward, into land they did not normally travel. Both young men recalled the land from travels seven or more years ago, when they were still children. They had not been back because their chiefs had found too much white man trail and too little game. After the heavy rains it was difficult to distinguish tracks of any kind.

Until one day they came to a trail that had been so heavily used that even the cloudbursts had been unable to obliterate it. They found it made a perfect route eastward. They would travel toward the morning sun until they considered that they were at the right place for a northern swing. But their second day along the trail they were stopped dead by a huge cloud of smoke floating over the next valley.

Young Buffalo stopped the little train in its tracks. He hid the women and the animals in a coulee and directed Big Chin to a concealed position above the women's hiding place. Young Buffalo then advanced over a long steep grassy slope. This was no wildfire sweeping across the high plains. He could not imagine what it was.

He crawled to the top of the hill and searched till he found a position that could look down into the next valley. But what he sought was not in a valley. It was on a hill across the valley, a brand-new wooden stockade with many buildings inside, some of them two stories. The fire came from a hill about three miles down the valley. He had seen white men at work before. They had chopped down numerous pine trees to build the fort, cut the branches away, and arranged them in huge piles before dragging the logs to the site of the fort. With the fort completed and the cut branches dried out, the white men were burning them in a huge bonfire, one of the biggest he had ever seen. Far down in the valley below the fort, a large herd of cavalry mounts was busy munching on grass.

At last he understood the reason for the visit the Sioux had paid them. The whites must be building several forts, pushing their way westward to protect the big wagons with the round tepees on top. The Crows had no fear of the long wagon trains. The wagons traveled trails south of Crow hunting grounds and they certainly were not going to war against the whites just because the miserable Sioux asked them to.

In fact, Young Buffalo thought, it might be a good idea to visit the fort and arrange a little trading.

"Braddock!"

"Yes, Sergeant," said the skinny private, walking along the catwalk to where the stocky NCO was standing, hands on hips, squinting out across the valley.

"What do you see out there?" the sergeant asked.

Private Braddock tightened his grip on his carbine. "I'd say they was Injuns, Sergeant."

"Oh you would. Well, you might know that it might

make a huge difference if you was to know what kind of Injuns these was.''

''Mmmm,'' he said. He never cared much for the sergeant's way of making every observation a classroom lecture for a slow pupil. But he had a horse, he had a bed, and he had three square meals a day—a vast improvement in the past few months.

''Bad Injuns, I guess,'' he said, sincerely hoping to please.

''Well, bad is relative,'' said the sergeant. ''And by our standards those are pretty good Injuns, though I'm sure a few well-placed shots could make them into better Injuns. These are Crows, and they've saved our bacon a couple of times over the years. Truth is, they hate the Sioux, they breed the best Injun ponies on the plains, and they could find a gnat in a haystack and probably tell you its name if it was their haystack, doncha know.''

Other nervous privates had finally seen what the old sarge had seen and were rushing to the wall facing the direction Young Buffalo was coming from.

''Boys!'' shouted the sergeant, ''don't get all itchin' to shoot one of these critters. I b'lieve the colonel might be interested in findin' out whether they have seen Red Cloud lately. Lieutenant, can we open the gate and let 'em in when they get here?''

''Hell, Sergeant, send someone for the colonel. You know he's the only one can make a decision like that. Lisenbee, why don't you get ready to load that cannon you got there, just in case the colonel is feelin' kind of ornery this day?''

Chapter 16

Young Buffalo had been taught how to act with white soldiers. He arranged the caravan in front of the double gate, about fifty yards away, and he walked forward, standing still maybe twenty yards from the gate.

The doors swung open and he could see, arranged before him, an officer with yellow stripes down the sides of his trousers, a half-breed in blue breeches and a rawhide shirt, and two carbine-carrying privates flanking them on each side.

He walked through the gate alone, advanced to the young officer, and spoke to the half-breed. The caravan followed a few moments later, and the gates closed behind them with a wooden thud.

"Crow," he said, simply. "Friend," and he raised his right hand. "Friend of white man."

Young Buffalo didn't like the lieutenant, didn't like him on sight. He'd seen that narrow-eyed look before, always in the head of an angry, mean-spirited creature with a diffused sense of revenge. As if to confirm the young brave's feelings, the lieutenant walked toward the nearest building, entered, and let the east wind slam the door behind him. When he emerged he had in tow a neat, spiffy officer with gold leaves on his shoulders.

"Two bucks, two squaws," the lieutenant was muttering, "and a whole herd of those little beasts they call horses.

Stinking buffalo meat piled on the backs of their horses. I told Billy White Hat here that I didn't want the fort bein' stunk up by their damned buffalo meat but he says these are Crows, and Crows are our allies. Is that so?''

The major laughed. "You're new out here, Lieutenant. Tell you what. Next time we go huntin' for Sioux and Cheyenne, you watch who's ridin' up ahead of the column, their noses twitchin' and their eyes stuck on the ground or the horizon. Matter of fact, we need these bucks if we can get 'em. Without Crows up ahead we got no more chance a catchin' Red Cloud than we have of catchin' them white clouds up yonder." He swept his gloved hand majestically across the sky. Major Ryan loved grand gestures. Now he turned to the half-breed, a young man with a Shoshone father and a now-dead white mother.

"Hey Billy, will you tell these boys here that we need scouts and we're willin' to pay 'em?"

"Yes sir," said the half-breed without enthusiasm. Billy White Hat was not much of a tracker and he hated that the soldiers knew it.

"You," he said. "What is your name?"

"Young Buffalo."

"Major wants to know if you'll scout for us."

Young Buffalo was not interested. "Got to take our meat and get home to our village," he said.

"No-no!" Big Chin said urgently. "Pay good money," he said.

Young Buffalo nodded. "How much?" he asked the half-breed. Billy White Hat relayed the question to the major.

"Thirty dollars a month plus a carbine and ammunition," came the reply.

"No carbine, rifle," said Young Buffalo.

"Rifle," the major agreed.

"When?"

"Seven suns, we leave fort," the major told Billy White Hat, who relayed the reply to Young Buffalo.

"Good," said the Crow brave. "We bring back meat, ponies and women to the village. You need more wolves, we bring them."

"You let them go they'll never come back," said the interpreter, and an argument followed.

Young Buffalo was firm. "We don't leave our women at the fort. Go to village first or we don't scout." He swept his left arm in a horizontal motion that left no doubt of his commitment.

"You promise to be back in one week?" the major asked. Billy White Hat snickered but relayed the question.

"Seven sleeps," was the answer. "We go now." And without further delay he walked his pony to the closed gate, followed by Big Chin and the women with the pack ponies. The major nodded to the lieutenant and the lieutenant ordered the gates opened. Within fifteen minutes the caravan was out of sight.

"Major, you sure you should have let those Injuns out to tell their friends we're fixin' to go after them?"

The sergeant cocked his head. "Lieutenant, you be out here a little while and use that head God put up there on your shoulders, you'll find out that the Crows would ride with the Devil himself before they'd ride with the Sioux. Gotta understand. The Sioux hate us because we push 'em around. If we stopped pushin' them around they'd stop hatin' us. With the Crow it's different. The Sioux hate Crow because that's the way it is. Much more honor bringing home a Crow scalp than, say, bringin' home your mizzerable head-a-hair. And the Crow feel the same way about the Sioux. Good for us, you see, if we got the sense to use it."

"Well, I don't trust any of 'em," said the lieutenant.

"I'd trust a Crow scout a heap more than I'd trust a lot of lieutenants I've seen in my life," said the cheeky, beefy sergeant, then, seeing the red rising in the lieutenant's neck added, "Present company excluded, sir." He nearly choked on the "sir."

There had been a time when many of the Crows did not know the value of money. That was a long time ago. By this time the better-informed ones knew that their scout wages were considerably more than a private's pay. But privates like Wayne Braddock were nearly as expendable as the second-rate cavalry mounts they rode. Good scouts were in desperately short supply, such short supply that in these early stages of the hunt for Red Cloud, the sergeant had to make some guesses about scout material.

This time he guessed right.

Young Buffalo and Big Chin returned to the fort with Blue Shirt and Would Not Listen in tow. They had actually recruited seven braves for the adventure, but Running Wolf insisted he could not spare seven braves what with the Sioux threatening to come down on them. He told Young Buffalo that if they had not been getting ready to join Gray Coyote's village for the rest of the season, then he would not have agreed to let any of them go. He knew that he had no right to detain his young men, but he pleaded with Young Buffalo not to take any others, and Young Buffalo agreed.

There were two pairs of Arikara securing the flanks. Young Buffalo and Big Chin were well to the right front, a half mile ahead of the column, studying the grass for signs of their deadly enemy.

Crows could do what very few white men could do: study the ground in front of them hour after hour, all day long. Young Buffalo never got bored on a scout. Mile after mile, slowly, painstakingly, he read the grass, and found not a blade out of position, and yet he continued to read.

His pony stopped. Pressure from Young Buffalo's thighs? A light tug on the reins? Young Buffalo would have said that he had told the pony to stop; told it with his thoughts. He was off the pony's back immediately, studying a small area of bent grass, walking forward in a deep crouch, his pony trailing behind him.

More bent grass.

Big Chin was off his pony, ten yards over to Young Buffalo's left. This was a fairly large party they had discovered, passing in the same direction, but how long ago? The answer would not be long coming. Horses defecate when they feel like it, fairly frequently, and the condition of the manure tells the story.

More than a day ahead. But who?

They remounted. The ground was softer here. The trail was clear, and there was something in the air.

Old smoke.

When wood burns, there is an odor. After the wood stops burning there is still an odor of burnt wood, but it's different from when it was burning.

Old smoke in the wind, which had been blowing mild air in their faces all day.

Time for caution. He put his hand up and the major stopped his column as silently as possible, but not silently enough. Young Buffalo hated the clanking of canteens and the squeaking of saddle leather on the army horses. He did not want them anywhere near him until his eyes answered the questions his nostrils were asking.

While the Arikara scouts loitered on the ridge line, Young Buffalo and Big Chin descended into a valley watered by a swiftly flowing river twenty feet wide, bordered by brush, grassland, and only a very few trees. They looked down the valley and caught sight of what had yesterday been a wooden structure, but was now little more than a heap of ashes. They could see fencing that had been pulled apart, and several red blobs that they knew would prove to be butchered cows. Above on the ridge, the Arikara scouts signaled for the column to come on, and by the time Young Buffalo and Big Chin had arrived at what had been a ranch-house, the cavalry was descending the hill at a heavy-footed gallop.

The husband, what was left of him, was tied to the last bit of fence that remained upright. His unseeing eyes gazed in the direction of the destroyed house. In front of the house the two Crow scouts found a woman and two baby girls. The woman was naked and scalped. Her breasts had been sliced off. She lay on her back, her limbs all spread, mouth wide open in a last cry of desolate pain. The two babies merely had their heads bashed in.

The man's eyes had been gouged out, perhaps right after he had been forced to witness the last agonies of his family. He too had been stripped and scalped, his privates cut off and forced into his mouth in a final act of disrespect by his killers, who had finished him off by firing about a dozen arrows into his body, which looked so white in the overhead sun.

"Get away from there!"

The lieutenant had galloped in ahead of the column when he saw Young Buffalo and Big Chin inspecting the body of the dead man.

"Get a-*way* from here," said the lieutenant, grabbing Big Chin by the shoulders and pushing him away. "You bastards don't loot no white man's body, not in front of me!"

Big Chin did not stand for anybody laying hands on him. Too quick for the eye, his knife was in his hand.

"Don't do it!" said his companion softly. Big Chin backed up a few steps and put his knife away. Young Buffalo did not know what the lieutenant had said, but could tell he was angry at them, though they had done nothing to deserve it. White men were strange, hostile people and there were still times when Young Buffalo wondered how his chiefs could tolerate such capricious allies.

Oh well. They had been studying the corpse because one could often tell the offending tribe by the nature of mutilations inflicted on the victim. It didn't matter. He had seen the arrows. Definitely Cheyenne arrows. But he would not volunteer any further information. If they asked, he'd tell. Maybe. If he calmed down. How he would have loved to help Big Chin cut the heart out of the disrespectful lieutenant.

Now he, Big Chin, and one of the Arikaras rode more than a mile ahead of the column. They were moving at a steady trot, gaining ground on the Cheyenne raiders, but still very careful, just in case the enemy had spotted them and were preparing an unpleasant surprise.

Ahead was a narrow pass that went through a deep notch. The scouts stopped nearly a mile away and studied it carefully. They could see no signs of life, and yet they agreed that something about it did not look right. They couldn't have explained to anyone—not even themselves—what it was about the place that troubled them so deeply, something they saw but could not define. Something.

The lieutenant wanted to know what that something was.

"I think they're just cowards," he told White Hat when the interpreter attempted to relay the scouts' feelings. "That one is just sulking because I wouldn't let him set there and gloat over that poor devil's body back there. As for the other two?'' he shrugged his shoulders. "I guess Crows are just scared of Cheyennes, don't you think?''

The half-breed looked at the lieutenant and said nothing at first. White Hat respected the instincts of the two Crows and the Ree, but he did not want the lieutenant yelling at him, pushing him around, or calling him a coward.

"I cannot tell what they are thinking,'' he replied, letting his pony walk away from the lieutenant so the lieutenant would not ask him any more stupid questions.

"It does not smell right,'' Young Buffalo insisted to White Hat, who passed the words along to the lieutenant.

"What smell, what?'' he asked, angry, frustrated, wanting hard information and getting something else he could not understand.

Young Buffalo pointed, not with his fingers, but with his eyes. The lieutenant understood, and stared hard at the notch. "Okay, I see,'' he said through White Hat. "Good place for an ambush. So? How do you know they are there? Go up there and find out.''

Young Buffalo nodded, then he and Big Chin rode off, not toward the notch, but back from where they had come.

"I told you!'' the lieutenant hissed at White Hat, bitterly, as if it were the half-breed who was riding off.

White Hat shook his head. "They're not deserting us. They'll be back in one hour, two at the most. Tell you what, lieutenant. They may be afraid of losin' their scalps, but they're not *very* afraid. Maybe just enough afraid that they never sleep real deep.''

The lieutenant kept his column camped two miles north of the notch while the sun crawled across the bright blue sky. He walked back and forth muttering into his black beard, snapping his quirt against his boot top, waiting.

Private Wayne Braddock had sneaked off into the brush for a quick sip from a tiny metal whiskey flask he carried between his saddle bag and his blanket roll. Braddock was still so new in this outfit that he had not gotten friendly with the other soldiers, who were mostly Yankees from Michigan and Ohio, and German immigrants. Braddock was a bit of a philosopher. He recalled meeting Young Buffalo on a dark

night at his campfire. The Crow warrior had seemed like a
ragged vagabond then, a useless beggar with no more purpose than Braddock himself. But Braddock had been watching the Crow at work all day, careful, methodical, like a
very good carpenter, making no mistakes, guided by his
experience, not his emotions. The Tennessean stretched out
on his back, his head on his blanket roll, staring up at the
sky, and thought back to a time when he was the respected
son of a rising cotton farmer in West Tennessee.

The year before the war started he remembered his father
going down to Mississippi to dicker with a slave trader
about buying a family. The slave trader had wanted to sell
the father and the oldest son. His father had turned the trader
down, angrily. "If you think I'm gonna buy two bucks and
then spend the next year waitin' for them to get over losin'
their family, you're out of your mind!" his father had said.

"I wouldn't worry about that," the trader had said,
coldly. "You jus' put them together with a coupla wenches,
they'll forget the old women folk soon enough. Trouble with
you, Braddock, you insist on thinkin' of them as folks. They
ain't folks."

He remembered the relieved expression on the faces of
the family as he looked back while he and his father were
riding away. Those poor people couldn't understand that this
trader was determined to split them up because he thought
he could get more that way. Young Braddock was angry,
but the real reason he was angry, he knew, was that he had
taken a fancy to the oldest of three daughters, who the trader
said was sixteen and who was not afraid to look straight
into Braddock's eyes, daring him to bury his soul into her
body.

He did not have time to wonder where that family was
today. He heard hoofbeats. The scouts were back. Naturally
he was interested in what they had found out. His life might
very well depend on them, and since he had joined the cavalry, his life had begun to mean more to him.

Young Buffalo grabbed the bugle before the bugler could
get out the first notes. He turned to White Hat to explain.
"Tell the lieutenant that the Cheyennes are camped below
the notch on the other side. There is one lookout at the

notch. I think if we are very quiet, we can wipe out these Cheyennes.''

White Hat explained Young Buffalo's thoughts to the lieutenant, who smiled and clapped Young Buffalo on the shoulder. ''That's the spirit,'' he said, and Young Buffalo did not enjoy the the lieutenant's approval.

Chapter 17

The soldiers hated being on foot. Their boots were not made for walking, yet they were being asked to trek more than three miles in a roundabout journey that would lead them to high ground above the Cheyenne encampment. The two Crow scouts had departed fifteen minutes before. It was their job to kill the single warrior guarding the notch. There were a dozen Cheyenne, mostly armed with bows, against forty cavalrymen armed with carbines.

If they could keep the element of surprise, and hold off on the attack until the Crow scouts ran off the ponies, the attack would be quick and deadly, and there would be weeping in Cheyenne lodges once their bodies had been found.

They crept through the tall grass until it petered out at a rock shelf a hundred feet below the notch. The grass was thick and they were well-concealed, but the guard was standing in the notch. There was no question of sneaking up behind him and quietly cutting his throat. He could see all the approaches. The only way to kill quietly would be with a bow, a deadly shot to the heart. That would take luck as well as skill. Hit a rib and it might not be a killing shot. Best to lure him as close as possible if they were to even have a chance.

In soft whispers they discussed the problem. Young Buffalo nocked an arrow and waited while Big Chin gave the call of a quail. At first the Cheyenne guard ignored the sound, but Big Chin kept it up, patiently, at intervals, until he finally had the guard's attention. Then he stopped.

The guard was looking more or less in their direction but they were well-concealed in the grass behind some thick brush. As soon as he looked in another direction, Big Chin resumed his quail call, just once, just a little off.

That had him! Not certain that he had heard what he heard, he began to walk quickly in their direction. He was holding a bow, not a rifle. Obviously he had been given this post because he was a low-ranking warrior. The others were probably enjoying a feast down the other side of the hill.

He was young, this watchman. They had probably told him to shout for help if he saw anything suspicious, but he wasn't about to do that unless he *knew* something was wrong. Young Buffalo knew the type, too sensitive to tolerate the derision that would follow when he told them he had heard a strange-sounding bird in the brush, and then they found nothing.

His fear of derision would cost him his life.

When he was within forty feet of their hiding place Young Buffalo rose up suddenly and let fly an arrow. The arrow missed the chest, sinking deep into the watchman's abdomen. He staggered and his mouth opened to cry out, but pain turned the cry to a soft croak. Big Chin was up, knife in hand, racing toward the staggering Cheyenne. He saw the warrior struggle for a deep breath just as he grabbed the youngster by the neck and buried his knife deep in his throat. Blood showered Big Chin as he gently eased the young man to the ground. While Young Buffalo signaled the soldiers forward across the valley, Big Chin quickly took the scalp, shook the excess blood out of it and tucked it in the waistband of his breechcloth.

They ran quietly up the hill to the notch, then crawled forward and looked down along the slope. At the bottom of the slope, about a hundred yards away, flowed a brackish creek. Beside it sat or lay ten Cheyenne braves in various positions of ease, some of them sleeping, some of them resting on their backs and thinking, others sitting cross-legged, chewing food and chatting. The two Crows looked around to see if there were any more they had missed. There were none. These men were very sure of themselves, very careless. Their ponies were grazing on the other side of the creek, with nobody guarding them.

Young Buffalo left Big Chin at the notch and ran back toward the soldiers, who were still a quarter of a mile away, advancing on foot. Through White Hat he explained the situation to the lieutenant, who marched his troops up to the tall grass near where Young Buffalo and Big Chin had ambushed the young Cheyenne watchman. He and Young Buffalo joined Big Chin at the notch, took a quick look at the situation, nodded, and ran back to his soldiers. He may not have had much experience fighting Indians but he had fought many small-scale actions during the Civil War, and understood immediately what had to be done.

He brought up the Arikara scouts and told them to make their way around the hill to the other side of the creek. Once the firing started, he said, their job was drive the Cheyenne ponies away, then come back like shock cavalry and help the troopers finish off the Cheyenne. The Arikara found their duties agreeable and scampered off on their mission. Then he took his soldiers up, not through the notch, but onto the rock ledges on either side. Soon he had thirty of them, boot to boot, just below the skyline, carbines cocked, watching the lieutenant for his signal. He raised his hand and brought it down. Thirty troopers raised up and fired a ragged volley that echoed across the valley. Most of the soldiers were not very good shots, but the Cheyennes were so close and exposed, and there were so many shots fired, that six Indians twisted in the dust and three more limped painfully toward the creek in a desperate dash for their ponies.

But the ponies were running away, and now here came three Ree warriors with rifles, whooping their war cries as they bore down on the fleeing Cheyennes. One Arikara got his man, and two others fell from more soldier gunfire. Miraculously, a single Cheyenne escaped across the creek, unhurt, with bullets screaming off the rocky ground behind him.

Young Buffalo and Big Chin stood at the notch, astonished, as the white men surged down the hill and proceeded to scalp and otherwise butcher their conquered foe. They were clumsy and maladroit at the business but before long arms, legs, fingers, and other things were being disconnected from the main torsos and either flung away or dropped into pouches the soldiers carried. Then the soldiers raced to where the Cheyennes had laid their possessions, everything from rifles and saddles to goods taken from their series of raids.

Young Buffalo walked among the bloody, fallen Cheyenne, and felt a strange hollowness in his stomach, about what he was doing out there. Surely the Cheyenne were the enemy, but he had seen the white men enough to know that they were no friends of the Absarokee. He knew the whites referred to all the tribes as Indians. He had never considered himself the same people as Sioux or Cheyenne. They were another people, different, cruel, often strange, nearly always hostile.

But he could not help but understand that they were more like him than the white men who were always taking more land, always building towns, chopping down trees, treating men of all the tribes like animals. It just didn't feel right to him, watching white men bend over the unresisting bodies of Cheyenne warriors, coldly butchering them, and Young Buffalo could not understand these feelings. The enemy of your enemy was your friend, but the white men did not feel like friends, even when they were feeding him and giving out ammunition and trinkets.

A shout arose from the far bank of the creek. The Arikara had flushed the surviving Cheyenne warrior. Instead of running through the tall grass, away from the camp, he was racing above the bank where the grass had been worn down by many elk and buffalo coming to drink. For a few seconds he and Big Chin watched, until they saw that the Cheyenne was outdistancing his pursuers.

Many horse Indians were not partial to being afoot, but Crow youngsters were taught to run before they were taught to ride. Young Buffalo and Big Chin took off down the hill with long confident strides, not at full speed but in a floating run that could carry them long distances. At first the Cheyenne continued to gain ground, and the Ree let him go, but the two Crows had won many a race in their lives by pacing themselves. Their feet flew across the rocky ground, fleet as the deer. Two jumps took them across the creek. A quarter mile ahead they could see the Cheyenne's head bobbing up and down as he labored to keep his legs churning. He was an older warrior, with too many years on the back of his pony and too many nights smoking his pipe in his lodge. His lungs were screaming out for air and his muscles were beginning to tie up. He dropped his rifle and pulled his knife, and took a look backward. Young Buffalo could see the pain through the warpaint. He did not go into a sprint to catch him; he played the Cheyenne as if he were a wounded deer, watching him carefully, watching the distance close. When he felt his own lungs begin to labor, he dropped his rifle, which in any event he had not reloaded.

He slowed slightly but still gained easily on the Cheyenne, whose shoulders were heaving with the effort of sucking air into his lungs. Soon the two Crows were only ten steps behind the Cheyenne. He took a quick look backward, then gave up his run and turned to face his executioners. His knife arm shook with fatigue, and his battle crouch was a sham. Big Chin stepped forward, seized the Cheyenne's arm, and easily twisted the knife from his grasp. Grasping the blade of his knife, he counted coup on the Cheyenne's shoulder with the handle, and Young Buffalo did the same. Then Big Chin threw the Cheyenne into the dust, face down, and put his knee on the Cheyenne's neck. Young Buffalo was not surprised. His stalwart friend wanted to scalp an enemy while he was still unwounded. Spent though he was, the Cheyenne flopped feebly around, resisting, then, in a final effort of courage, he turned over onto his back and pointed to his chest.

"Bury your knife here!" the gesture said, boldly, and with respect, Big Chin complied.

Back in the Cheyenne camp, the Rees were singing their victory songs, but downstream Young Buffalo watched his friend make his cut and yank the scalp from the Cheyenne warrior. He was suddenly aware of bees buzzing in the nearby tall grass. He heard a fish break water in the creek.

The wind was freshening from the west. He could smell the purple wildflowers. He could smell the blood and the sweat of the dead Cheyenne.

Big Chin kept the Cheyenne's knife and offered his friend the ammunition pouch. Young Buffalo refused it. "The Cheyenne is yours," he said, "and so is all he possesses." Big Chin studied the dead man's moccasins, worn and useless, as was his loincloth. The two friends climbed to their feet and took their time returning to camp. Big Chin was elated by his victory, but Young Buffalo was depressed. He saw the future clearly. With the eyes of the Crows, and the bullets of their guns, the white men would someday defeat the Sioux, and on that day they would also conquer their allies, the enemy of the Sioux, the people of the long-beaked bird.

When they arrived at the camp, Big Chin smiled at the lieutenant and waved the fresh scalp at him. The lieutenant had one also, which he waved back. They were buddies now, members of the same club, a club Young Buffalo had no interest in joining, not today. For half the troops this had been their first action and they were nearly drunk with the excitement of victory. Some had donned the feathers of the dead men, while others danced around in an awkward parody of an Indian victory dance.

Young Buffalo felt ashamed. He walked to White Hat and told the half-breed to tell the lieutenant that his scouting was finished, that it was time for him and Big Chin to return to their village. When White Hat relayed the message, the lieutenant grew angry, walked up to Young Buffalo so the two were chest to chest and told him that if he did not finish out his term, not only would he not get paid, he might get shot for desertion.

Young Buffalo did not know what desertion was, but he knew anger when he saw it, and he saw it, suddenly, on the faces of all the troopers. Never mind that he and Big Chin were responsible for the victory, they were, like the soldiers, not free to go.

They continued the scout for two more weeks. Young Buffalo had to endure nasty looks from the lieutenant, who understood that his best scout had abruptly lost his appetite for the chase. But he could prove nothing, and when they returned to the fort, the two Crows got their money and departed so fast that the sutler did not have a chance to take it away from them.

On the long journey back to the village, Big Chin noted his friend's silent mood and respected it, although he did not completely understand. Boisterous as he was, he kept his silence until they found the village on the Rosebud four days later. It had been a quiet, prosperous hunting season for the village, and when the two scouts returned, the village was happy for the opportunity to hold a feast and a scalp dance.

Caught up in the excitement, nobody noted the silence of their most honored young warrior, except their chief, Running Wolf, and White Hot Smoke. Long before the festivities had ended, Young Buffalo and White Hot Smoke walked back to their lodge and lay down on the soft hide of a buffalo cow. She stroked his forehead, then ran her hand down his right cheek, but said nothing. She had found that if she did not ask, but showed she was ready to listen, then he would talk.

He talked.

"The white men," he said, "are not our friends."

She let his quiet declaration hang in the air for a few moments. When she was with him she seldom responded without first considering his words.

"Who are our friends?" she asked.

His silence was even longer. "Our people," he said. "A few Shoshone. People of the pierced noses. Maybe." He thought again. "We can rely only on our own."

She did not respond. She knew there would be more.

"My grandfather said that a long time ago we and the Sioux were brothers. They should still be our brothers but they are not because they wish only to take what is ours. They are our enemy because they choose to be our enemy. If they chose to make peace with us our chiefs would smoke the pipe with them."

"But did they not come and try to make peace with us?" White Hot Smoke asked earnestly.

"Pah! They came to turn our faces from the whites, so

they could defeat the whites and then turn on us."

"Could they defeat the whites?" she asked.

Young Buffalo thought for a moment, then he laughed so suddenly that he startled his young wife. "You know, I believe they could, for a while. The white men are powerful, slow, blind men. Without us to be their eyes they could never find their enemies. The Cheyennes have been running free, killing the white men who break the soil and care for the white man buffalo. It was Big Chin and I who found them. There would have been no battle without us, and the Cheyenne would now be riding through the place the white men call Colorado, killing more white farmers."

"I do not understand what is troubling you so," she said. "If you help the white men kill your enemy it is good, whether or not the white men are your friends."

"I am not so sure. The Cheyennes are the friends of our enemies, and so they are our enemies. I should have rejoiced in the death of each of them. I should have danced with the Arikara. I should have drank with the soldiers, and yet I could not. When I saw the white men cutting the flesh from the slain warriors, I felt sick to my stomach."

"I do not understand," White Hot Smoke responded. "Our people cut flesh from our slain enemies."

"When we do it, we honor Great Spirit," he said. "When they did it, I watched the look on their faces. I expected them to eat the fingers and ears. I believe that the Sioux, the Cheyenne, the Crow, the Kiowa, the Pawnee— maybe we should be together against the whites."

"Sioux killed your father!" she admonished. "Sioux killed two of my brothers. I am not ready to love the women of the Lakota people."

"Neither am I!" he cried with strangled passion. "I know that I will fight the Sioux again, maybe at the side of the white men. But with my last breath I will believe that the tribes should be together against the whites."

Their flap was open. One passing by might visit. The one was their chief, Running Wolf.

Running Wolf, like other village chiefs, did not stand on ceremony. He was an active man. If he wished to talk with someone he might invite him for dinner, he might ride with him, or he might simply pay a visit. Running Wolf was a great hunter and a great warrior. The Absarokees were known as the finest horse breeders on the plains. Running Wolf had so many swift, brave buffalo ponies and war ponies that it took half the children in the village to keep the best of them exercised and strong. But he also gave away ponies, and invited those who were down on their luck in for feasts, so that he was by no means the wealthiest man in the village.

"I am pleased that you and Big Chin did so well on your scout with the soldiers," he said, seating himself in the place of honor pointed out by Young Buffalo. "It gives me a good feeling when I can see who will be tomorrow's leaders."

Young Buffalo could not respond. When he was on the hunt, his chief was the man he could defer to in comfort, but in quiet talk by a lodge fire he could feel awestruck by the great chief who always seemed to know the right things to do and say. Running Wolf understood. Running Wolf understood so much.

"Tell me what you think of the soldiers," he said, knowing that when Young Buffalo's mind was on his job, he would know what to say.

Young Buffalo found his tongue. "They are not men like the tribes are men," he said. "They complain about the food. They complain about their chiefs. They complain about how long they must ride their ponies. How can a man complain about such a thing? They do not honor their god. Sometimes they even yell out his name when they are angry. They think that we are like lizards and snakes—that is how they think of us."

He could see Running Wolf staring into the fire, absorbing the words of his finest young warrior. Then the chief looked straight into Young Buffalo's eyes.

"You must hear what I say now. They are the most important words you will ever hear from me. Do you understand that they have given us land to live on? Land that is ours and only ours?" he asked.

"They have given us nothing," Young Buffalo retorted, his awe forgotten. "The land is ours. We took it a long time ago—'' he stopped suddenly in response to a sympathetic wave of Running Wolf's hand.

"Yes—yes," said the chief. "Do not talk, listen, and all will become clear. You must believe what I say. One man may not be strong. Another man may be strong as a buffalo. But if the weak man is not one but ten, and if the ten all have fine rifles while the mighty man has only a knife, then the mighty man must die, or he must learn to get along with the ten weak men. Do you understand what I am saying?"

Young Buffalo nodded.

"For every Absarokee man, the white men have ten." He thought for a moment how to express large numbers. "Not ten," he said. "Many more than ten. Many, many more than ten."

Young Buffalo said nothing.

"My son," the chief continued, "I do not truly mean the white man gave us this land. The Great Spirit gave us this land. But the treaty people said that they would keep white men off the land if we promise to make it our own. It is plenty for us, although it has the lines white men draw on their writing skins, which is something we have never heard of. If we fight the whites, they will forget the treaty and take our land away from us."

"Unless we whip them," Young Buffalo interjected.

The fire flickered in the chief's steady, calm eyes. "We can whip them today," he said. "We can whip them tomorrow, maybe, but to keep our land we must whip them forever. The Creator made so many of them." He shook his head. "So many of them. And He gave them such good guns. They cannot fight but they can shoot. They look like the masters of all. If we stand in their way they can ride over us the way their wagons ride over the land. But if we remain their friends, if . . . All we must do is remember that the Sioux would kill us all if they could. We may not know who our friends are, but we certainly know our enemies."

"They are the Sioux," Young Buffalo agreed. "But when I saw the soldiers taking scalps and fingers from the Cheyenne—then my heart felt sick. It did not seem right, the soldiers standing over the fallen Cheyenne, cutting with their knives while the Ree danced. I should have been happy to defeat a troublesome enemy, but I was not, not fighting alongside soldiers who do not trust us, who look at us like we are locusts."

The chief did not respond immediately but Young Buffalo could feel his sympathy.

"In battle a great war chief is always watching for a weakness in the enemy," he said. "He also watches for weakness in his friends lest they betray him and become the enemy. When you fight the Sioux alongside the whites, you weaken our forever enemy, and you also learn much about the people that some day might become the enemy."

Young Buffalo looked up from the fire in surprise. He had never heard a Crow chief suggest that someday they would leave the whites and go their own way. It was a thought he had harbored himself but because he was so young he assumed that he must be mistaken.

Chapter 18

Though Young Buffalo was still very young, Running Wolf knew his favorite protégé had "horse medicine." Of all the ones without fires—animals who were not humans—it was the horse that the Crows loved and revered. All the ones without fires had great powers that the Great Spirit did not give to humans, but the horse was special. And Young Buffalo was special with a pony. Not only was he adept at selecting the best ponies for racing, hunting, and war, it seemed that he could take any pony and get more out of it than other braves.

Young Buffalo loved horse trading, but the men of Running Wolf's village did not want to trade with Young Buffalo because, even if the trade was good for both, Young Buffalo was so adept at working with ponies that his always showed better.

The Crows had their own way of hunting buffalo that worked best in their home country, where they had transformed several areas into buffalo jumps. One massive buffalo jump could mean a winter of good eating for the fortunate band, and Blue Shirt had discovered a good-sized herd several miles above Grapevine Creek.

The buffalo jump had to be carefully planned. Nearly everybody in the village took part, one way or other. Running Wolf was as good a strategist in the hunt as he was in battle. He sent Would Not Listen and some of the older boys out to the jump to place markers, and he sent Young Buffalo, Big Chin, and Blue Shirt to keep an eye on the buffalo and get them started on the signal.

The jump itself was a flat mesa that ended at a sheer, sixty-foot cliff. To the right as one approached the cliff was a steep upward slope, too steep for buffalo to climb. The mesa itself was a quarter of a mile wide. The buffalo would have to be channeled or they would scatter across the mesa and the jump would fail. Would Not Listen and the boys made a line of boulders the size of small melons leading toward the cliff. Ten yards from the cliff, just outside the row of rocks, they erected a safety wall to keep any ponies from getting too much into the spirit and trying to make the jump with the buffalo.

When the rock work was done, Would Not Listen rode back to camp and returned with Running Wolf and eight of the older men. Meanwhile seven more warriors joined Young Buffalo, waiting behind the buffalo for the signal.

Though the buffalo sensed that the Crows were not far away, most of them continued to nibble the sparse grass with an occasional cow swiveling her head, trying to see whatever was making her uneasy. But buffalo eyes were not much good for seeing anything farther than a few yards.

Young Buffalo took a quick look at the sun, which would be behind them, a good thing because he and his men took their vision very seriously. A single gust of wind blew brown dust into his nostrils—a good smell for a man who loved the challenge of getting the job done. Buffalo jumps did not always succeed like they were supposed to, and leaders could lose face if the buffalo veered at the last moment and fled safely from the scene of their planned destruction.

Two rifle shots echoed across the rocky hills. All was ready. Time to start the ponies; time to start the buffalo. Arranged in a wide arc, the Crows moved forward slowly on their ponies. They wanted the buffalo to sense the location of the danger, so when they started running they would run away from the horsemen, toward the precipice. Forward walked the ponies, then into a slow trot. The buffalo sensed, then smelled, then finally saw the line of hunters moving toward them. Some of the more experienced animals were beginning to move now, but there was no consensus until the leader started out, not straight ahead away from the hunters, but on an angle toward the steep slope on the right. That was all right as long as the hunters rode along their flanks and kept them from turning the wrong way. Young Buffalo moved toward the front of the herd, fired his rifle close to one of the bigger bulls, and moved him a few degrees closer to the jump. Now the herd was in motion, gaining speed, headed for the steep slope. Then the leader sensed the upward slope ahead and straightened the herd out, away from the slope, toward the clear horizon that was in fact the jumping-off point. They were making noises now, noises of discontentment as they began their fatal run, gaining speed, running in a black-brown, woolly mass. The hunters closed in on their rear, firing their rifles, whooping, waving blankets, and now the herd was truly frightened. They were running hard for the horizon, desperate to escape the men behind them, much too frightened to sense that the real danger was to their front.

Young Buffalo breathed a sigh of relief. The buffalo were channeled into an area a hundred yards wide, between the steep slope on their right and the row of boulders to their left. The roiling dust, the smell of the herd, the low, terrified cries, and the whooping of his companions were all music to Young Buffalo.

Several buffalo on the left must have sensed the new peril, because they turned toward the row of boulders and attempted to break through there. The older men barred the way, waving blankets and launching shrill screeches that turned the buffalo back into the main herd.

Now came the great danger for those driving the herd. The mounted men must press closer, increase the stress, put the herd in such a state of fear that they would ignore the fearful unknown ahead; and yet the men must stop their ponies before they followed the herd over the edge. Most of the men dismounted, snapping their blankets, sprinting forward, shooting their guns, continuing their chilling screeches, running, running, and the buffalo lowered their heads and surged forward as hard as they could to escape the fearsome devils behind them.

"There!" Young Buffalo cried out. "Jump!" But they almost did not jump. At the last moment the leader and others near him saw the danger and slid to a halt at the edge of the cliff. The ones behind them did not stop, but galloped forward and swept the leaders with them in a plunge that ended on the rocky ground below. Row after row followed, and some that were not killed by the fall were crushed by those that followed. In ones and twos and fours they hurtled into space and ended their run in a massive pile of bodies below, some still in death, some writhing in pain. All who were not dead were stunned and badly hurt. Below stood one more group of men from the village, mostly men too old and too stiff in the joints to man the row of boulders. It was their job to advance to the moaning, writhing pile and finish off the wounded.

More than a hundred buffalo had made the jump. No more than a dozen had won their freedom by charging past the blanket-snapping men at the row of boulders. One of the commands of the medicine maker was that only those buffalo who made the jump were to be killed. The others were to be allowed to live.

Far to the left was a steep narrow trail down the bluff. The women had already arrived below with their ponies and plenty of rope. The men would soon be making their way down the path from the mesa. Then they would use the ropes to separate the buffalo carcasses enough for the women to work at the wearying, bloody chore of skinning and butchering the buffalo. Young Buffalo found White Hot Smoke and the two of them began to haul away at the body of a young but fully grown cow, using a pony for the heavy work, sliding the cow far enough away from the rest to give White Hot Smoke room to work.

The work of skinning and butchering was hot and sweaty. The women labored with cheap butcher knives that did not hold their edge very well. Before long they were up to their elbows in blood. Huge flies buzzed around them, landing on the carcasses but also on the sweaty foreheads of the women. Above them, watching them cut and saw, the buzzards and hawks circled, certain that when their turn came there would still be plenty of gristle and meat left to slake their appetites.

The men had done their job and rewarded themselves by cutting out blood-soaked kidneys and livers, which they proceeded to devour raw, feeling the force of the animals surge into their bodies as they tore juicy chunks with their teeth and chewed fiercely.

The jump had taken but a few minutes. The butchering took hours, and that was just the beginning. Now they loaded the meat on the backs of the ponies and wearily led the animals to the village. Backs and arms aching with fatigue, they stretched the hides out and staked them to the ground to dry, and worked the tanning mixture of buffalo livers and brains into them. Then they began to slice the meat in preparation for drying. They had to work fast. This meat was an important part of their winter food supply. And there was more: bone for needles, awls, and other tools; liver fluids for curing the hides; sinew for bows and bowstrings; nearly everything that had been a buffalo was useful for the people.

But not quite everything. Beneath the cliff where a hundred buffalo had made their final flight, buzzards and coyotes sparred for the meager leavings trapped in an enormous pile of buffalo bones that were already beginning to stink with decay in the afternoon summer sun. Beneath this pile were the crumbled remains of previous buffalo jumps. The sun finished its long journey across the big sky and sank behind the mountains, leaving the silent tangle of buffalo bones glowing blue-white in the moonlight.

Above the bones floated the distant sounds of the village, celebrating the successful hunt with a feast and a dance. Most of the celebrators were men. The exhausted women had long before bathed their aching bodies in Grapevine Creek and returned to their lodges to sleep their long, black dreamless sleep. The following day would be a long one, getting the hides and meat ready for the next move. Three days after that they would be knocking down their tepees and loading their ponies. It was time to move again, and the hard work of moving day was woman's work; all this and nursing babies or perhaps giving birth, cooking, mending, making clothes, nurturing children and a hundred other necessary chores. There were times when the work was so hard and endless that there wasn't even time to reflect on just how hard it was, or how easy their men had it when they weren't being gored by buffalo horns or slain in battle by the Sioux.

Braddock did not find the village of Running Wolf by chance. Desperate as he had been he should have known better than to enlist in an army of Yankees. Army was army. He hadn't liked serving in the ranks of the Confederacy; had liked it less when a bullet had bit him at Shiloh. Perhaps he had forgotten what it was really like to spend his days following useless, foolish orders given by dimwitted sergeants and self-important lieutenants. What was worse than to have do something stupid and useless just because someone with stripes or bars said you had to?

AWOL itself was no big deal. The northern plains were endless and the army was stretched too thin to pursue deserters all over hellandgone. Consequently there were desertions every month, and they were just part of the reality of military life on the plains. So many deserters meant more men to recruit, and the recruitments always fell short, leaving the forts even more undermanned than they had been when they'd first been built.

For a month Braddock had hoarded supplies, worked his horse to keep it in shape, and planned his bolt for freedom. He had intended to leave by himself, but when three other malcontents had announced their intentions to desert, he began to reflect that survival alone on the plains was never guaranteed. His buddies, and the alcohol they cooked in a secret still a mile from the fort, were the only things that had kept Braddock sane over the six months he had spent in northern Colorado with the cavalry. With them, why, escape might be more than escape, it could mean some good times.

The horse herd had cropped so much grass around the fort that the animals had to be corralled nearly half a mile away from the post. Travis Scott, the most resourceful of the deserters, had discovered a storeroom full of discarded saddles, blankets, and bridles. Late one Sunday afternoon they had walked out of the gate with tack on their shoulders, without attracting curiosity. Indian activity had been sparse in the area and if a few privates wished to exercise their horses on a free Sunday afternoon, well, why not? Only they did not ride, they ditched their equipment in a dry creek bed and covered it with dead tree branches and straw.

A week passed. They accumulated more supplies: spare canteens, canned foods, hard biscuits, spare ammunition. They had planned well. None of them had guard duty the coming Friday night. Their quarters were located on the east wall, where the ground was soft. They had easily dug a small hole under the wall from the little room adjoining the sleeping quarters.

Now, slowly, carefully, quietly, the four soldiers wriggled under the wall and headed out for their rendezvous with freedom. There was no moon out. The sentry hollered "Halt! Who goes?" but by then the men had scrambled away into the dark, heading out to the horse herd. There they ran into terrible problems, namely soldiers who were actually awake, even if they weren't walking their posts. Scott, who had assumed leadership of the group, suggested that they vanish into the grass and wait.

"The night is young," he said. "Those boys'll be asleep in an hour, bet my canteen on that."

They waited, and sure enough, soon they could see sentries leaning up against trees, then nodding, then kneeling, then finally, falling asleep and rolling over onto their backs. The four men broke from their hideout, cut the lines of some of the horses, saddled them, and led them away from where the sentries were deep in slumber.

They led their horses into the nearest valley and walked with them for fifteen minutes, then mounted up and moved them at a patient walk for another half hour. They found a well-worn trail that led them between two rugged hills. They moved single file through the notch, and once on the downhill side, Scott took the lead, galloping his horse across the narrow valley below and up a gentle slope. A bright half-moon arrived at last, and when Scott reached the top of this hill he turned to the other three soldiers, who were riding more carefully, waved his broad-brimmed hat, and whooped

.out into the night. Braddock kicked his chestnut gelding into a fast trot, then a gallop, raced up the hill, came to a halt beside Scott, and told him to shut up.

"We must be a good three miles from the fort, Granny," Scott said. Scott called every man who worried about anything "Granny."

The other two soldiers, named Eldon and O'Hara, were New York boys still new to the saddle and they barely felt comfortable in any gait beyond a walk in the daytime. They feared ridicule even more, otherwise they would be leading their horses till dawn, anyway.

"Look, Travis, we'd better put as much distance between us and the fort by morning—ain't no time for celebration, all that nonsense," said Braddock.

Scott snickered. He was a veteran soldier who had quit learning the day after he had mastered mounted drill.

"Damn it, Granny, you think they're gonna find us? We been ridin' mostly over rock and the only Ree trackers they got left are those two drunks, Yellow Eyes and that other one."

Eldon and O'Hara had caught up to them and the four were all sitting astride their mounts on top of the hill illuminated by the glaring half moon.

"Boys," said Braddock, "I guess I'd dawdle too if this was some little game, but if, just if, them fools catch us, they will take us back to the fort, line us up against a wall and shoot us."

Scott snorted and shook his head. "Hell, when was the last time you went out in a patrol looking for deserters?" he asked. "I'm tellin' you, they're so worried about the Sioux that they don't send out no small patrols no more."

"Boys, I ain't sittin' up on this hill flappin' my tongue the rest of the night," Braddock replied, urging his mount into a slow trot down the hill. They had been riding east, but when he hit a small creek at the bottom of the hill, he followed it northward. Eldon and O'Hara noted Braddock's determination and decided that he, not Scott, knew what he was doing. They followed Braddock without a word. For all his bravado, Scott had no desire to be left alone on the plains in the middle of the night so he followed too, at a distance, casually, as if he didn't really care whether he rode to freedom or back into the arms of the U.S. Cavalry.

Not until dawn arrived did Braddock dismount by a creek that cut a deep enough valley to hide the men and their horses from the surrounding countryside. He tied up his horse and unsaddled it, lay back on a blanket, uncorked his canteen, then pulled out a hard biscuit and commenced to gnaw, keeping away from a painful tooth on the right side of his mouth. Eldon and O'Hara camped just across the stream, Scott a hundred yards upstream. He did not unsaddle, nor did he eat, but immediately collapsed and fell asleep on some very rocky ground.

Three hours later Braddock awoke, his body taut. He never woke up without a reason. He looked over at Eldon and O'Hara, sleeping undisturbed ten feet away from him. He looked down the creek and spotted Scott's horse. Scott was close by, on his back, his hat over his face to shield his eyes from the midmorning sun. Even as Braddock watched, Scott stirred, removed his hat from his face, and sat up. He was feeling the same thing that Braddock was feeling. Something was amiss that he could not figure out.

He climbed to his feet and made his way to the creek, not to drink, but to urinate. No bushes for Scott. Everything he did was flamboyant in its own low-class way, even urinating in a stream.

He caught a glimpse of Braddock staring at him and, far from being self-conscious, he waved at Braddock with a big smile on his face as he watched his stream arc halfway across the creek.

He never got a chance to finish. A single shot from beyond the far bank sent him sailing into the air, arms spread outward. No cry escaped his throat. He landed on his stomach in the creek, arms flapping like a fish on dry land. Eldon and O'Hara were on their feet immediately, their hands fumbling for their saddles and trying to cinch them on their horses.

Their activity drew fire, bullets thudding into the soft dirt around them as they scrambled awkwardly into their saddles and climbed the river bank. In the meantime Braddock was able to saddle up quickly without having to dodge gunfire, and took off after his companions.

Eldon and O'Hara never had a chance. As recruits they had the worst horses and they could not ride well in any event. Braddock had been riding since childhood. His horse was strong and deep-chested. Over the bank he went, and in a dozen jumps he had overtaken his cohorts. He sent his horse into a stretch-necked flat run over the level ground, his long stride putting vital distance between himself and his pursuers. They were only now sprinting for the horses they had given to holders, who were bringing the animals up to meet them.

There were eight of them, enough to capture four escapees but not enough to deplete the fort's garrison. Their horses were fair, not great, and so was their horsemanship. Still, once they sighted Eldon and O'Hara they were able to close in quickly. So intent were the two deserters on hanging on to their galloping steeds that they did not dare to look back, nor could they have raised their hands to surrender if they had wanted to. They were overtaken quickly by a scalphunting corporal named Krueger, who rode close to Eldon, pulled his sidearm, and demanded that the deserter surrender.

Wide-eyed with panic, riding harder than he had ever dared, Eldon never saw Krueger, but rode on, his eyes fixed straight ahead, his hands clutching the reins like white-knuckled vises. Krueger shouted again for the man to surrender, but if Eldon heard, he gave no sign. The corporal wasted no further time. He cocked his Colt, raised it to within five feet of Eldon's head, fired—and missed. He pulled back the hammer, fired once more, and was rewarded with a shower of brains and blood. O'Hara heard the gunfire, saw the skull of his buddy explode and promptly dropped the reins of his horse and raised his hands. Freed from restraint, his horse stretched into a real run and pitched O'Hara onto his head, breaking his neck.

Now there was only Braddock, but he had put a quarter of a mile's distance between himself and his pursuers, and was now coasting at an easier gallop, saving his animal for the steep hill that loomed ahead. He had counted on the impatience of the corporal and his patrol, and he was right. With only one deserter left, they ran their horses hard and as they saw themselves closing, they flogged their animals for even more speed. They wanted a short chase. They could catch him on the hill, they were sure.

They were almost right, which made them very wrong. Braddock's horse climbed the hill with ease, less than a hundred yards ahead of Corporal Krueger and his men. Still strong, the animal took the downslope without effort. Krueger's patrol, on the other hand, spurred their flagging horses, struggling up the hill, and three-quarters of the way up, the animals were about blown. At the top, the corporal stopped long enough to catch a glimpse of Braddock, already well down the hillside.

Krueger urged his horse down the hill but the tired animal ignored the spurs and picked its way down the slope, its knees almost buckling. Krueger finally got sensible. "Slow it down, men," he said. "We have his trail and there's nobody out here gonna take his side. He's got a long way to go to get away, and we're gonna get him, don't you doubt it none."

Chapter 19

Braddock may have been a stubborn, hardheaded son of the Tennessee cotton culture but he was not incapable of learning. He had gone west to make a new life and he had failed again and again. If he failed now, he would have run out of opportunities.

He kept his mount to a steady pace and assayed his chances. He had more experience than his pursuers; he had more horse than his pursuers. Against him was the undeniable fact that there were eight of them and one of him. If they used the land to flank him, or if they took turns taking runs at him and wearing down his gelding, they could catch him.

One other thing. When he had joined up he had kept his rifle. On duty he was forced to carry a carbine, but when he decided to desert he had chosen the range of his rifle over the lighter weight of the smaller weapon. Now, if he chose a good position he could outrange his enemy. Of course, he didn't really want to make war against the army, even if they were mostly a bunch of Yankees. Desertion was one thing, killing his fellow soldiers was another. So confident was he that he could outrun the soldiers that he determined not to pull his rifle. If he did not fight, he reasoned, it became a race, not a war, and they would be more likely to give up a race than a fight in which they had taken casualties.

All these things he thought as the miles stretched behind them. They had come so quickly he suspected that they had not taken rations and camping gear. His rations and gear were slim, but soldiers liked to travel in some comfort. They had killed three of the four and would prefer to avoid the long chase if they could. They were a hundred yards away now, struggling, laboring. He asked for a little more speed and the gelding responded. Slowly the soldiers receded, but they did not give up. He continued the accelerated pace until they had fallen more than a quarter of a mile behind. Ah, this was going to be a long chase after all. If they lost sight of him they would track him. Maybe they *had* brought some rations along.

All right then. He was not about to give in, return to the fort hog-tied, and get shot for his efforts. He was moving northward now, out of Colorado up into Montana, out of Cheyenne and Arapaho country, north to the Crows. His friends. The army's friends. He was still wearing his army uniform. His civilian clothes had been falling off him when he had taken the oath. The oath. Wonder what God would think about the broken oath. He laughed. In this Godforsaken country—that was it. God had forsaken this country. Of what value were oaths?

He had brought his horse down to a more leisurely pace but the soldiers were content to follow, and were not closing in. Ahead was a notch. Once he got through there he would be out of their sight for a while. If he could pick up the pace there, and they could not see him when they made it through and looked out at the next valley, maybe they would give up.

Only way they can catch me is if my horse goes lame, he thought, and with the thought came worry. Horses do go lame, always at the worst of times. He watched the trail in front of him carefully, looking for stones and animal holes. Then he began to pray. Oh damn, that oath! If God was not heeding violated oaths in the West he certainly wasn't about to consider a desperate, hastily assembled prayer from a deserter. From his father he had received the idea that his relationship with God was a give-and-take affair. A little charity here, a little honesty there, a little prayer of praise just to let God know you were thinking of Him. They all weighed on your side if you were in a tough spot and were begging for a little divine intervention to get you out.

But all this consideration had not made Braddock a better man. Instead, he always put off. God, I'll send a little prayer tomorrow. God, I'll pray as soon as I find a church to pray in. These people out here ain't much for churches you know. Maybe next time I get to Denver. I know you'll understand. Charity, of course, was out of the question because he never had anything to give. The one thing he did understand better than a lot of his more sanctimonious contemporaries was that Indians were God's people too. During their pursuits of hostile Cheyennes, Braddock had managed to spend time with the Crows, especially Young Buffalo. If the Crow warrior had recalled their previous encounter he gave no indication, but he did manage to teach Braddock a few signs.

His fellow privates had given him a little hell for his nonconformity. "Gonna be a squaw man?" "Gonna cut the seat out of your breeches tomorrow and start ridin' around em-bare-assed?" That pun had convulsed them for days. Why would a white man spend so much time with a redskin? They couldn't understand it. But then, neither could he. There had been something that had drawn him to Young Buffalo, and now he knew what that something was. It was the need to have a friend outside the army structure. He had known on the day he'd enlisted that he was not going to be able to stay in uniform for long. He just wasn't made that way.

Onward he rode, carefully saving his mount. Without dismounting or stopping he reached into his saddle bag, pulled out a biscuit and gnawed on it. It was hard, almost inedible. But if he could pry an edge loose and suck on it until the moisture had penetrated, then he could chew.

His mouth was almost too dry to moisten the biscuit. He pulled out his canteen, pulled the cork with his teeth, tucked the cork in his shirt, and drank as he rode. There, that was better. The cork went back into the canteen, the canteen over the saddle horn, and he bit hard into the biscuit. There it was, the story of his life, teeth against hard army biscuit.

This time the biscuit won. That molar must have been fixing to shatter. The biscuit finished the job.

Undiscouraged, Braddock spat out the piece of tooth and recommenced to gnaw on the biscuit. This time he cut loose a fairly large piece, which he sucked on and sucked on until he could chew it. He dropped the remainder of the biscuit into the saddlebag and turned his head. His backtrail was empty.

Far from feeling better, he felt unnerved by the empty backtrail. As long as he could see them he knew where they were. Now, how could he be sure? He left the trail and pounded along a rock shelf for a while, then, to save wear and tear on his horse, he dismounted and led the horse over the stone, down to a creek wide enough to hide tracks. It was a broad creek for the summertime, bordered by cottonwoods and scrubby cedar underbrush. The creek wound in all directions and often doubled back on itself but its general direction was north.

He felt a slight jolt and turned to find an arrow buried in his saddle. He had not learned much about tribal lore but he knew that striped wild turkey feathers on an arrow probably meant Cheyenne. Oh, sweet Jesus. Now was the time for the prey to pray. Behind him were four Cheyenne warriors, flogging their ponies, less than a hundred yards away and gaining on him with every stride.

He leaped into the saddle and spurred his horse, hard. No sense saving the mount now. Space. He needed space. They must have been riding a ways too, because when he asked the gelding for more, the Cheyennes began to fall back.

He jumped off the horse while it was still in motion and led it up a hill to the top of a rock that afforded a great view in all directions. He wedged his lead into a tight crevice, pulled out his rifle, and snatched a bag of ammunition off the saddle horn. These Cheyenne obviously did not have much respect for soldiers. They kept coming, though they must have seen him raise his rifle to his shoulder. He chambered a round and got a good sight picture on the nearest Indian, and squeezed the trigger. The rifle bucked and through the smoke he could see the pony leap into the air and throw its rider. He hated to do that to a pony but he had to make his shots count. Riders were hard to hit. Horses were easy. The pony caught the bullet in the flank, and once it had unhorsed its rider, it was off in search of some place that didn't hurt like this bullet hurt.

With the élan and bravery that set them apart as a people, the three remaining Cheyenne braves rode forward to where the unhorsed rider was shaking off the effects of his sudden collision with the ground. Two of them raced toward Braddock's position, rifles at the ready, while the third hooked his arm under that of the unhorsed rider and pulled him up behind him.

Braddock had no intention of killing or wounding one of the Cheyennes and getting them any angrier at him than they already were. Besides, as he squinted out into the sun that was beginning to loom low and red on the western horizon, he could swear that he saw riders. Could be bad. Could be good. And good could be not so good. Bad meant more Cheyennes and if that were the case he might as well slice off his own scalp and hand it to them. Good could be the troopers, but then, the troopers were as hungry for his life as the Cheyennes.

He watched and waited, wondering how he had ever gotten himself into such a fix that the sworn enemies of the plains *both* craved his destruction.

The Cheyennes pulled up and turned back toward the west as soon as they saw that their comrade was safe. Their charge had only been a diversion. But now they saw the riders coming too, and Braddock knew the newcomers were soldiers by the way the Cheyennes turned south and headed for a tall rocky outcropping that would provide good cover in case the troopers came after them.

And they did, at first, in a headlong, strung-out charge that could have been disastrous for them had the Cheyennes not been too surprised to react. But then the troopers spotted the bucking, bleeding pony that Braddock had shot and the leader of the detachment signaled a halt. The Cheyennes fled into the rocks and disappeared like smoke in a prairie wind.

Braddock could picture Sergeant Tolliver discussing the problem with Corporal Krueger. "We're out here to catch deserters, not Indians, Corporal. Who fired the shot? Who wounded that pony? D'ja see where they were headed before they spotted us? I'll betcha Braddock is up on that hill. Maybe his horse is down. Maybe . . .''

"Damn," Braddock grunted. He had hoped that the Cheyennes and the soldiers might take each other's minds off him. He crawled back into the clump of trees where he had left his horse, led it down the reverse slope, and rode northward at a hard, steady clip.

He listened carefully as he rode, hoping to hear the rattle of carbines echoing off the rocks, but he heard nothing. He could only conclude that he was a more powerful enemy to the Republic than the Cheyennes, who with their Sioux brothers were making life horrible for settlers up and down the South Platte River. He pushed his gelding a little harder. Just a while longer, he thought, and we'll be able to rest. He tried the usual tricks for losing a trail: rocky ground and creeks. He could not understand how the troopers had been able to cling to his trail for as long as they did, unless they somehow had an idea of where he was going.

The shadows grew longer minute by minute until at last he descended into a valley so deep in shadow that he could almost consider it night. He found a creek, tasted the water and found it acceptable, if not great, let the gelding drink, and then tied it to a bush fifty feet away from the creek. There was a little grass, which the animal began to crop, but Braddock had also brought a small bag of oats with him, and these he began to feed the animal. "You deserve better, old scout," he said. When he had been issued the gelding, he had been told that it was called Lefty, but he quickly became convinced that the horse didn't know its name. So he called it a succession of nicknames, and he was certain that the creature could respond to the tone of his voice, if not to the sound of its name.

Tired as he was, he could not sleep. With time to consider his fate, he remembered that if he were caught he would be lucky to live long enough for the trial, the guilty verdict, and the execution. He lay on his back for hours listening to the night sounds, never hearing anything that sounded remotely like human beings, much less the clinking of canteens and the rubbing of leather on leather. He must get some sleep, and an early start. His best chance would come by running his pursuers into the ground. Perhaps they had already run out of food and turned for home, but he could not be sure of that.

Still, if he were to sleep, he would have to believe. Yes, they were not equipped for the long chase. Yes, they would be concerned that the Cheyennes would get their friends and run them down. It occurred to him then that if they could go after an eight-man party of soldiers then it would not be unlikely that they would hunt him down, alone and vulnerable as he was. No, he didn't think that would happen, although he could not come up with a reason why it wouldn't.

He turned over on his side and let serious fatigue finally drag him under.

He woke up and heard nothing. No birds, no scurrying critters, no toads, no nothing, and he knew he was in trouble. He held his breath and listened to the silence. He opened one eye and saw nothing. Still dark. He could not take a breath. Something was looming over him. He felt a cold wave sweep down his back. He had to do something, even if it got him killed.

Underneath his blanket lay his Colt. He fitted his hand into it, then jumped up, sending his blanket flying. Awakened by the sudden noise and movement, the gelding whinnied. He whirled around, first left, then right, cocking his pistol and pointing it into the darkness.

There was nothing human anywhere close to him.

He looked around more carefully now, and in the moonlight he could not see anything worth worrying about. He had no idea how far away dawn was, but with his heart beating like the pistons of a 4–4–0 railroad engine there was no way he was going to find any more sleep on this night.

He froze. Heavy breathing, behind him, followed by a nudge behind his head. He pulled his hands away from his Colt and began to raise them, then scoffed at himself. He understood, finally, that he had been awakened by the gelding, which had somehow worked itself loose and instead of heading out for freedom was scavenging for the sack of oats, which Braddock had been using as a pillow.

His nerves were vibrating like big cottonwood branches in a windstorm. Might as well get along, under a bright moon, but which way? This valley, he recalled, moved northeast to southwest. He could follow it north till it hit Elk River, then head east until he struck the Bighorn. Honestly, he had no idea how he'd recognize Crow country when he hit it, but hit it he would—he had to, his life depended on it.

He was getting tired of his life depending on such chancy events as finding such-and-such river before the Sioux—or in this case the soldiers—found him. He had grown up in a real house on a real farm with a real mother and father and a couple of real slaves. He had fought in a real war, had survived by the grace of God and had deserted from two armies less than ten years apart.

As he walked his pony north in the chill, predawn air, chewing on a piece of hard biscuit, he remembered a warm bed in his father's house. His father was gone and the bed was made warmer by the little trashy girl who lived with her five dirty brothers in a shack down the road. She was not dirty, he remembered, and he thought it was because she was looking to climb up the social ladder a bit by coupling with him, a landowner's son.

He remembered how he felt with her, how she loved to snuggle, and rub his back and do other pleasant things to him. She had that mean little mouth that trashy girls always seemed to have on them, but he liked mean-pretty, liked it real well. He liked her knowledge, and her ambition. Clean a trashy girl up and she can make your blood run downhill all right.

His father's house was just a heap of ashes now. How the mighty had fallen. He was fleeing from the U.S. Army, ready to settle for life among a village of heathen redskins who spent much of the year coated with bear grease and had never eaten a pork chop in their entire lives. For a moment he felt so lost, so desolate, that he wanted to give up and lie down and let the Lord take him, but then he remembered how hard it was to die. Otherwise he would have never left Shiloh, where death was easy, no more effort than sticking his head up and taking a swarm of bullets from the sunken road. Youngsters from all over Arkansas had died on the field that day.

He had died there too, though he didn't know it then, and didn't know it when he arrived home to find everything gone. No, it dawned on him in stages, as each failure followed the other, that he was alone and without hope of ever reclaiming the kind of life he had enjoyed before half of Tennessee had marched off to war against the Union.

He tilted his canteen back and drank, and saw the new dawn and let it work its magic on him. He had gotten to the point where he was angry at the dawn because it made him feel good, and he knew he shouldn't. In an hour or two the good feeling would be gone, but for now he would have to tolerate the cheerful message that dawn brought him.

"C'mon!" he flicked the reins and managed a trot out of the gelding. He knew that if the soldiers hadn't given up the chase, they were either still sleeping or dawdling over their bacon and coffee. Small detachments under the leadership of sergeants dawdled a lot. The sergeants were not all that interested in provoking battles when it was possible to lead their troops out into the hills, follow a few trails, and return to the fort with the good news that all the Sioux and Cheyenne had been intimidated by the new fort and had vanished into the outlands, never to return. The sergeants knew it wasn't so, and the officers knew it wasn't so, but good sergeants were hard to come by and the officers were satisfied with the lazy but savvy noncoms they could call upon in a tough spot.

The sun rose cool and turned hot. His coat came off. His sleeves rolled up. His head began to bob, and then in the mid-morning heat he drifted off into semi-consciousness and let his horse show the way. The gelding had ideas of his own. He was thirsty and displeased because Braddock had forgotten about him. He sniffed out the creek, walked toward it, and began to drink. Only the loud slurping brought Braddock back to life before his horse had gotten itself a bellyful of cool, alkaline water that might have put the horseman back on foot. He kicked hard at the animal, failed to move it, jumped off into the creek, and with numerous curses dragged him back onto dry land. Quickly he tied his horse to a willow bush, filled his canteen, drank, refilled the canteen, climbed back into the saddle, and rode on.

He was no longer alone. Two pairs of eyes watched him from a nearby crag, and followed him until he was out of sight up the valley. Without haste both men mounted up and followed his trail, staying out of sight. They were careful, these two, wary of all possible ambush sites, wondering what he was doing alone on his way north, where there were no whites or big gold strikes. As the shadows closed in on the valley they picked up their pace until they caught sight of him up ahead. Once they had a chance to study him they realized he rode a U.S. Cavalry rig and wore a white cavalry hat. They had seen many other deserters before. He had to be another. This was useful information. They had been around soldiers enough to know that unlike Indians, who believed that if a brave wanted to quit his band that was his business, the white men got angry and dragged deserters back for more service, or punishment, or both. They could not understand that kind of thinking, of course, and certainly did not understand why men would want to be part of a people that would do such a thing to them. They would certainly not capture the man and try to bring him back, but they must be wary, because they knew that soldiers might be following him. Many bluecoats did not know a Crow from a Sioux, nor did they care.

They followed the lone soldier until he made camp for the evening, then they took advantage of the remaining daylight to head up on the ridges and study the backtrail. They did so for an hour, found nothing, and decided to visit the soldier, who maybe had stolen some bacon when he had deserted. Both Big Chin and Would Not Listen were inordinately fond of army bacon, when it was not rancid.

On the way back up the valley the two men debated whether to ride in noisily, singing and calling out to the man, or sneaking in and showing their peaceful intentions before he had a chance to get frightened and hostile. They opted for the silent approach, reasoning that if they approached noisily the white man might get frightened anyway and then only bad things would happen.

To their delight the unmistakable odor of bacon was drifting down the valley as they tied their ponies upstream from the white man's camp. They walked casually toward the camp until they were less than two hundred yards away, then they crept forward carefully, crouching, silent. The white man was sitting on a rock in front of a smoky fire, eating hot bacon directly from the frying pan, soaking a biscuit in the fat until it was soft, then taking a bite and washing it down with strong coffee that drew the two Crows like carrion drew vultures.

They crept closer. Maybe it was the crackling of the bacon in the pan. Maybe he was exhausted. Or maybe his mind was elsewhere, but he did not hear the two Crows approaching him from the rear.

When they were close enough to pounce, Big Chin grabbed Braddock's arms and pinned them behind his back while Would Not Listen took a small stick and ran it across Braddock's throat as if he were cutting it with a knife. Braddock sucked in a huge lungful of air but before he could react in any meaningful way, Big Chin had him in a big, affectionate bear hug and Would Not Listen had used his stick to fish a slice of bacon from the pan. As for Braddock, he had thought his life was over, and was so relieved that he danced Big Chin around the fire even though he and the Crow had not had much to do with each other during the times the warrior was scouting for the army.

Then he stepped back and attempted to sign a message to Big Chin. "Take me to the big Crow village." His signing was so clumsy and limited that Big Chin found himself staring at Braddock's hands like a child watching a magic show.

"Tell me," Big Chin replied slowly, using vocabulary he had learned in late-night talks with the soldiers. "Tell me with talk."

"I need to find Young Buffalo," said Braddock.

"Why no more soldier?" asked Big Chin, studying Braddock's ragged non-uniform.

Braddock was at a loss for an answer. How could he

explain that he was always joining up because he wanted to fight, and always deserting because he hated to soldier?

"Like to fight like Indian, not like soldier," Braddock replied, and from his point of view, this was no lie. But Big Chin had a devious turn of mind.

"Ah," he smiled. "Want squaw man?" he said, missing some words but conveying the thought. He knew that many soldiers on the plain had to go for a long time without a woman, except for sometimes the "pay women." He knew about them too.

Braddock looked past the campfire into the night. "It would be nice to have a woman," he said.

"Crow woman make good wife," Big Chin said, and again he was being devious, because what he had on his mind was his sister She Bear, who had been living in his lodge since her husband had died in a fight with the Atsinas a few years back. She Bear was not bad to look at, but she had earned her name with her disposition, and Big Chin was trying to find a way to get her out of his tepee because she was forever sowing discord between him and Wild Berry. Perhaps she would be happier in her own lodge, maybe with the white man, who might some day take her not only out of his lodge, but out of the village—maybe even away from the valley of the Elk River. Then he would have some peace at home.

"Come, morning," Big Chin said, making the sign for morning as he said it.

"Morning," Braddock repeated, signing as he said it, atrociously.

He must have learned his signs from the Arikara, Big Chin thought, not because the Rees necessarily signed any worse than anybody else, but because to Big Chin's way of thinking, that misbegotten tribe was incapable of doing anything well.

Chapter 20

Young Buffalo was not sure that he was glad to see Braddock. On one hand, he seemed to be a good fighter who was not afraid. On the other hand, the way the soldier chiefs treated Braddock showed they did not care for him very much. Young Buffalo did not always understand why white men acted toward each other in certain ways, but he sensed that Braddock's sloppiness counted against him.

"Did the soldier chiefs let you go?" he asked Braddock, once he had been given space in Big Chin's tepee, at the latter's insistence.

Braddock thought for a moment. He was not a liar by nature, but he was given to selective truth when he felt that his future depended upon it. Still, he felt that Young Buffalo would guess the truth anyway, so he elected to tell it the way it was.

"I did not want to stay with the soldiers," he said. "Fort all closed in," and he hugged himself to show how he felt. "Like to be free," he added, knowing that Indians should understand that kind of feeling.

Young Buffalo did not understand. Why would a man become a soldier in the first place if he did not want to feel closed up? Young Buffalo would no more think of putting himself inside a fort than he would think of crawling into a box and burying it in the ground.

Young Buffalo brought Braddock to Running Wolf, not

because Running Wolf had the right to decide who lived in the village—he didn't—but because Running Wolf had the ability to see into a man's heart.

Running Wolf and his two wives always had good hot food in the kettle for anyone in the village who was hungry, and he supported seven souls who lived in his lodge, which was the biggest and finest in the village. Braddock had seen his food snatched from the frying pan by Big Chin and Would Not Listen. He was so hungry he almost could not focus on Running Wolf's questions enough to provide cogent answers.

"So, you run from the soldiers and you want me to make you welcome here even though you know that we are the soldiers' friends," the chief said sternly, with the help of Blue Shirt, who had a gift for languages and had learned much English in the course of his scouting experiences with the army.

During the years Braddock had spent on the northern plains he had met Crows, Arikara, Shoshone, Sioux, Arapaho, Assiniboin, Blackfoot, and Cheyenne. Nearly every one of them had refused to show emotion before him or any other soldier he knew. Running Wolf was different. He viewed Braddock with obvious distaste. This was the man he had to persuade.

"When you look at me, you see a white man," said Braddock. "Look at me closer. My hair, my eyes, my skin. Do you not see that I have the blood of the red man?" he asked.

"Ah, yes, what you call 'Indian.' Which 'Indian'? I would like a white man more than a Sioux."

Running Wolf's response was so devastating to Braddock that he was slow figuring the words that might let him in.

"My people came from the other side of big river. Very powerful people. The white men made them move to the land on Red River to the south."

"If them so powerful why white man make them move?"

"White men are more powerful, more powerful than any Indian tribes."

Running Wolf nodded. "That is why we do not fight

white man. We fight with him, against our enemies."

"That is what my people did," Braddock replied. "Until the white man did not need us any more. Then he took our land. He took all our land. Gave us land instead that we did not want." For the first time in Braddock's life he talked about the Creek people as "us." Never in his life had he thought much about his Creek blood. Nobody had ever told him anything about his great-grandfather, how he came to marry a white woman, how the generations of dilution had brought respectability. None of that had meant a thing to Braddock. Until now, trying desperately to find a place among the Crows. How many lies had his family told early on in their quest to find a place in Tennessee in a white society?

Running Wolf was no fool. Nor was he impressed by Braddock's redman blood. He'd never heard of the Creeks and had he chanced to be visiting the Indian territory where the Creeks lived, he probably would not have liked them and they would have liked him less. But Running Wolf believed in live and let live among his own people. He respected Young Buffalo and was very fond of the ebullient Big Chin. If they want him to live among them, they must have their reasons. Very well. The man came with a good rifle and ammunition, a fine Army Colt, and some soldier experience. Young Buffalo said he was a better fighter than most of the soldiers. Another fighter in the village at a time when the Sioux were threatening mayhem was not to be taken lightly.

From the day he arrived, Braddock was determined to "go Indian"; that is, to vanish into the Crow culture to the extent that if the village met up with soldiers he knew, they would not even recognize him. He let his hair grow, wore a loincloth and leggings, put hoops in his ears, traded his wide-brimmed army hat for a floppy black hat with a high crown and a big eagle feather. He did not have much of a beard but he shaved it nearly every day.

And he was determined to take a Crow wife, soon. Most Crow women did not look beautiful to him but he had not known a beautiful girl since his fiancée, now more than a dozen years removed from his life. And Big Chin's sister She Bear was still very young, with a nice shape, a pretty round face, and a pleasant smile—when she smiled. There was the rub. She almost never smiled. She looked at him with longing, almost lust. Braddock could not remember the last time a woman had looked upon him that way, and her desire excited him. Still, there was something about her, something he could not quite figure, that made him cautious. One evening she had made her bed close to him, and in the middle of the night he had felt her touch, heard her soft words that he did not understand, and very nearly pulled her under his blanket. But he was unfamiliar with Crow customs. If he slept with her, did that mean they were married? He had come to the Crow to be free and maybe find a way to prosper in business the way squaw men often did. If he took the wrong woman he might find himself on the run again, and this time, where would he have to run to?

So he pretended to be unawakable and after awhile She Bear gave up with what Braddock took to be a snort of disgust and crawled back under her own blanket. When he felt a little surer about her, maybe he would be the one doing the midnight crawl into her bed.

The next day such a possibility became very remote.

Perhaps she was angry because she had felt rebuffed the night before. Perhaps she was battling nature. Perhaps she was just experiencing a little more discontent then usual. The following morning she threw a magnificent temper tantrum, and the unfortunate object was Wild Berry. With the responsibility of marriage and the daily dominance of her husband, Wild Berry had lost much of the vicious temperament that had caused her to be named after a poisonous fruit that drove people and animals mad just before death. She Bear repeatedly mistook her increased outer calm for submissiveness. She never seemed to learn. On this morning she did it again.

The day started out calmly enough, with the women bustling around preparing breakfast while the men lay in bed for an extra forty winks. The smell of coffee was so thick and rich that Braddock considered Big Chin's tepee to be just about heaven. It seemed that Wild Berry and She Bear had agreed the day before that Wild Berry was to fashion a new pair of moccasins for Big Chin and She Bear was supposed to mend some of his leggings. She Bear was content with the arrangement until she saw the leggings; then she let out a wail that might have been heard halfway down Elk River to the country of the hot shooting water. Fortunately the two women were standing just outside the lodge at the time.

"Sure, you give me a job like that because you saw what a mess he had made of his leggings!" she snarled. "A real wife would cut a new pair of leggings for her husband, but just for spite you give me these rags and expect me to make something good out of them! I'm surprised he hasn't thrown you out yet!"

"Shh, try and let them sleep a little longer," said Wild Berry quietly, but Braddock could hear the anxiety in her voice. He liked that woman, so sensual and mischievous yet so patient with her unpredictable husband.

"Don't you take that tone with me," She Bear growled back at Wild Berry, who had ducked back into the tepee to stir the kettle. She Bear followed her back in, and the rest of the argument was carried out in sibilant hisses, most of which Braddock missed. The hissing got louder and louder, at least on She Bear's part, until at last Big Chin rolled out of his bed and told She Bear to get out and stay out until she learned to speak properly to his wife.

Abruptly she turned her wrath on her brother. "You marry this woman and suddenly it no longer matters that your sister is alone, without a husband," she said venomously.

"I have tried to find you a husband," he replied. "Nobody even wants you as a second wife because they want their lodge to be peaceful." He turned and looked meaningfully deep into the shadows of the tepee, where Braddock lay rolled in his blankets, pretending to sleep. "I think he is a good man," he said quietly, "but why should he want you when he wakes up to your shouting and your anger?"

"That is the husband you have chosen for me?" she sneered. "Who wants him?"

"Who wants you?" Big Chin retorted. "We have lost

men in battle, in the hunt, to disease at the forts. There are no unmarried men for you and no men or their women would let you in as a second wife because you are so much trouble. He may be only a poor white man but he is a man.''

"But what kind of man?" she asked heatedly, recalling her rebuffed advances. "His blood is too thin for a woman! And you, my brother, my big, stupid brother—"

Her voice was rising again as her bad temper once more took control. "And this woman from the village of Gray Coyote who cannot speak our tongue properly and who thinks that only she can make moccasins for my precious brother. What kind of a man are you to put up with such a woman?" She was about to give a long commentary on Wild Berry's cooking, Wild Berry's hide curing, perhaps even Wild Berry's lovemaking, but Wild Berry had finally run out of patience after two years of criticism and complaints. Too late to stop her, She Bear watched in disbelief as Wild Berry picked up She Bear's bedding and hurled it through the open door-flap into the dust outside. Then she reached for two of She Bear's bundles, pulled her arms back, and with an underhanded motion sent them out after the bedding. Then she folded her arms and turned to Big Chin's angry sister.

"You do not say such things to my husband," she said. "You are not welcome here any longer."

"I?" She Bear rose up tall and rigid in self-righteous dignity. "You throw me out of my brother's lodge?"

She turned to Big Chin. "Who is boss person here?" she challenged.

"Not you, my vicious sister," he responded. "Go back to our mother. Tell her you are sorry for being mean to her. I want you here no more." She was not moving, so he helped her toward the door flap with a kick in the rump.

She Bear grabbed hold of two lodgepoles and attempted to pull down the tepee, but she was unsuccessful, and one more lick sent her out the doorway into the sunshine, where several in the village were standing by watching the drama play out. She was too proud to give in to defeat. She grabbed the poles that controlled the smoke flaps, pulled them down, and stalked away without deigning to pick up her meager belongings. She did regain her self-control enough to keep her mouth shut as she walked past the smirkers on her way to her mother's lodge.

Chapter 21

Braddock had been unable to follow the argument but sensed that his indifference had been the fuse that had set off her powder. He wanted to apologize to Big Chin, but within a minute after She Bear was gone Big Chin began to laugh, great belly-shaking laughter. Wild Berry joined in, her musical treble a pretty counterpoint to his thundering bass.

Tears were rolling down Big Chin's face as he turned to Braddock. "When she came to you last night why did you not take her under your blanket?" he asked, his dark eyes dancing with mischief.

"I—I wanted to—I wasn't sure it would be all right."

"All right?" Big Chin roared. "It would have been all wrong. She would have clawed your back to ribbons." He stopped laughing long enough to catch his breath. "When her husband was still alive we could hear—she had those mean claws tearing up his back and he was such a brave man. Not wanting to cry out, you know, too big a man to show pain. 'Nnnhhh! Nnnhhhh!' Big Chin imitated the pained, subdued grunts of his late brother-in-law, and that brought back the laughter, shaking, quaking laughter.

" 'Nnnhhh! Nnnhhhh!' That's just the way he sounded, like a warrior the Comanches are torturing trying hard not to show the pain." Now his laughter turned into a whoop. "Imagine such a way to make love. I think when death came to him he welcomed it because he could finally sleep good without being ripped apart in the middle of the night.''

Braddock noted that Wild Berry was keeping her thoughts to herself. She had not relished throwing She Bear out, and though her husband was making her laugh, she had hated the confrontation. For his part, Braddock could not help but be disappointed. Still he was horrified at how close he had come to being a sacrificial victim.

Big Chin knew his sister would be back no later than the following day so he scheduled a hunt for himself, Blue Shirt, and Braddock. He asked Young Buffalo and Would Not Listen to come along, but both men were busy. Young Buffalo and White Hot Smoke lived in the next lodge with his mother, and he was not pleased to see Big Chin preparing to head for the hills so suddenly.

"You're going to leave Wild Berry here to face that sister of yours all by herself? How could you do such a thing?"

"She can take care of herself just fine," said Big Chin. "Now, it would be fine with me if you might step in and—"

"And what? I'd sooner face a Hunkpapa village than She Bear when she's having a bad day."

"Then you would not help Wild Berry if my sister started to fight with her?"

Young Buffalo stared down at his moccasins in deep thought. "You don't stay too long away," he said emphatically to his friend.

"I be back two, three day at most."

Big Chin solved his problem in a most unusual way—that is to say, he took both Wild Berry and She Bear on the hunt.

Blue Shirt brought along his wife too, a very young woman named Star Appearing. They made their way out of the village, traveling north with four extra ponies heading for a place where they almost always found buffalo at the end of the summer. The dispositions of both Big Chin and his sister improved as the village vanished behind a hillside. These two were much happier in the solitude of the hills, without the bumptious bustle of the village to disturb their tranquillity.

Six young riders on good ponies trailing unburdened pack horses could make pretty good time. Thirteen hours of riding found them less than a day from their destination. They camped contentedly by a clear stream with good water for the ponies. The men relaxed while the women set up camp. Blue Shirt produced a small quantity of whiskey. There was not much whiskey around the village. Running Wolf frowned on it, and as long as he kept his men away from the whites, few of them would make any great effort to procure it.

The women prepared dinner, a good meal with broiled fresh buffalo meat and corn. For a while the men talked and smoked, but they were still young enough that when their wives took their hands and led them away, they followed the women into the shadows. Then only She Bear and Braddock were left by the fire.

Each had reason to dislike the other, yet each found the other attractive. For a time they stared at each other, and then She Bear smiled. Braddock was pleased by her unexpected good nature. They began to speak, and sign, awkward for both of them, but each made the other understand, and here was the sense of their conversation.

"Are you still angry?" Braddock asked.

She hung her head, ashamed, and shook it. "I could not help it," she said. "I am lonely."

"Did you get angry before your husband died?"

I have always, she thought, but she could not share her shame with this dark white stranger. She looked down at the ground and said nothing.

"Come sit by me," he said. She obeyed, and was glad when he reached out and brought her closer to him. She felt his face warm against hers. Felt his lips against hers, and let him slide her dress from her so he could feel her skin against his bare chest. It felt good, so good. Why had she hated him so?—oh yes, it was because he would not do this the last time she came to him. He pulled her down and they spent long, slow minutes exploring each other. Each one wanted to make it last. Each one wanted the other to have good feelings. Each one had a reason to be kind, to be gentle, to be loving. This was an invitation to the future, a sample offering with no guarantees, but with hope.

He could feel her tremble, a good tremble. He could see her eyes wide, unblinking, in the flickering light of the fire.

He took her hands in his and stopped his movement. Her eyelids flickered.

"Do not claw my back or I will pull your arms away and satisfy myself and you will never have me again," he said. She knew only a few of the words, yet she understood their meaning. She damped her excitement just enough to enjoy the power of the Tennessean as he brought her toward fulfillment. She could feel him, too, the desire, the need for her, the hunger for her.

Her fingers began to curl as her excitement and her movement increased, as she rose to meet him, and she threw her arms around him, squeezing tightly, digging her finger-nails into the palms of her own hands. The pain was exquisite, and after she reached her peak, her long climax dissolved into gratitude for him, for the unexpected under-standing, for daring to demand gentleness from her, for tak-ing such obvious delight in their union. And in their mellow moments of repose immediately following, she wanted to pledge her eternal submission to him if only he would take her as his, but an inner voice told her that if she surrendered, his gentleness would turn to cruelty.

Yet the next morning, when the women were serving the men an early breakfast, Big Chin and Blue Shirt and their wives immediately noticed a difference. She Bear was at-tentive to the needs of Braddock and she had a look of peace on her face that none of them had ever seen in her. That was not quite true. Big Chin remembered seeing that look on the face of his sister when she was a child, when after a sickly winter she had eaten her first large meal. He knew what had happened during the night and was not yet sure how he felt about it.

Braddock was a mixture of conflicting emotions. On one hand he felt satisfied after the evening's activities. But something was wrong. He should have enjoyed the way she had cut a choice piece of buffalo hump, roasted it carefully, then cut it in two and served him the bigger, better portion.

Instead he felt annoyed, as if she were proclaiming their union without asking him how he felt about it. He wanted to tell her to get the hell away from him, that he would cook his own meat, thank you.

His feelings of annoyance annoyed him. If he did not want a woman who made sweet love to him at night and served him a loving breakfast in the morning, then what did he want? He felt that he had only two choices: find a good Crow woman and settle down with her, or spend the rest of his miserable life wandering the West in poverty until he either starved to death or a predator claimed him.

But he simply could not help the way he felt. This woman had satisfied a hunger, slaked a thirst, but had not filled his heart. He remembered how he had felt about his fiancée before the war.

No, if he were to be honest, he could not remember how he had felt about his fiancée. Not really. His confusion just made him more ill-tempered, but he kept his feelings hidden as he sank his teeth into the choice morsel she had given him. Nobody noticed, because neither of the other men showed much appreciation for the services their women were rendering them.

After breakfast the women packed and they all moved out, the men considerably ahead of the women as they followed the valley of an unnamed creek toward a canyon where they never failed to find game at this time of the year. Their eyes, attentive to the sparse yellow grass that stretched before them, failed to catch the straight line of a gun barrel on a bluff above them. This was Crow hunting ground. It had been Crow hunting ground for generations. While the Sioux and others sometimes nibbled around the edges, there was no reason to believe that after the last punishment the Crows had inflicted upon them the Sioux would take the chance of angering their traditional enemies yet again.

But warriors of the plains often do not conform to the wishes of their chiefs. In this case, five young men had come into the Crow lands on a challenge from the mischief-making uncle of one of them. Their goal was simply to bring back the scalp of an Absarokee, no less, no more. But once they had reached the heart of Crow country they were so pleased by the bounty of game that they almost forgot their purpose, as they hunted and gorged themselves. It was a sad accident that they discovered Big Chin's party before some alert Crow scout discovered them and put an end to their good times.

The valley was narrow at this point, so the young Tetons hidden above found themselves within easy rifle range of Big Chin's group. And all except one of them had late-model rifles. The Sioux had stolen many white men's weapons from the farms and villages they had been raiding in Colorado. How satisfying to put them to good use against the hated Crows.

The young Sioux were impetuous and careless. Their badly planned ambush should have gone awry and their scalps should have wound up drying in the lodge of a Crow marksman, but this day everything went their way. Their first volley knocked Big Chin and Braddock out of their saddles, and the second wounded two of the three women.

Braddock felt the bite of the bullet as it burned through his thigh. Somehow he held on to his rifle as he hit the ground. He crawled behind a bush and began to scoop dirt in front of him, although he was at first not certain of the direction the firing came from. The gunfire had missed Blue Shirt, who had immediately found the location of the shooters and quirted his pony hard to put a quick three hundred yards more between himself and the bushwhackers. But he didn't make it. The rifles cracked again, all aimed at him, and this time one of the bullets found its mark. His rifle flew in one direction and he dropped into the grass in another, with blood flowing from a hole just above his hip.

Blue Shirt was a battler. He reclaimed his rifle and snatched a bag of ammunition from his pony before he sought out the creek bank and found cover there. She Bear had dismounted and run to where Big Chin lay, picked up his rifle, and was laying down fire in the direction of the ambush.

By then the soldier had reasserted itself in Braddock's breast. He did not feel the pain of the wound. He reasoned that they must be close to have hit so many of their targets. His sharp eyes scanned the nearest bluffs and quickly found the painted faces. He cocked his hammer, laid his sights on one of them, squeezed the trigger. The face disappeared.

Blue Shirt had also found the ambushers, and opened up with a good Spencer rifle. Braddock saw a body slide halfway down the hill and lodge against the trunk of a stunted pine tree.

That was all.

The two men waited but a few minutes before they broke cover to see about Big Chin and the women. What they found was heartbreaking.

Big Chin lay still from a bullet that had entered an eye socket and taken a part of his skull with it as it exited. Wild Berry was unconscious from her fall, covered with blood from a bullet that had entered and exited her neck. Star Appearing was bending over her with a doeskin cloth, working hard to staunch the flow of blood.

Braddock limped over to where Big Chin lay. Big Chin was dead, and She Bear was draped over her brother, barely conscious herself. Even while she was emptying his rifle at their attackers, her life had been draining from her through a wound in her upper chest. Braddock watched helplessly as she stared at him without speaking. She smiled at him, a secret smile, as if only he and she knew the truth, that she had been ready to love somebody before a bullet found a home in her. Then her dark eyes closed, her labored breathing grew shallow, and then stopped altogether.

Chapter 22

Many of the plains Indian tribes customarily used the travois to transport goods, wounded people, and the elderly from place to place. The Crow prided themselves on their horsemanship. In most Crow villages, everybody rode.

This little group had to compromise their customs if they were to make it home. Of the four survivors only Star Appearing was unwounded, and of the three others only Braddock was capable of movement. His leg wound could hardly be called superficial, and soon stiffened up so badly that every step was agony. He took the sharpest hatchet they had and limped down to the creek bank to chop down young trees. The hatchet had a decent edge on it, but it was not made for this kind of work and it took him two hours to chop down four trees for legs, then another for a cross member. Did the Cheyenne travois use a cross member? He did not remember, but it seemed logical.

In the meantime, Star Appearing worked hard packing moss into the wounds of Blue Shirt and Wild Berry to stop the bleeding before it was too late. She worked with a rifle on her lap, looking around frequently, worried that the Sioux might return and finish their bloody job. She gave her patients water and decided their wounds maybe were not as bad as they might have been.

Braddock tied the logs to the saddles of two ponies and brought them back to Star Appearing, who immediately be-

gan stretching buffalo robes between the logs to serve as
beds for the wounded. They had already loaded the dead
over the saddles of the two ponies before the bodies had
stiffened into a straight position. Critical as their situation
remained, Braddock's heart ached for Big Chin, who had
taken him into his home, and even more so for She Bear,
who had been his tender lover for one night on this earth.
Now that she was gone he felt certain that he might have
tamed her down enough for them to have a good life. In
death all the hardness had left her face, leaving a sweetness
she had never known in life, at least not until the last night
she lived.

Star Appearing was too concerned about the fate of her
husband and her lifelong friend to think about the dead, but
she saw the tears on the white man's face and thought,
"This man may be too soft for our kind of life."

But as she watched him work in spite of his grief, she
changed her mind. He mounted his pony and led the two
ponies bearing the bodies up the closest rock hill he could
find. He had seen Indians bury their battle dead by dropping
them into deep crevices and covering them with rocks to
protect them from scavengers. He carried his rifle at the
ready. He knew that the Sioux could come back, but still
he persisted in his dangerous chore, and that impressed the
wife of Blue Shirt. He discovered a narrow trail that led up
the hill and followed it until he found a fissure that would
work.

"Commit this soul to your keeping, Oh Lord," he said,
to his own surprise. Except for his mother, his family had
not been much for church, and the prayer was of his own
authorship. With a grunt he pushed the body of his short-
time friend over the edge into the crevice.

He was surprised at how light She Bear was. She had
loomed so large when her temper surged, but she could not
have weighed a hundred pounds. He held her for a moment,
stared at her face and almost kissed her, but changed his
mind.

"She ain't in there," he muttered to nobody, and
dropped her body down the crevice, remembering to repeat

the prayer for her, wanting to distance himself from his grief but so far unable to do so.

Star Appearing had done a good job on his leg, and was lucky too. There would be no infection in the wounds of her patients. Considering her inexperience with travois, she had done a good job there as well, and before long they were on their way home, leading two ponies pulling travois. They knew that if the Sioux attacked, some hard choices would have to be made.

Both Wild Berry and Blue Shirt had regained consciousness. They made no sounds until their world came into focus. Blue Shirt, who was stronger, asked the questions, and Star Appearing, without halting the procession, answered them. Although Wild Berry wanted to scream out her anguish in the time-honored mourning rituals of her people, she knew that she could not indulge herself, not then. Instead she let her weakness pull her back into unconsciousness. Blue Shirt remained conscious, and Braddock gave him a skin of water, but the warrior said not another word the entire day.

Three days later the little group made their way into their village. Some people went into mourning, gashing themselves and wailing, while others vowed revenge. Coolly, quietly, Young Buffalo and Would Not Listen were meeting with other braves both young and not so young, making preliminary plans for riding southward to strike the Sioux.

But Running Wolf had different ideas. He called a council for that night, and in the red glow of the falling sun he announced that he had made a deal with a tall hat to supply the army with as many scouts as they needed for as long as they needed.

"The White Father beyond the river has heard our cries and is sending many soldiers to wipe out the Sioux," he announced after the pipe had been passed around. "He has said that there will be so many soldiers from so many directions that the Sioux will be trapped, and then they will have to give up everything."

The warriors attending the council listened in silence. They were pleased that their white friends were determined to make war on their sworn enemies, but the older ones had been around for too long to believe that anybody could get rid of the entire Sioux plague in their lifetime.

"Our chiefs have been asked to send the white men our best scouts. They say that with their good guns they could finish off the Sioux but they need the eyes of the Crows to find them. They said that we do not have to fight the Sioux, we need only find them for the soldiers."

Young Buffalo shook his head and laughed, quietly, sadly, but inside himself only. He had been around the whites enough now to see that the whites would never understand the Absarokee. To believe that the chiefs could just order their warriors to join the soldiers—how foolish! A warrior is his own man. The Crows do not make slaves of their fighting men like the white men do. And to think that the Crows would not want to fight the Sioux! The Absarokee warriors live to fight the enemy. And the Sioux were the Crows' greatest enemy.

For a moment he put away his grief and laughed out loud, and nudged Would Not Listen. "They think we fear the Sioux," he said, but Would Not Listen shook his head.

"You do not believe this is so," said Young Buffalo, as he stood up to speak.

"Ah, my young brother," said Running Wolf, who was always pleased when Young Buffalo stood to speak in council. He wanted Young Buffalo to succeed him some day as village chief, but Young Buffalo was a quiet man among the many. Had Big Chin lived, and had he grown wiser as he had grown older, he probably would have carried the pipe for the village. He was known by everybody, and loved for his ebullient good nature. Big Chin might have made a good village chief, especially with Young Buffalo as his advisor, but now, without Big Chin, Young Buffalo must step forward.

"I know the white men," he said, and paused so his fellow warriors might understand that he really *knew* them. "I watch. I listen. And now I tell you of their hearts. Some of the older ones are good fighters. Many of the younger ones are not. It does not matter. No matter what happens it does not matter. The great chief Red Cloud defeated them but it does not matter. If they have us to lead them to the Sioux they will beat the Sioux. But then we must do as they say. We should not fight on their side against the Sioux.''

There were looks of astonishment among the warriors. One of them rose, that tough, stringy old battler named Two Rivers, who was a terror on the battlefield but who seldom spoke in council.

''Has my brother Young Buffalo lost his fighting heart, that he says we should not fight the Sioux?'' He did not speak much, but everything Two Rivers said always sounded like a challenge, so Young Buffalo was not offended.

''I did not say we should not fight the Sioux,'' Young Buffalo replied, with the stony calmness that always pleased Running Wolf.

Some of the warriors murmured. Honest speech was prized as a great virtue among the people of the long-beaked bird, and Young Buffalo was considered among the straightest of talkers. He heard the murmurs, and he smiled.

''I did not say we should not fight the Sioux,'' he repeated for effect. ''What I said was that we should not fight beside the white men against the Sioux.''

That kind of hairsplitting could only infuriate a simple soldier like Two Rivers. The man was under sixty-six inches tall and weighed less than a hundred and thirty pounds, yet his stone-hard arms could drive an arrow through the body of a buffalo. He was a dark bronze color and though he had won many honors in battle he wore but a single feather in his long, black, unbraided hair. His reason? Every fight for him was a fight to the death. It was his desire to kill as many of the enemy as possible before he fell, and he did not want his death to be trivial—a chance long-distance shot from the rifle of a young Sioux brave hungry for glory. Let his death come from a Hunkpapa warrior who came to fight him face-to-face with a spear or a hatchet.

For years this stone-age anachronism had fought alongside Young Buffalo in battle, pleased by each of the young man's coups, pleased even more when the young man felled a Sioux. Unlike most warriors, Two Rivers did not quest after the prestige of touching a live enemy. He saw the land as home for either the Lakota or the Absarokee, but not for both. And now, to hear this young fighter lying and denying filled him with rage. He did not have to speak. His anger radiated from him like a bright aura.

"My wise old brother, I do not like to see you waste your anger on me," Young Buffalo said, almost smiling. "But if we fight alongside the whites, it will not be as a people, but as a few men against many. We would be at the mercy of the bluecoat leaders. And I am telling you they are not good leaders. There are few of us, yet enough to defeat our enemy in battle. The white men are so many they can afford to waste lives. We cannot."

He had Two Rivers' attention, and his curiosity, but he had not convinced him, so he walked closer so that the old warrior might hear his every word.

"Hear me, wise old brother. What I say is true. We must find the enemy for the white man. We cannot tell them what is the right thing to do; they will not listen. So after we find the enemy, we must leave them to fight the Sioux on their own."

"And if the Sioux should whip the soldiers, and take their rifles, what happens then?" asked the old battler. "They will take the new rifles and use them to murder our women and children."

"If they whip the white men once, that will only make the white men angry. They do not care about the lives of their soldiers. There are so many white men they can just bring more."

Now he walked away from the council, to the lodge of his late friend Big Chin. The men all watched him as he entered the tepee, then emerged, with a feeble, sad-faced Braddock leaning heavily on him. The warriors were silent, and polite. They trusted Young Buffalo, and waited to hear more from him.

"I bring my friend Brad-dock to you, not to listen, but to speak, so you will understand."

He let Braddock stand by himself. With great effort, the Tennessean managed to remain upright.

The two communicated in an awkward patchwork of Crow, English, and sign.

"I have asked him to tell us about the soldiers. He told me when we fought the Cheyenne that he had fought in a great war where there were many soldiers—go to the great forests of lodgepole pines and see the trees in the mountains, count the trees on all those mountains and there will be more soldiers."

"Hah!" Two Rivers' guffaw was almost rude. "And what happened to all those soldiers? Did they all die? I have not seen them. Go to a fort, what do you see? This many soldiers in a big fort." He held up his fingers, and closed his hands several times to show ten, twenty, even fifty soldiers—nowhere near enough to whip the Sioux even if they could fight.

Young Buffalo nodded and resumed his communications with the ashen-faced Braddock. Braddock responded in kind. The other warriors craned their necks with curiosity but waited patiently.

"Braddock said that when the war was over most of the soldiers took off their uniforms because they were not warriors."

"Not warriors?" asked Two Rivers. "What then? Women? Men who are like women? I do not understand."

"You have seen the white man farmers; they are not warriors and they are not women. That is how it is with the whites. I do not understand either, but that is how it is with them. He said that there are only a few soldiers because the white men do not believe they will need more soldiers to whip the Sioux. But if it happens that they *do* need more soldiers to whip the Sioux, then they will *get* more soldiers to whip the Sioux."

"That is good," said Two Rivers.

"But he says the men who lead the soldiers are not good leaders. That is why he left them to come to us. And that is why we must not fight alongside the soldiers."

Running Wolf had been pleased to listen. A good chief does not tell his people what to think. He lets them find out. Then they will believe, and when he tells them, they will follow, willingly. But he had his own questions.

"If we let our best scouts go to help the white men find the Sioux, then we will be too weak to fight the Sioux ourselves. Do we just stand idle while our enemy has one hand busy fighting the whites?''

Young Buffalo struck a thoughtful pose. The question was a wise one, of course, but Young Buffalo had been pondering that question himself, and so the answer was not long in coming.

''If the soldiers find a small village we will stay, for the battle will not take long. If the soldiers find the big village, then we will go home. If they need us again, then they can send someone to find us.''

''And how will the white men feel about us if we do not stay to help them fight the enemy?'' asked Two Rivers.

Young Buffalo stood in silence for five long minutes, such a long time that Running Wolf believed he hadn't heard the question. Just as he was about to ask Two Rivers to repeat his question, Young Buffalo made his reply. His voice rolled out from deep in his throat, in a long sad rumble.

''I do not care what the whites think of us,'' he finally replied. ''They are pleased to think badly of us most of the time anyway. Let them think what they wish, as long as they are the ones trading lives with the Sioux. The lives of our fighters are very important. We will not give them up easily.''

Chapter 23

This was a time to wait, a time of uneasiness for a people used to creating their own destiny. Running Wolf tried to keep the warriors home, to stop their private wars.

He kept a special eye on Young Buffalo and Blue Shirt. They would be plotting revenge for the death of their friend and brother, Big Chin. Death was a constant in the villages of the plains tribes—disease, childbirth, the hunt, and the warpath took their toll. But the people were never casual about death in battle. When a loved warrior was slain, especially when he was ambushed while in peaceful pursuits, the people of Running Wolf felt compelled to seek revenge. Revenge to the people of Running Wolf was not merely an eye for an eye, but a blow meant to convince the cowardly enemy that it was foolish to harm the people of this village. Often Running Wolf encouraged revenge raids, so long as they were planned and executed to succeed. But this was not a good time for haphazard action. The chief felt that something big was going to happen soon, and it was important that his people's strength be spent wisely.

Big Chin was especially loved in the village. Children followed him around. Women loved his sunny disposition and his love of chatter and gossip, so odd in a warrior. The old people also loved him, because he was never too busy to pay them a visit, eat a bit of their food, and tell them of old friends he had seen in the villages he had visited.

He was always visiting other Crow villages. He always said he had cousins there. There were always four or five girls he dreamed about on his hunts. He was a man who had never been able to make up his mind until the day he had met Wild Berry.

As for that desolate girl, she did not slash her hair or her legs, nor did she fill the night with anguished cries. While Braddock attended her every day, feeding her, changing her dressings, she showed little or no response. Once her mind had fully returned to her she almost stopped getting well. She did not want to eat. She would spend all day staring into the fire, expressionless, trance-like, not denying his death, not denying her loss, simply denying her heart and mind the ability to feel anything at all.

She would surely have starved to death had not Braddock forced her to eat. Food or no food, the feeling among the older women was that she would perish if she did not awaken from her trance. Fortunately there was a little something deep within her monitoring her world, and that something gradually became aware that she was carrying Big Chin's child.

The message seeped into her slowly, like water trickling along a creek in summer, but as it did, she began to show signs of life. First her eyes started following Braddock as he moved around the tepee, doing women's chores, which caused some comment in the village. But the food would not last forever. Sooner or later he'd have to go out hunting. Running Wolf had come by several times offering food, but Braddock knew that the chief had to feed a lot of people and he refused help. One evening he leaned close to her and said, softly, "You must come back to us so I can go and get food for us. I will take care of you but you must help me."

She did not understand his words but she heard the kindness in his voice and she touched his hand with hers. She then signed "thank you," a sign he had learned from Young Buffalo when they scouted together.

He adjusted her buffalo robe. Autumn was almost here and the chill winds would soon be coasting down from Canada. She took his hand and placed it on her belly. Although it was still fairly flat, he understood what she meant.

"That is good," he said. "Now you must get much better fast so I can take care of the both of you."

The antelope stew was steaming hot in a camp kettle. During the days before the fatal journey he had watched her cooking, fascinated by her ability to take a little of this, a little of that, a chunk of this, a few fresh leaves of that, throw it in a pot of boiling water, and always come up with something savory and delicious. He had studied her cooking methods and now he copied them, with impressive results.

He spooned the liquid from the mixture into a wooden bowl, sat her up, and let her sip. Was she ready for something solid? He would let her make that decision. He had no idea. Nor had he any idea who to talk to for advice. Young Buffalo and other young men were away, some hunting, some scouting for the army. He would have liked to talk to wise Running Wolf, but he was still intimidated by the village leader. The Crow language was coming slowly to him, and most of the people still felt strange. Their ways were so different from the ways he had learned as a child.

She sipped for a while, then stopped. She tired easily; she probably wanted to rest now. But no, she signed that she wanted more. He gave her more, and to his surprise, she spoke her first words since the ambush, and the words were English. "Thank you," she said.

Two lonely-looking tepees stood exposed to the early autumn winds. The flap from one opened and a man and woman emerged, both wrapped in warm buffalo hides.

The past week had made all the difference in the world. She was eating solids now, and she had given him a smile—her first—on the previous day. He had responded by going out hunting, and bringing back a deer.

The village had picked up and moved, as they did frequently during the summer. With the autumn they would move less frequently, and then, come winter, they would set up more permanent quarters, in a sheltered valley, tucking themselves away from the bitter winds of the high country.

Braddock and Wild Berry ducked into the neighboring tepee, home of Young Buffalo and White Hot Smoke, who was ripening toward motherhood. Young Buffalo had decided to stay for a while for the sake of Wild Berry. Though he and White Hot Smoke liked Braddock, neither had great faith in his ability to care for Big Chin's widow, and they were determined not to lose her as they had lost him.

Braddock was surprised at how hard Young Buffalo had taken the loss of his friend. Everything he had seen and heard about these people had convinced him that they did not feel deeply, the way white men did. Oh yes, they had emotions that ran hard along the surface and occasionally erupted into violence and cruelty—his father had told him that, many years ago. That was why Andy Jackson had thrown the Indians out of Alabama, Tennessee, and Mississippi; that was why Andy Jackson was the greatest American this side of George Washington. That's what Braddock's father told him.

But Young Buffalo did not fit the descriptions he had heard of the Crows, or any other Indians for that matter. Young Buffalo was like Running Wolf, looking to take care of the poor people—and there were some very poor people in Running Wolf's band, people who were old, or widowed, or just plain rotten hunters.

And now Young Buffalo was there to take care of Wild Berry, which offended Braddock. He had tried to get them to go with the rest of the band, but the young chief—for that was how people were thinking of him now—and White Hot Smoke refused to move until Wild Berry was also ready to travel.

Today was her first day out. White Hot Smoke had cooked a stew of elk, a brew to give strength to those barely well enough to eat hardy food. Wild Berry was given the seat closest to the fire, and there she sat, carefully, for she was still sore, and frail. Young Buffalo noticed the gentleness with which Braddock helped her seat herself, and he did not miss the glance of appreciation from Wild Berry. He felt a surge of anger that this white man had the nerve to step into the lodge of his dead friend. He was not worthy. He was only a sloppy, bad soldier who had deserted the bluecoats when he had had enough of army rules. Young Buffalo did not respect rules imposed upon him from outside, but he believed absolutely in the rules that had been fed to him with his mother's milk. A man had to have rules from somewhere. This man did not fit in with his own kind, so why should he fit into the hard world of the Absarokee?

Yet he had survived the Sioux attack and, according to Blue Shirt's wife, he had fought bravely. Alone she surely would not have been able to hold off the miserable Hunkpapa dogs. He had had a keen eye and a steady hand when anything less would have cost the lives of six people instead of two. Young Buffalo had noticed, too, the sadness in the eyes of Braddock. The white man must have cared a lot for Big Chin, or perhaps even She Bear, though he could not imagine anybody forming an attachment to She Bear.

And now he watched as Braddock showed sweetness and kindness toward the woman who had once almost been the woman of *his* life, a happy, mischievous girl who had become the perfect mate for his garrulous friend, his brother. He felt a vise clamp tight in his chest, felt the unquenchable hatred for the Sioux that Crows had felt over so many years. How strange, he thought, that the instruments of his revenge must be the white men. Not such a long time ago, when the Sioux had come to annihilate them, they had sent the men of the Teton back to their hills licking their wounds and weeping for their dead. The story of the battle had been told so many times over so many campfires that it seemed to him it had been fought by legendary giants like his grandfather and his grandfather's grandfather. But no, he, Young Buffalo, and Big Chin, and so many others who had been his warrior cohorts had fought and won that battle.

So why must they now depend on the stumbling, bumbling, clownish soldiers to fight their next battles for them? He did not understand why it was so, yet he knew it was so. "We cannot beat them alone," he had told his people.

But why not? It was not that the Crows were growing weaker, but that the Sioux were growing more desperate. Very desperate, if they were going around asking the Crows to join them in war against the soldiers. None of the young men had gone to the old chiefs and asked why they did not join the Sioux. To join the Sioux was unthinkable. The Sioux had always been the hated enemy, and the white men— Here Young Buffalo's thoughts ran into a stone wall. The white men were said to be their friends, but they had taken so much land from them. Tribes did not remain friends when one tribe took land from another. Why were the whites any different?

He spent days pondering the question as he sat by his fire, as he hunted for both lodges, as he scouted carefully, seeking signs of their hated enemy, until finally, one morning, Braddock emerged from Big Chin's lodge and announced that Wild Berry was finally strong enough to travel.

They could travel easily, because most of Young Buffalo's thirty-seven ponies were with the village's main herd, nibbling the grass about a day's travel down the Elk River. Only a half dozen pack horses, carrying lodges, personal effects, and food, trailed along with the four riders.

Young Buffalo felt as if he had an arrow in the belly as he looked back at the last village encampment where he had seen Big Chin alive. The pain traveled from his belly to his throat till he thought he might choke on his sadness. He rode on about a hundred yards ahead, not just to watch for enemies, but so the others would not see the tears.

Not until they had put two sets of hills and two valleys between themselves and the old village site did the pain begin to lift from his throat, replaced by the usual deadly calm that made him so respected among his people. Let the Lakotas come, all of them, the Hunkpapa and Miniconjou, the Oglalla and Sicangu, the Itazipcho, the Sihasapa, and the Oohenonpa. He knew them all, and hated them all; why had the Creator of life made so many of them?

They traveled slowly for the sake of Wild Berry, but the second day she seemed much stronger, spending much of the time riding beside and talking to her lifelong friend White Hot Smoke. Toward the end of the second day they began to see signs of the next village encampment, and around dark they topped a ridge and looked down on the new camp, with its circle of tepees glowing warmly from the fires within. Young Buffalo could not help but feel that warmth travel to his chest, as it always did when he returned to his home village.

To the north he could see the dark mass that had to be the herd, cropping the ample autumn grass. He wanted to turn north, to visit his favorite war ponies, but the women were tired, so instead he led them into the middle of the village, where they found their places and began to erect their lodges.

In the dim light of an outside campfire, Young Buffalo spotted his friend Blue Shirt approaching. He could tell from his friend's walk that something was troubling him. He thought perhaps his friend might still be mourning the death of Big Chin, but as Blue Shirt drew closer Young Buffalo knew that something more was causing him worry.

"Running Wolf is missing," Blue Shirt said by way of greeting, before even inquiring about the health of Wild Berry.

Young Buffalo nodded and awaited the details.

"He went out hunting yesterday morning with Seven Horses. Each followed his own deer track, saying they would meet at the place where they parted company. Seven Horses followed his deer for—" he held his hands three feet apart to show how far the sun would move while Seven Horses was following his deer "—then lost it and returned to the place where they were to meet. He waited till not long before sunset, then followed the track of his chief, but lost it in the dark and returned to the meeting place. The next morning he looked again but lost his trail at a small creek. He kept looking for the rest of the day, then traveled all night to get back to the village. Tomorrow we must go looking for him. I am afraid."

Young Buffalo said nothing, but his heart was filled with dread. Running Wolf would never stray long or far from the village, especially during times like these. On the other hand, the chief might have given away so much that he might have had to hunt to replenish his lodge's food supply. Young Buffalo was tired. He needed rest if he was to think clearly. Still, as he lay down beside White Hot Smoke that night, sleep evaded him. Too much was going wrong. He relied on his warrior's discipline to close his eyes, relax his mind and body, and will him into a sleep that lasted only until the first purple light of dawn.

Only three of them rode north the next morning. The village could not afford to be missing any more warriors.

Of the three, only Young Buffalo was a warrior of the first rank. Seven Horses was way past his peak; in fact not far from a time when arthritis and bad eyesight would make him more of a hindrance than a help in the everyday life of the village. The third man was Braddock, whom the village still did not trust, but Young Buffalo knew that he was reliable in a fire fight.

As they rode, Seven Horses explained in detail what had happened. Had he heard any gunshots? No. Any loud noises? Any signs of white men, or red? No.

Perhaps his pony had thrown him and run. Perhaps he had been bitten by a snake. Either way, Seven Horses should have found him, but he had not. And if Running Wolf was hurt, where was his pony?

By noon Seven Horses had led them to the place where he and Running Wolf had scheduled their rendezvous. There was no sign of their chief, but there was still a faint track of the chief's pony. They followed the track to the stream, then rode downstream and spread out in an attempt to pick up the track. They were moving into a canyon rimmed by huge rocky ledges. While the others continued to seek out a trail, Young Buffalo was drawn to a spot high on the ledges where hawks were circling. He spotted a meager trail that led up between some rocks toward the birds, left his pony below and climbed the trail, but when he got to the top all he found was a steep drop-off. He pondered the question of what was drawing the birds, then dismounted and walked toward the ledge. An area above the ledge had a little grassland, and into the soil that held the grass, someone had driven a stake, and attached a rope. The rope led over the ledge.

Young Buffalo tugged at the rope. There was considerable weight on the end of it. He walked to the ledge and looked over. Swaying in the afternoon wind, fifty feet down, was a body, the body of a Crow warrior. An old Crow, that was certain. As he watched the body swinging in the wind, he could see that it had been scalped. The head was tilted back so far that he could determine that the throat was cut, a signature mutilation of the Sioux. Though the scalping had distorted the muscles of the face, and parts of it were covered with dried blood, there was no doubt that the man at the far end of the rope was his chief, Running Wolf, the finest man he had ever known. More than a dozen arrows had been shot into him. But why then had they hung him off a rock face, to dangle in the breeze while the vultures and eagles fed off him?

The tears came freely now. He did not care who saw him. His chief, so tough yet so wise and good, was now a thing, hideously butchered by the Sioux and hung off a cliff as eagle bait—ah!

The Sioux must still be close by. He thought of their war bonnets, the long rows of eagle feathers that trailed down their backs. They would be waiting, somewhere, for eagles to perch on the arrows they had shot into him, then at short range they would kill the birds and retrieve the feathers for their own war bonnets or for trade.

He took a deep breath and collected himself. Mourning was for later. Action was for now. He leaned over the edge and saw a ledge below on the face of the cliff. On a hunch he skirted the edge until he found another rope that trailed down the face of the cliff. Immediately he understood. The Sioux devils were down on that ledge, so close to where the body hung that they could have almost grabbed the birds with their bare hands. He reached down to pull the rope up and leave the Lakota braves stranded down below, but then he paused. If this was the only way up for them, then why not wait for them to come up and dispose of them one by one?

He rounded up Braddock and Seven Horses and showed them the fate of their chief, but he did not give them a chance to vent their grief.

"His killers are down there," he said, softly, pointing to the ledge. "We can have them all, no matter how many of them there are."

The two men agreed.

In the late afternoon they sat atop the bluff, waiting for the rope to move, like a nibble on the end of a fishing line. If the Sioux waited till dark to ascend, that would be better. They would come up one by one and fall prey to knives and hatchets. Seven Horses lay with one hand on the rope, poised to feel the telltale vibrations of the climbers, and when the sun was red on the western horizon, he nodded to Young Buffalo. The rope had been seized below. Now they could all see the rope moving. They waited, quietly, until a face appeared where the rope hung over the ledge. Still they waited. The face had endured a difficult time. The Sioux warrior was too tired and distracted to notice much as he clawed his way to the top of the bluff.

The *whoosh* of a descending trade hatchet was the last sound the Sioux warrior heard in this life. He slumped, lifeless. They let his blood pour out into the earth and waited for more Sioux to climb the rope, but none did.

"Maybe he was the only one?" Seven Horses asked, but Young Buffalo shook his head. No one man could have bested Running Wolf. He was too smart and strong for that.

"Well then, maybe he was the only one down below."

Again Young Buffalo shook his head. He did not bother to explain his train of thought. Enough that he was certain others were down on that ledge.

Seven Horses was not so sure.

"I will prove to you that they are below," Young Buffalo said, and with one quick downward swing severed the warrior's head from its body. Seven Horses descended the hill in another direction and came back with a rope in his hand. Young Buffalo took the rope and tied it as best he could to the long braids of the dead Sioux warrior. Seven Horses had also brought up a small bag full of crow feathers. Young Buffalo took a handful and stuffed it into the mouth of the dead Sioux, a sloppy job that left the corpse looking more like he had eaten a dead crow than his enemy had humiliated him. He scalped the Sioux, then as an afterthought he drew his knife and popped the Sioux's eyeballs from their sockets, letting them dangle on their muscles. He then lowered the head of the Sioux warrior, quickly, to a height even with the ledge below. If there were more Sioux down on the ledge, they would react.

When the head of the dead warrior reached the level of the ledge, and twisted to show his brothers the horrible things that had been done to him, the Sioux were too well-disciplined to cry out but one of them did grab the rope, pull the head to him, and cut the rope. "They are down there," Seven Horses said superfluously, and while the Sioux were occupied, the Crows pulled their chief up and cut him loose.

Young Buffalo looked down again. He could see the ledge but not his enemies. They could only escape by climbing the rope. They were trapped—unless there were Sioux warriors in the area who knew where they were.

Chapter 24

Young Buffalo and Seven Horses cared for the body of their chief, then sat close to the edge of the cliff and discussed the situation in low voices. Braddock lay close by, his head overhanging the lip. It was his job to see if in the fading light the Sioux might attempt to climb the rope, but he was also listening to his cohorts, doing his best to understand what they were saying.

"We could just cut their rope and leave them to starve to death," Seven Horses suggested, but Young Buffalo wanted none of that.

"I want to go down there and kill them and throw their bodies down to break on the floor of the canyon below."

"But they will be hard to get at," the old warrior pointed out. "We would have to come down by rope, and they will be watching for us."

They thought for a while, quietly, while the wind blew across the valley and freshened their faces.

The wind.

Young Buffalo drew his knife and began to cut handfuls of yellow grass that grew in spots on the mesa where they sat. Soon they had a respectable pile for a starter. Then he and Seven Horses walked down the path on the other side of the hill until they came to a spot where a windstorm had felled the scrubby trees that clung to the side of the hill. There was plenty of deadwood there, rotten and dry, perfect for fire. They brought up a few armfuls apiece, then went back and cut some live wood. They selected from the dead-wood, live wood, and dead grass, and made up a large pile which they wrapped in a length of rope. Braddock had some lucifers. He scratched one and touched it to the dead grass in the bundle. Once they saw the fire spreading to the dead-wood, they began to lower the rope that bound the burning pile.

The wind that blew across the valley fanned the fire into a formidable inferno, which they lowered until it was a few feet above the ledge, right where they expected the Sioux to be standing. By now the live wood was beginning to burn. The wind should have been blowing fire and live smoke into the faces of the Sioux, but the Crows on top of the bluff did not hear the expected coughs and cries of discomfort. They heard nothing but the crackling of wet wood.

"What, have they found another way out?" asked a dis-appointed Seven Horses, but Young Buffalo put a finger to his mouth. They listened carefully, and as the crackling fire began to die down, they could hear a faint, echoing cough. Seven Horses scratched his head, puzzled, but Young Buf-falo nodded with understanding. "There must be a cave down there—that's it. That's where they are. The ledge must be wider than the mouth of the cave. If we go down there when it's dark, we can creep in on them and take care of them for good!" His voice was soft but filled with choked emotion. With the coming of dawn he would see their bod-ies shattered on the rocky floor of the canyon.

Both men now joined Braddock, leaning over the rim and staring down at the ledge. They were studying it, carefully, because they did not intend to descend until dark, and they wanted to know the path of their descent as well as possible so they could work by feel.

Young Buffalo waited until dark, then continued to wait for at least three more hours. There was a thin sliver of a moon, nothing more, which was fine with Young Buffalo. He positioned a new rope that would not be visible to the men in the cave, then signaled Seven Horses to descend to the ledge. Although the older man had known a time when he told Young Buffalo what to do, there was no question of

Young Buffalo's right to lead into this battle.

Seven Horses grabbed the rope and disappeared down the face of the mountain. Next Young Buffalo signaled to Braddock that it was his turn to descend to the ledge. Braddock had dreaded this moment. He had fought bravely at Shiloh. He had been a tough trooper in the army's skirmishes with Red Cloud's Sioux. His timely, well-aimed gunfire had probably saved himself and three other people the day Big Chin was killed. But his courage melted where heights were concerned.

"I can't go down there," Braddock said in a pleading voice. "Too high up."

Young Buffalo could be understanding where understanding was necessary, and possible. But he had never before known a man who was afraid of heights. In the dim moonlight he simply got up in Braddock's face with the grimmest, angriest, most implacable expression Braddock had ever seen on the face of a man.

"You will go down that rope now," demanded Young Buffalo.

In a babble of English, Crow, Cheyenne, and sign, Braddock asked him why they didn't just leave the Sioux in their cave on the ledge to starve to death.

"The enemy is down there," Young Buffalo explained, simply, as if to a child, punctuating his statement by cocking his pistol.

It wasn't the cold hard threat of the gun, it was the power of Young Buffalo's command that brought Braddock to the edge of the cliff and sent him down the rope.

Once he had climbed below the edge of the cliff, Braddock froze.

He had few qualms about facing the Sioux in a desperate hand-to-hand battle at midnight. He was prepared to kill. He was prepared to be killed. He was not prepared to dangle in the dark until his arms grew too tired or his hands grew too sweaty and he slipped off the rope and fell many feet to the rocky valley floor. His dreams had been haunted by such falls, since his early childhood.

After a few paralyzed moments on the rope, reason took over. If he did not climb down and search for the ledge his arms would only grow more weary and his chances of avoiding the fatal fall would rapidly dwindle to zero. He could already feel the perspiration sliding down his back. If his hands got wet like that he might as well let go and see if he could fly. Gingerly he began to climb down, taking care to look at the face of the mountain as he descended. He must not slip past the ledge, or he was sure he would never be able climb back up.

The night was so dark he could barely see the grim figure of Seven Horses as he reached way out into space and grabbed the rope and pulled Braddock to the ledge. The two men now stood together on the ledge, ten feet from the mouth of the cave, and waited for Young Buffalo to join them.

Seven Horses put a finger to his lips. "Listen to the cave," said the sign, but Braddock was too preoccupied with his precarious perch on the ledge to pay much attention to the old warrior. Still, in the silence, he could hear soft-spoken words coming from the interior of the cave.

Braddock could feel the rope wiggling. He moved aside, his back pressed against the wall of the cliff, and watched Young Buffalo as he stepped easily onto the ledge and joined Seven Horses in listening to the sounds inside the cave. From the sounds they surmised that the cave could not be more than four strides deep, nor was it very wide. There were three or four of them, and they were sitting down. Although the descent of the three men had been careful, they had made enough noise that careful warriors should have heard them. But the Sioux had come to the conclusion that their enemy would not hazard an attack when all they had to do was wait for their prey to come out and try to make their escape, so they were not paying attention. Young Buffalo knew enough of the Hunkpapa dialect that he could understand some of what was being said. "How do we get down from here?" was the primary subject.

Young Buffalo had no desire to make this a lengthy project. He had the guns and he had the element of surprise. He would do the job quickly. In absolute silence he stepped past the opening to the cave, and knelt on the other side. Then he motioned for Braddock and Seven Horses to kneel on their side of the cave entrance. He drew his revolver and they drew theirs. With sign he explained to them what they had to do. Then he waited for a few moments, until he was certain that both of his men were ready. He nodded his head and at the same time they cocked and fired their weapons, quickly, six times apiece, not more than two feet off the floor of the cave.

Above the crashing echo of the gunshots came the shocked cries of wounded warriors. Those who were not hit by the direct shots were hit by the ricochets. One man not immediately killed rushed for the opening of the cave, his own weapon blazing, but stunned as he was, his furious rush only brought him out on the ledge, where a firm push by Young Buffalo sent him over the precipice. He did not scream as he fell; the attackers heard only a fading moan as the warrior entered eternity.

Young Buffalo saw no need to rush in immediately. Nobody else was coming out. Calmly he reloaded and the others did the same. They cocked their weapons and fired again into the cave, more slowly this time, scattering their shots into every corner they could imagine. When they were finally finished, they lay silently, listening. Young Buffalo held up one finger, meaning that only one man was left breathing, and he was moaning softly.

Braddock had more matches. They crawled in and Braddock lit one. The cave was even smaller than they had thought. There were three men lying face down, two of them dead, one of them breathing but unconscious. Young Buffalo made a quick examination and was surprised to find no bloody wounds. He must have been knocked unconscious by a ricocheting bullet or a chunk of rock sent flying. Young Buffalo spoke a few quick words to Seven Horses, then tore a piece of shirt off one of the dead Hunkpapas and used it to bind the survivor's arms behind him. He did the same with the Sioux's legs. Then he and Seven Horses went to work with their knives on the scalps of the two dead Sioux. When they were done they pushed the bodies out the entrance and over the edge. If they were going to get any sleep they would need space, both physical and spiritual.

Braddock was exhausted. Feeling secure in the cave from

any long plummets into the valley below, using his arm as a pillow, he did not care what his cohorts intended to do now. He was determined to get some sleep.

Yet it seemed to him he had hardly closed his eyes when he was being bumped rudely by Young Buffalo. He sat up suddenly, saw salmon-colored dawn through the opening to the cave, and his stomach gave a sudden lurch. Outside was that narrow ledge, and a rope he would have to climb to reach safety—if someone had not stolen the rope in the middle of the night.

It was not Young Buffalo who had shaken him. Young Buffalo was sitting by the opening, calmly taking a bite from a strip of jerky. The jostling Braddock had received came from their Sioux prisoner, who was thrashing around like a large, violent inchworm, striking out at the nearest target with his bound ankles. Braddock was his nearest target. Annoyed, he simply moved over to the next rock.

Seven Horses was less civil. He grabbed his army-issue Colt and pounded a knot or two into the head of the prisoner, who groaned and stopped struggling. Young Buffalo walked over to the prisoner and began to talk to him in a bad but understandable Lakota dialect. The Absarokee language was related and occasionally a Crow word crept in, but all in all Braddock could see that a dialogue was beginning.

Young Buffalo asked first about the ambush that had claimed the life of Big Chin. The prisoner thought for a moment, then denied knowledge. Young Buffalo then asked about Running Wolf. "Ah," nodded the prisoner. "That one, that chief. Yes, we knew he was a chief. He didn't need feathers. He was a chief to his toes. Killing him was a great thing."

Young Buffalo did not think it was such a great thing. "Four warriors to kill one old man?" he asked. "So it has always been with the Lakota."

The prisoner did not respond. He was too proud to tell Young Buffalo that there had been six against one, and that Running Wolf had killed two Sioux before he finally fell with an arrow in his chest and another in his belly.

Young Buffalo's lust for blood and suffering had been fairly well quenched when the third dead Sioux warrior had been pitched off the ledge. With the mercy worthy of a great war chief, he offered the young Sioux a warrior's choice.

"The others want you to feel their knives," he told the prisoner. "They want to scalp you while you still live. You see that one? The one you kicked? He is a *Wasichu*. He thinks the way to prove he is a great man is by cutting out your liver and eating it while you still live to watch him. The other, the old man, my uncle, was a brother to the chief you killed. He wants to drag you behind a pony, and cut off a small piece of you every time the sun moves, so that your blood and your body makes a trail from here to the Greasy Grass."

The young prisoner did not change the mask on his face, but the quick flutter of one eyelid told Young Buffalo that his words were being heard.

"I want to see if a Lakota can die as bravely as an Absarokee," Young Buffalo continued. "You are unwounded. We can take you outside and you can join your brothers down below. If you do it bravely we will celebrate your courage and we will not cut your scalp."

When he heard Young Buffalo's speech he suddenly felt warm and unafraid. "Your words are good," he said. "If you will untie me I will die like a great Lakota warrior should die, and you will praise me."

"That is good," Young Buffalo said, and he told Braddock and Seven Horses of his talk with the prisoner.

Seven Horses was not pleased, but Braddock was fascinated at the chance to watch someone who was unafraid of a long fatal drop into a rock-strewn valley.

In the soft pink and blue of early morning they helped him out to the ledge. Young Buffalo cut the bonds that held his wrists, while Braddock cut the cloth that bound the prisoner's ankles. Quick as an eyeblink the Sioux bent down and grabbed Braddock's arm, but Braddock was too quick for him. He jerked his arm away and backed up against the wall behind him. Alone on the edge of the ledge, with no further chance of taking an enemy with him, the young brave launched himself out into space in a neat dive, head down, arms extended, as if he expected to cleave water below.

Young Buffalo and Seven Horses watched approvingly. "You knew his heart," said Seven Horses. "You are a great young chief."

Braddock was not interested in the conversation. The prisoner had come very close to bringing him along on his great leap into the unknown, and he would take a while to recover. Young Buffalo then told Braddock that they had done what they came to do, that the time had come for them to leave.

"I suppose you want me to go first?" Braddock asked.

"You go now," Young Buffalo said, impatiently. "Now."

The rope hung out away from the ledge, so far into space that he would have to leap for it. Why couldn't one of them go first? It would swing some as they climbed it, and then he could reach out and grab it.

"You first," Young Buffalo repeated impatiently, adding several Absarokee syllables.

"What is that?" Braddock asked.

"I call you new name," the young chief explained. "Means 'Afraid To Be Tall.' "

"Oh hell," said Braddock, who could not have cared less about a new name. He had been less frightened charging the Hornets' Nest at Shiloh than he was at this moment.

"You so tough you carry my gun," he said, handing Young Buffalo his pistol, and before Young Buffalo could object, Braddock leaped out into space, grabbed the rope, felt it slip, then hold, and began to climb. In the soft light of dawn the top of the mountain looked a mile away. He caught a grip on the rope with his moccasins and was relieved to feel them hold as he straightened his legs and climbed. He reached with his arms and pulled, folded his body, gripped with his feet, and repeated the process. He knew better than to look down, but he didn't feel any too good when he looked up either, so he kept his eyes ahead of him, focused on the rope, and continued to ascend.

At last he reached up and felt solid rock. For one brain-numbed moment he could not figure out what to do next.

The ledge on top had no good handholds, but there was the rope, stretched across the ground to the stake that held it. But would it continue to hold him, or would it pull out just when he thought he was safe? Hell, these Indians know what they're doin', he thought, reaching out for more rope and using it to pull himself onto the plateau atop the bluff.

Now he was glad he'd gone first. He checked the stake and began to shout down to Young Buffalo and Seven Horses when he heard a scraping noise behind him. For an instant his body froze, then on instinct he ducked. A hatchet flashed past the corner of his eye, followed by the heavy impact of an arm on his shoulder. He grabbed the arm and jerked it as hard as he could. The rest of the body was already in a downward motion—the tug merely finished the job, pulling the attacker over his shoulder. The Indian bounced on the ledge, then, with his fingers extended in vain for a grip, slid over the edge.

The Sioux said something very short as he slid, then he was gone.

A moment later, Seven Horses appeared, and boosted himself up on the ledge. Young Buffalo followed in quick order.

"Who was that?" he asked, jerking his head in the direction of the precipice.

"He didn't tell me," a shaken Braddock replied. By this time he had had a bellyful of high jinks in the sky. No telling how many more Sioux were prowling around these mountains. Fortunately his two cohorts felt that they had taken sufficient revenge on their enemies to head for home. They gathered up the body of their great chief, carried him down the hill, tied him onto a pack horse, then mounted their own ponies and urged them forward in a fast walk.

"Go home fast," said Young Buffalo, meaning all of them.

Braddock did not have to be told twice.

Chapter 25

When Young Buffalo became chief of Running Wolf's village, good fortune smiled on the people. The Crows had a treaty with the white men that had shrunk their land holdings but had left them with the best hunting grounds. Meanwhile, the Sioux chiefs and their allies, the Cheyennes, were so involved in conflict with the *Wasichus* that they left the Crows alone. Disease stayed away from their tepee flaps and hunger was rare. There was always talk of war—sometimes real, sometimes rumors, mostly from the south—but for this Crow village the cycles went on in peace.

Three new children came to Young Buffalo and White Hot Smoke—two of them boys. Three children also came to Braddock and Wild Berry—one of them a boy, son of Big Chin, and two girls. Braddock proved to be useful to the village. His trading skills were only fair, but his knowledge of English was so important in their dealings with whites that his status in the village increased with the passing years.

Wild Berry and Braddock's time together had begun cautiously; she, still filled with grief, he, wondering if he would be able to share a lodge with the ghost of Big Chin.

Over their first months together he had listened to her cry in the night. He would bring her an herb tea that would help her sleep. He slept close enough to her that she would know he was there, but not too close. When she gave birth to Big Chin's child, Braddock was out hunting, and stayed out for days while White Hot Smoke and Star Appearing made a big fuss over the burly baby boy with the large jaw.

When he came back he listened in the night as she nursed the greedy, hungry man-baby. She told her friends that Braddock slept close by but did not touch her and they all assumed that he was being kind. How could they know that he had no hunger for her, that he was still mourning his brief love with She Bear, the woman whose heart nobody had ever touched? Except that he knew that one night out on the high plains, they had touched each other, and meant it deeply.

Wild Berry was pathetically grateful to the man who shared her lodge. He proved to be a good hunter, and a fair trader. When the tepee covering needed a new buffalo hide to replace one that had worn out, he was there with the tough hide of a big old bull buffalo. When the stew pot needed filling he would bring home a freshly killed antelope, and when he disappeared for a week, he came back with the best coffee she had ever tasted, and plenty of sugar too. He did not rise within the village hierarchy, but he was learning the language, and his closest friends were Young Buffalo and Blue Shirt, the best-respected of all the young men.

By day he and Wild Berry were cordial as they passed each other by on their way to their chores. During peaceful times, men hunted, bred and trained the fine Crow ponies, and talked of great matters in council. Women did everything else. So they did not see all that much of each other during the good weather seasons. The first winter she was busy with the baby and he was busy with his thoughts. She noted that he could sit still for hours at a time smoking his pipe, or doing nothing, just thinking, maybe. She was satisfied just to have a life with no more difficulty than the unending hard work. Some of the men made it much harder for their women.

And then, finally, one night, more than a year after Big Chin and She Bear had been killed, while he lay in his blanket close enough for her to know he was there, he decided that the time had come for him to come to her.

He chose his night well, a chilly fall night when his

warmth might be welcome. She heard him as he crawled to her and lifted her cover. She felt his body next to hers, felt his arms around her, gently, asking for no more than her warmth. But she was ready to give much more. Her arms went around him, and she began to kiss him. The tears came, a quiet, welcome release as she kissed him, and touched him. He was overwhelmed by her feelings, and let her do as she wanted. He spoke softly to her, in English she did not understand. The gentleness of his voice both soothed and encouraged her to do what pleased her until she was ready for him to complete her by doing as he pleased, and yet as he took over he did not hurry. This kind of love was new to him, so rare and precious that his own life would be precious to him from this day forward—his own life and the life of this beautiful bronze widow. When they were done, he lay on his back, hands behind his head, and thought about Tennessee for the first time in many years. He imagined himself on hot summer nights, in a simple cabin with a front porch looking out on grass fields that rolled on down to the Tennessee River. He saw himself on that porch with this woman, this "Wild Berry." Why not? His ancestor had once shared a Mississippi front porch with a Creek woman.

These were fine times for this village of the long-beaked bird. Their buffalo herds were not yet being hunted to extinction like the herds to the south. They saw no gold-hunters haunting their reservation. The mighty Sioux were suffering from weakness within. Some of their most powerful chiefs had given up their freedom to settle on agencies, and thereby earned the contempt of those chiefs who kept their bands free to roam their country. But the white men were determined to subdue all the Sioux, so the so-called "hostiles" had little time available for the vocation and avocation of raiding their cousins and enemies, the Crows.

Because Young Buffalo was young, he could make the braves understand. "Do not raid the Lakota villages. Not now. The white men will call for scouts, and that will be the time to win glory and coups. You must wait. You must wait."

They waited. And the old men agreed that Young Buffalo

could become one of the greatest of all the Absarokee chiefs.

And then, one day, another Sioux emissary appeared. He came with only one other, and his message was the same as the one they had received years ago.

"The whites are taking all the land. They put our people on bad lands and behind walls. They treat us badly and they will do the same to you. You must join us and the Cheyenne and Arapaho, and throw those people back to the other side of the big river. Worst of all, they have lied again. The treaty said that they would not go to the *Paha Sapa*, our sacred Black Hills. They lied. The yellow-hair chief led many men into the *Paha Sapa*, and there they found the yellow metal that makes the white man crazy."

Some of the Crows had been afraid that this would happen. They had always known that if the white men went to the Black Hills the Lakota would fight, and try to take land from the Crows to make up for the loss of their sacred place.

Sacred place? Young Buffalo knew better, but he listened politely.

"When the plains are hot, we always refresh our spirits in the cool woods of the *Paha Sapa*, given to us by Great Spirit so long ago."

So long ago? The Lakota memory was a strange one. The Crow keepers of stories told of the wars in the days of their great-grandfathers between the Lakota and the Kiowa—it was then, not way back in the mists of time, that the Lakota received their precious *Paha Sapa*, not from Great Spirit but by the grace of their great numbers. Young Buffalo kept his face stern and unmoving, but he wanted to laugh out loud.

"The soldiers went away and the other white men moved in and cut down our trees and made the water in the streams bad to drink. They kill all the game and shoot at our people if they see them near their towns. It is too much, and we will have war against this evil people."

Young Buffalo listened to the emissary but did not speak. Instead he let tough, leathery old Two Rivers do the talking. Two Rivers was a compulsive warrior. Only the sting of battle made him feel alive, and one did not have to know him to know the kind of man he was.

"We have fought the Lakota for longer than anyone can remember," the old warrior began. "I love you as enemies. I would not like you as brothers. Because you have been bad to the whites they have taken much that is yours and made you suffer. We have held the white man's hand from the beginning and he has not been false to us. Maybe if you learned your lesson you would not suffer so much."

By this time Braddock had learned enough of the Crow tongue to understand what was being said. He wanted to come forward and tell Two Rivers that he was foolish to believe that the white men would keep their promises. He wanted them to hear from the lips of a white man that Yankees would not stop until they owned everything.

While the Sioux and the Crows talked past each other, Braddock let his mind drift back to a day in the fall of 1860, when he and his father rode over to Jackson to attend a meeting in the courthouse. When they arrived, dozens of men sat on benches to listen to a gentleman from South Carolina explain why it was important that all the states of the South unite now that the North had elected a Republican President.

"There are among you a few who do not hold slaves," the man told them that day. "You think that this is not your fight, but you are wrong. The Yankees do not know how to let others go about their business. They must control all the trade, all the ships, all the railroads. On your way home tonight, think of the last summer you spent among the beautiful fields of Tennessee. Then think of the filthy, stinking streets of New York and Philadelphia and ask yourselves why the bankers who made those horrible places should have the right to have power over us. Have we not created a way of life second to none on earth? Will we give it up to the moneychangers? Never, I say!"

The gentleman from South Carolina had asked for victory in a war that hadn't even started yet. What he and all the others had gotten instead was defeat, a defeat of which Braddock had sampled a bitter portion down at Shiloh. Now it was the Indians' turn to go down before the irresistible power of the Yankees. He wanted to stand up like the gentleman from South Carolina and beg his people to make cause with the Sioux and all the other plains tribes, to drive the Yankees back across the Mississippi, before it was too late and the buffalo were all gone. Ah yes, his Crow brothers might not yet know what was happening to their brothers the buffalo, but he had seen the buffalo hunters coming in to some of the forts farther south, their wagons piled high with hides. He had heard the hunters swear that in a few short years they would finish off the herds completely. They seemed so proud, sometimes tapping their Sharps rifles affectionately as they told of prairies red with hundreds of stripped buffalo carcasses.

And yet Young Buffalo could point to their beautiful domain, thousands of square miles signed over to the Crows as long as the grass grows, the most beautiful place on earth, theirs forever because they remained steadfast in their friendship for the whites, who had never attacked their villages. And they remained steadfast against their eternal enemies the Sioux, who wanted to wipe out every man, woman and child who lived under the wings of the long-beaked bird.

The Crow chiefs were wise, and probably right, he thought. The South fought the Yankees with every ounce of courage it possessed, only to be overcome. The Indians too were bound to go down before the whites, no matter what side the Crows fought on. He was like the others in his village. He wanted to be on the winning side, and he wanted to kill the Sioux because the Sioux were their great enemy.

Young Buffalo kicked some sticks out of the fire, ending the council. Braddock turned and walked home. What a beautiful sight: his home, the hearthfire glowing softly through the hide covering of his woman's tepee.

He ducked through the door-flap and watched Wild Berry as she stitched some ornamental beading into his spare pair of moccasins. So intent was she on her work that she did not look up as he entered the room. When he sat down beside her she started, then smiled, then frowned.

"I do not want you to go to the whites to fight the Lakota," she said. "Plenty others to fight Sioux. You help to take care of this family. Teach them the good things. I do not wish to lose another husband."

He sat and watched her as she stitched. If a white man had come to him and asked, "Do you love this woman?" he would knot his brows as if he would not understand such a question. It was as if he were asked, "Do you love your hands, or your eyes?" She was part of him. Were he to lose her, he would grieve for many moons, until he was finally used to having lost her, but till his death his mind would go back to the contented days when he still had his hands—or his eyes—or his woman.

Yet now he was going to have to hurt the woman who was a part of him.

"When they go, I will go," he said. "They do not like Mitch Bouyer or the other men who speak two tongues. Young Buffalo believes that the ones who speak two tongues and live with the soldiers speak to please the soldiers. Young Buffalo needs someone who will say his words straight and will not be misunderstood. Is there anyone else you know who can do this?"

Wild Berry paused in her chore, looked at him for a moment, then bit the thread she was stitching. She knotted it and looked back at him.

"Then you must promise me something," she said. "You must not sacrifice your life for the white men. You are no longer a soldier. You are a Crow. The white men would not sacrifice their lives for you. Do you hear me?"

He smiled back at her, and waved his hand around the interior of their lodge, dimly lit by the flickering flames of a small fire to which she now fed a few dry sticks.

"Do you think I would give this up so easily?" He pointed to the three sleeping children. "Do you think I would give them up? Do you think I would give you up?"

"I know you put yourself between us and the Sioux and if it meant your death, you would not care so long as it meant life for us," she said. "But if you die fighting for the white men, then when the Sioux come you will not be here to stand between them and us."

His face became grim. "The Sioux will never come again!" he declared. "When the white men are finished with them there will not be enough Sioux warriors left to harm a single Crow child."

"Oh, have the whites suddenly become such ferocious warriors? When they win battles, it is always against women and children. When they meet the Sioux on the battlefield—"

Braddock shook his head. "You are right and yet you are wrong," he said. "When I was a soldier we met the Sioux and the striped arrows several times and we beat them."

"And who had the most men? Did you ever face them when they had more men?"

"Sometimes they had more men," he insisted.

"And yet you still whipped them?" she asked incredulously. In the time he had been with her they had never talked about the battles he had fought when he was still a white man.

"We had more guns," he replied. "More guns, better guns. Sometimes the big bang guns," he added, referring to the small artillery pieces they sometimes brought with them.

"Sioux make good warrior," she said.

"Young Buffalo and Seven Horses told me of the many times the Crow fought the Sioux and whipped them."

"Crow better warrior," she agreed. "But Sioux strong and brave too. Please, my husband, I can see you must go, but be smart, do not be foolish. I must have you with me. For the children, I would have to live with my heart broken. You are not so cruel you would have me do that."

"I cannot make medicine to tell me if I will come back," he said, gently. "But I will be careful. I do not trust the soldier chiefs. I have never trusted the soldier chiefs. If they are foolish, I will not stay."

They were camped on the Rosebud when they received another emissary, this time General Gibbon, who was known to the Crows as "The Limping Soldier."

"The Crow people have been our faithful friends forever," Gibbon said through his interpreter. "For many years the Sioux and their allies, the Cheyenne and the Arapaho, have been stealing your horses and your women, fighting your warriors, and trying to grab your land from you. The time has come to put an end to all this. We are gathering many men to go out and whip the Sioux, the Cheyenne, and the Arapaho. I want your best wolves to come to my camp, where we will meet with The Other One and Son Of The Morning Star.''

The Other One was General Terry, a big soldier chief. Son Of The Morning Star was Custer. Braddock and Young Buffalo both decided to ride with Gibbon. They knew that Custer would get them into a fight, and both men wanted to sink their teeth into the Sioux, who had given them so much grief.

The next day two other men came to the village and said that Three Stars needed men to go with him and fight the Sioux. Three Stars was General Crook. Most of the Crows in Young Buffalo's village thought Crook was the best of the generals. The white men told the Crows that the President himself had ordered Three Stars to ask the Crows to help him. The Great White Chief in Washington was big medicine. If he was asking for help, that meant that the whites were serious about whipping the Sioux.

The taciturn Two Rivers stood up to speak and all eyes turned toward his scarred, leathery face.

''I have been fighting the Lakota for too many moons,'' he said. ''I am tired of fighting the Lakota. I want to fight them one more time, and whip them one more time. With the whites we can whip them so bad that they will never bother us again. This is the gift I would leave to my children.''

The next day Two Rivers departed with many of the other warriors from his and other villages, not just to scout for the whites, but to whip the Sioux once and for all.

Chapter 26

Two Rivers had reached the bend in the road. His body was still strong and hard. His hand was still steady and his eyesight still good enough to kill a deer at 100 yards.

But the years of hunting and war—the wounds, the cold winters, the pounding his body took when his ponies thundered across the plains—these things, as well as age, were carving the edge off his skills and his powers. On cold winter mornings he sometimes felt so stiff that he had to labor to climb up into the saddle. His knees and hips sometimes pained him so badly that he, once the swiftest-footed of all the Crow warriors in his village, could barely break into a run.

Every year he wondered if his powers would return with the warm weather. This year they had returned. Next year? Two Rivers never worried about next year. He knew his time would come, knew that some day his light would be extinguished. For all his belief in a hereafter that provided perfect hunting for good Absarokee warriors, a part of him believed that when his light went out he would be left in eternal darkness. The thought did not trouble him because he felt he was so tough that given a little time he could conquer anything.

Two Rivers and the others rode for two days over the hills and valleys that led to Goose Creek, where Three Stars and his men were camped. Around noon they topped a rise and looked down on a soldier encampment, with its white tents in arrow-straight rows. The camp was filled with soldiers, mules, and wagons. In all his many years he had never seen so many soldiers in one place.

He and the others were thrilled by this display of power, whooping and shrieking as they tore down the grassy hill, charging the camp as if they were the Sioux themselves. Fortunately Three Stars' scouts had alerted the camp of the Crows' imminent arrival, so nobody panicked, but a bugle blew and like blue stones in a kaleidoscope, the soldiers rushed around in random patterns only to arrange themselves in straight lines. The Crows came to a halt on a rise just above this parade ground, and watched with amazement as an officer gave a command and the soldiers stepped off in perfect cadence. The Crows had seen soldier cavalry many times and were not impressed, but these were walk soldiers, and many of the Crow warriors had not seen the precision marching of infantry.

There was cavalry too, in troops with beautiful horses in matching colors, and a band with polished brass horns that gleamed in the midday sun. They played fine music, this band, and the walk soldiers stepped perfectly to the beat. In spite of his great experience, Two Rivers was impressed, and his heart swelled at the thought of going into battle with all these wonderful-looking men in their fine blue uniforms. For the moment he forgot that, though some soldiers could fight well, others could fight no better than young children. This was beautiful, a sight to tell his grandchildren about when he returned home.

Maybe it was the sight of all those handsome, well-armed troops marching like a mighty machine, or maybe it was the fine music of the marching band that cleaved the air and echoed off the surrounding hills. Maybe it was the promise of a decisive battle against worthy foes they were determined to beat, or maybe it was just the magic of a beautiful spring day. On that rise overlooking the parade, they painted their faces, decorated their ponies, uncased their weapons, and remounted. Then, screeching the war cry of the Absarokee, they raced down into the camp, firing their guns straight up, throwing themselves over the sides of their ponies. Some stood up on the saddles of their ponies, arms folded, while others leaped off and remounted without their ponies breaking stride—feathers streaming in the wind, feathers quivering and bent backward and the fierce colors of the war-faces gleaming in the bright sun.

And the marching solders—ah, the marching soldiers halted in their tracks and the band faded to silence! What was a cavalry parade next to a headlong Crow battle charge down a hill right into the center of camp?

The warriors did not ride through camp but swerved suddenly to the right and rode an entire circle around the camp, one hundred and thirty-five strong. The Crow warriors were there not for their eyes alone but for their strong arms and their battle wisdom. For a minute the officers could not react to the performance of their allies, so awestruck were they, but at last an order was shouted. The walk soldiers began to fire volley after precision volley into the air, a respectful salute to the power of the long-beaked bird. It was a moment of communication between two peoples who shared the culture of the war-soldier, and respected each other for what they shared. Each fed off the power of the other, and felt the war-spirit rise from deep in their breasts.

And finally, when the last salute had been fired, they stopped at a spot close to, but not too close to, the straight lines of soldier tents, and there they made camp. A young horse-soldier lieutenant rode slowly into camp and requested that the pipe carrier, Plenty Coups, and the other chiefs come with him to meet with Three Stars.

General Crook welcomed him and the other chiefs with firm handshakes all around. Plenty Coups noted that Crook did not wear a big smile like many other whites when they came forward to shake the hand of an Indian. Three Stars' habitual expression was sour and serious, as if a smile were a distraction to the business at hand, which in this case was killing Sioux warriors.

"I am glad to see you." He paused. "I had hoped that you would have come three days past. And the Shoshones still have not come. Have you heard any news of Chief Washakie?"

Two Rivers wondered why the whites always thought

there was some sort of message system among all the Indians that kept them aware of each other's whereabouts at all times—as if they didn't have enough to do just to survive from season to season.

Crook introduced the chiefs to the officers and the officers to the chiefs and a lot of hands were shaken as the officers and chiefs attempted to outdo each other in dignity and bearing. It took a while for all combinations of handshakes to get done, and Plenty Coups noticed that General Crook was continually looking around.

"We will start when Washakie arrives and not a moment later," he told Plenty Coups, and even as he spoke Shoshones began to appear over the hill opposite the one used by the Crows. The soldiers went into the same drill as they had when the Crows had arrived, including the review, the marching band and the echoing rifle volleys. The Shoshones were already dressed in their fighting fashions, and now the Crows joined them in a wild pony run, circling the camp twice. Then came the war drums, and the war dances—Shoshones and Crows together working themselves up into fighting trim, while the soldiers looked on.

When the dancing ended, the warriors lined up and received their ammunition. Two Rivers was dumbstruck. They gave him as much ammunition as he could carry, more cartridges for one fight than he had shot off over the past three years, and he could see that every other warrior was receiving the same. He understood that men with enough ammunition to fire at will could outgun twice their number who must make every shot count. There were rations too: hardtack and bacon, enough to support a village through an entire winter. How rich these whites must be to be able to give away so much so casually, he thought, and he pitied the Sioux and Cheyenne who must take their hard-won weapons and old buffalo meat and go up against these miraculously armed and fed soldiers.

Custer and Gibbon were already in the field. Crook expected a message that night but no message came in. Crook sent for Plenty Coups.

"We leave in the morning," he said. "I want you to take nine wolves and ride to the Rosebud. The Other One, the

Limping Soldier and Son Of The Morning Star are all out there somewhere. You must find them. Leave tonight and we will follow when the sun rises.

Two Rivers was one of the nine men that Plenty Coups chose to go out as wolves. As they climbed the first of the succession of high hills that led to the Rosebud, he could hear the wolves and coyotes howling in the distance.

They were not wolves and coyotes, he knew that immediately, and so did Plenty Coups. So the Sioux would know where Crook's troops were right from the beginning. Two Rivers was a cautious man, but he was not worried. Covered with mud that made them look like wolves, he and the others moved across the hills, out of sight of each other. But he knew they were there, because like the Sioux they talked across the night with the sounds of wolves, coyotes, owls and other night animals.

The old warrior felt comfortable with the night, protected by it, confident that his enemies were not his equal in the dark. They crossed one hill after another, one valley after another, one stream after another, and *then*, suddenly, the dawn was coming, pink and factual.

Ah, to his right where there wasn't supposed to be anybody, he saw a Sioux war bonnet bobbing up and down along a creek bed. When the creek bed got shallower the entire Sioux appeared. Two Rivers did not want to be seen, but it was too late, so he signed to the Sioux warrior that he should go home while there was still time.

He saw the Sioux warrior toss his head back good-naturedly. He did not say anything, but smiled at the Crow veteran and signed, simply, "We will see."

The Sioux warrior disappeared down the dry creek bed and Two Rivers continued forward. On his right he could now see a scout whose name he did not know—the scout was so well covered with clay, Two Rivers would not have been able to distinguish him from the ground around him had he not been looking for him. Two hundred yards farther to his right he could see Plenty Coups signaling with his blanket to come over. Two Rivers mounted his pony and rode over to where the young chief was dismounted, on one knee, examining the bodies of two dead horses.

Any scout would have known immediately that the two horses were cavalry mounts, even though they had been stripped of all they had been carrying. Both were covered with blood, theirs and that of their riders.

"These were messengers," Plenty Coups explained. "Here is as far as they got. Son Of The Morning Star and the Limping Soldier do not know where Three Stars is or where he is going."

Two Rivers nodded. This seemed like a bad omen. There was no doubt in his mind that the Sioux were all around him. He could not have explained how he knew. What he could hear. What he could not hear. Fresh horse droppings. Maybe something he smelled.

Plenty Coups sent the other wolves along, while he waited for Crook to arrive so he could tell him that there was trouble ahead—and maybe behind.

As the day wore on Two Rivers prowled the hills, carefully, his senses tuned way up. With the darkness the coyote calls returned, along with the wolf calls, and the owl hoots, all around him. He had never felt so boxed in and, alone as he was in the dark, he had to wonder whether everybody else knew what was happening. He and his pony retraced their route. He rode carefully, knowing that if his pony took a bad step, his chances of seeing another dawn would be poor. The night sounds were ominous. In spite of his toughness, his long years of battle experience, he was wound tightly, expecting any moment to feel the bite of an arrow in his back.

After about an hour of careful riding he could hear the noises of Crook's thousand-man army over in the next valley. Oh, no, he thought, they're camping right on the Rosebud. A bad place to camp, in a valley with their backs to the river. Whites thought such places were good places to camp, but the Indians placed no great faith in the security of rivers.

He came into camp and found Plenty Coups sitting with Crook and his officers. He tied up his pony and walked to the fire to report. Though he felt a strong sense of imminent danger, he waited silently while Crook spoke with his adjutant, and only spoke when Plenty Coups turned to Frank

Gruard the interpreter and explained that Two Rivers was one of his best scouts and had just come in.

"They are so many . . ." said Two Rivers. "They would not be out now, so many, if they did not mean to attack."

Two Rivers knew that Plenty Coups knew, but he also knew the way white men thought: a scout just come in from the field might know something that they did not. He waited while Gruard explained the situation to Crook.

"We have a big army here," said Crook. "Let them come. We will be ready for them."

Plenty Coups shook his head. "No, no. You have a big army but they—" he tried to explain that the Sioux and their allies, the Cheyenne and the Arapaho, had numbers an Indian could not conceive of.

One of the officers, a Major Dawes, scoffed and suggested that the Crows were losing their nerve. "Maybe they should go home, General," he said. "Might be a better fight without them."

"Major, these men do not fear battle, they just don't believe in throwing their lives away," Crook replied. "If Plenty Coups here says there's a heap of Sioux out there, he knows what he's talking about. We're gonna pull out in five hours, while it's still dark, see if we can surprise 'em. Our job is to find Custer and Gibbon and not get killed before we do."

The soldiers should have been ready when the Sioux attacked. It was early daylight and they had been on the march for several hours. Maybe they were too tired or maybe there were too many young soldiers riding the horses.

The Sioux came from several directions, riding hard, whooping like all the demons of Hell, almost on them before they could be soldiers.

The Crows reacted. Following Plenty Coups' lead, they rode out in front of the soldiers and broke the Sioux's charge with a charge of their own.

But the enemy had been through all this before. They did not run, they simply split in half and drove around the Crow vanguard. The soldiers were easy, tasty morsels for the Teton meat-eaters. The cavalry panicked and retreated. Only the walking soldiers, seeking cover in willow thickets, held on. The Sioux and their allies went after the horse soldiers, raining arrows down on them. The cavalry horses were wide-eyed, some with fright, others with pain, bucking and plunging, leaving their soldiers in the dust—ripe prey for a warrior wielding a hatchet or rifle butt. This was survival time for the Sioux, and no time for coup sticks or hand touches. Soon the cavalry and the Sioux were so mixed up that the Crows dared not fire into the melee for fear of hitting the wrong people.

Two Rivers had an old muzzle-loading rifle he had relied upon for years to hunt game with, but he loved to go into battle with a mouthful of arrows that he could pull and shoot faster than anybody could shoot a rifle. From the back of a moving pony he could not hit anything much farther away than twenty yards. But in this battle the enemy was close enough to touch.

He was a holy terror. His first shot caught an Arapaho right through the heart. The Arapaho was dead before his head hit the ground. His next two shafts each caught an enemy's pony, and a fourth shaft killed one of the warriors he had unhorsed.

He could feel the Sioux retreating, slowly, grudgingly, still shooting, still fighting, but gradually giving way before the unexpected fury of a hundred Crow warriors in one place.

Then, as he looked right and fired an arrow into the flank of another Sioux pony, a big soldier horse, crazy with fear, ran into his pony, knocking Two Rivers to the ground.

Stunned as he was, he still held onto the lead of his pony. The Sioux saw him on the ground and soon the bullets were kicking up dust all around him. His pony was running for all it was worth, dragging him across the field until they were clear of the main action, at which point he regained his feet, and finally the back of his mount. His bow was gone but he still had his rifle. Quickly he turned his mount back toward the roiling, dusty battle.

What he saw was not encouraging. Dead horses and horse soldiers were everywhere. But the walk soldiers had found cover and held fast, and the Sioux had had enough of charging the volleys that flamed out from the willow thickets. Mostly it was the Crow charge, so unexpected when they had the whites falling back, that halted the Sioux in their tracks. They had left the field in good order, bearing most of the wounded, but ten bloody scalps adorned the waistbands of their Crow enemy. The Crows had lost only one man, and although Two Rivers was disappointed with the fighting of the horse soldiers, he was happy to see that the Crows could still prevail against a big, tough Sioux charge.

Old and grizzled and tough as he was, he was moved by the slaughter on the battlefield. Crook had a big job retrieving all the wounded, who filled the air with groans and screams. Crows usually kept silent no matter how much pain they had to bear. Since Two Rivers regarded all warriors as men, he assumed that if the soldiers cried out from their wounds, it meant that they must feel pain more acutely than Indians did, and he could not help but pity them for it.

Although he was stiff and aching from his fall, he ignored what he considered to be the ordinary wear and tear of life to help the wounded Crows, Shoshones, and soldiers. The soldiers brought up mules to carry the dead and wounded. Walking the field, Two Rivers found a much better rifle than the one he owned lying by a dead Sioux pony. The army had issued considerable ammunition before the fight, and though most of it was no good for his muzzle loader he took all they would give him, hoping he might find a weapon that the ammunition would fit. Oh well, if it did not fit, he might still be able to trade it to someone who had bullets that fit his beautiful new rifle.

The sun was very high now. He and the Crows returned to Goose Creek where they and the soldiers had traded brave parades the day before. Here, Three Stars would lick his wounds and his soldiers would wonder how it was possible that the Sioux could hand them such a licking. All the soldiers knew that though the Sioux had left the field, it was the soldiers who had the most holes in their ranks by far.

At Goose Creek, while the soldiers collapsed into post-battle fatigue, the Crows and Shoshones prepared to go back home. They had done their job—found the enemy, fought them, and probably saved the soldiers from disaster—but many wondered just how the whites were going to subdue the Sioux if they could not stand up to them in battle.

A dust-covered General Crook was shaking hands with the chiefs, bidding them goodbye. Two Rivers had no desire to press the flesh of Three Stars or any white man at this time. He was different from many Crows who prided themselves on the white men they knew. The old warrior had no more wish to seek out the companionship of the soldiers than to socialize with the Sioux. He did step into a chow line for some hot food, which he ate quickly, and washed it down with some water from Goose Creek. He found a few handfuls of oats for his pony. Then he checked the animal out for wounds or lameness, watered it lightly at the creek, and without so much as a wave, headed northward. His work was done. Killing Sioux was always good. Slowly he pointed his pony homeward and let it take him there. Only when he got home would he discover that the fall from his pony had broken two of his ribs.

Chapter 27

There were actually a few men who had served with Braddock five years before who were now serving with him again as the Custer column bumped along on its westward run from Fort Lincoln to the country of the tall mountains.

But dressed mostly in buckskins, with his dark hair long and braided, and his earrings, and his face burned brown from living with the sun and the wind, he was unnoticed among the dozens of Arikaras and the handful of Crow scouts who rode along with Son Of The Morning Star. He lunched away from the soldiers, with the Crows, and never said a word of English to anybody, and he never expected any of his old cohorts to recognize him.

Over his years with the Crows he had come to agree with the assessments of many Crow warriors—that the white men did not know how to listen to their senses. Nothing out there on the land seemed to alter their preconceived notions of what the Indians would or would not do.

Young Buffalo did not know much about the organization of cavalry units and it never occurred to him to ask his friend Braddock about it. He did note that there were five groups of men in Custer's command, and that each group rode like-colored horses. The idea of every man in a company having the same color of horse appealed to Young Buffalo's artistic sense, but he also thought that if he was as rich as the white men he would have good fast horses for each of the soldiers, instead of horses of the same color. Nobody had an eye for horses like the Crows, and he could tell by looking at the animals' chests and legs that some of the horses were much better animals than others. Leave it to the whites to worry about the color of horses, he thought.

He thought they were lucky to have so much food, and was happy to gorge himself when he had the chance, but it didn't take him long to figure out that there was also a lot of liquor in the canteens of Custer's troopers.

Once they were out in the field he did not spend a lot of time near the soldiers. He was generally far ahead, looking for signs of Sioux. But one afternoon he returned from his scout to find that the army had made camp on an old Sioux camping ground. There were a number of funeral scaffolds on this ground, and the soldiers didn't mind taking them apart and relieving the decomposed bodies of any interesting artifacts and trinkets that might have been enclosed in the blankets wrapped around the bodies.

If in the process the scaffold fell and the body tumbled into the dust, the soldiers just left it there. Young Buffalo was dismayed by such soullessness on the part of the soldiers, but he never discussed his feelings with Braddock. He knew Braddock only so well, and no more. Perhaps Braddock would have shrugged his shoulders and said, "Well, they're only dead Injuns and dead Injuns don't kill nobody!" Young Buffalo hated arguments, especially with ignorant people, so he left the camp to look for recent Sioux signs, which he had yet to find.

He found tracks, many tracks, and four hundred sets of lodgepoles being dragged by travois, but the horse droppings were weeks old. He came back and reported his findings but everybody, including himself, considered them unimportant. Whatever the Sioux had been doing then, they were doing someplace else now. He turned in early.

He was up even before the cooks were lighting the fires for the camp kettles. He did not know what had awakened him and he was not pleased to be up so early. To him, his body was like a vessel, and every hour he slept poured new energy into that vessel. Puzzled, he rolled out of his blanket, stood up, shook the blanket out, and wrapped it around him.

Across the valley he could hear coyotes, real ones, not Sioux.

He was not reassured. The stars were brilliant on this pre-dawn. They were too brilliant, almost as much like suns as like stars. Then, before his unbelieving eyes, they began to whirl around until they were aligned in a pattern he understood but did not like. Locked in this pattern, they began to run to the west, then they stopped suddenly and ran back to the east. They stopped again, and suddenly got brighter, so much brighter that he had to shade his eyes.

Now they began to fade, but before they faded out altogether, they began to drift toward the horizon, or toward the ground; he could not tell which.

Whatever had been going on was unnatural, and unnerving—no less so when he found himself still curled in his blanket, awakened by the sound of cooks setting the kettles in the fire pits. A dream was as real as reality, perhaps more so. He did not know what the dream meant, but whatever it was, he did not like it.

The next afternoon they found newer tracks, much newer. He and one of the Ree scouts returned to the soldiers and brought a pair of captains to try to figure out what the tracks meant. They did not know and hated that they did not know. Not knowing made them angry and frustrated. "Is this all you could show me?" asked a tall captain with a long, extravagant mustache. "You're supposed to know the Sioux! Tell me what in hell they're doing, where they're going, understand?"

"They very close," said Young Buffalo. "I be careful."

The officer eyed Young Buffalo with a disrespectful sneer on his face. "I know you'd be careful," he smirked. "I thought the Crows were men! But I see you do not want to fight them."

What Young Buffalo did not want to do was argue with the captain, so he pretended not to understand. He just walked his horse away, as if he had accepted the captain's assessment. He knew why the trails were such a mess; bands of Sioux and Cheyenne were coming from all points of the compass and gathering—somewhere not far away. But if he told them this, explained that the Sioux and Cheyenne were having their biggest gathering he had ever seen, the captain might have called him one of the white man names that meant someone who is afraid of fighting.

So instead he rode back to the column and told the Ree scout. While he was there he ran into a grim-faced, nervous-looking Braddock.

"Too many Sioux out there," he told Braddock.

"That ain't the half of it," said Braddock. "Old Iron-butt says that once the Sioux see us they'll run, so he wants to attack in a hurry, before the Sioux are able to escape."

As a scout, Young Buffalo was riding probably two or three miles for every mile the column rode, and he had to dismount frequently to study the Indian signs. In fact, sometimes he was walking more than he was riding because the closer he was to the ground, the more trail he could see. He was tired, but Crow warriors don't stay tired when there is a need to do more.

So when Custer announced that after dinner they would be making a night march across the mountains, Young Buffalo simply unsaddled his pony, took a few bites of hardtack and dried deer meat, washed it down with a few swallows of water, and found a shady overhang away from the noise of the camp where he could get some badly needed sleep. Braddock tried to follow suit, but he couldn't help feeling jumpy about the fight that was sure to come the next day. Custer, he thought, was an idiot. All generals were idiots and so were ex-generals. Braddock had never been a coward. He had a matter-of-fact aversion to dying. He had gone into battle at Shiloh because he had been too young and dumb to know about the stupidity of generals. As soon as he understood, he took french leave of the Arkansas militia and never came back.

He would never leave his buddies in the middle of a fight—that would be letting them down—but he for sure wasn't going marching off toward certain death because an idiot general wanted his share of glory. Now this Custer, he was one of that kind. Fight to the last drop of blood, his or his men's.

So Braddock lay in the shade of that rock ledge, his head pillowed on his saddle bags, his hat over his face, trying to decide if the time had come to get back to his family.

He counted the reasons why Custer and his command were doomed: One, too many Sioux. Two, too much booze on the trail. Three, not enough good troops. Four, too much Custer. Five, stinking single-shot carbines. Even some of the Crows had repeating rifles, and he knew that the Sioux and Cheyenne had been finding ways to get more repeaters. There was no way of knowing just how many Sioux warriors had the soldiers outgunned.

So he counted the reasons, like other men count sheep, and tired as he was, the scare in his belly calmed down and he slept.

They were up before the troopers and they had at least one row of hills behind them before the soldiers headed out with bellies full of bacon and hard biscuits. Braddock had seen them the night before, caring for their ponies and trying to get comfortable for the evening. They were dead beat from the day's marching and he knew that Custer was going to march them into the ground today too. He wanted to talk to Young Buffalo about it, but they were wolves now, and wolves did not hold long conversations when they were out looking for Sioux.

Actually they were not looking, not yet. The leader of the scouts, an Arikara brave called Dull Knife, had them riding toward a hilltop that would later be called "The Crow's Nest." The acute vision of Young Buffalo was already legendary and Braddock had borrowed a good pair of binoculars from Captain McDougall's supply train. It was still dark when they arrived at the top of the mountain, but behind them a blue blush on the eastern horizon announced the imminence of dawn.

The older warrior waited with Young Buffalo and Braddock for the sun to reveal the future to them. Braddock tried to believe that when the day was bright he would focus his binoculars in all directions and see no trace of the Sioux and their allies. He tried to believe, but he could not. The sun was now over the horizon and the land below was taking on a blue shadowed look. Gradually the blue grew pale, then disappeared altogether, leaving them to contemplate the empty hills and valleys below.

Then Young Buffalo signaled that he had seen something and Braddock's stomach went cold.

"There, you see, beyond that bald hill in front of us," said Young Buffalo, pointing so precisely that Braddock aligned himself with Young Buffalo's extended arm and studied the valley of the Greasy Grass as it wound its way in and out of the low hills. There was a bit of a haze, but they could still see a good distance. Braddock saw some motion in the lower left corner of the binoculars and moved them in time to see a Lakota warrior mounting his pony and vanishing into a thicket.

"Ah, they're watching us, so what?" he said.

"Not them," Young Buffalo replied stolidly, though he was annoyed that after years with the Crows Braddock still did not know what to look for or how to find it. "Look where I pointed, way off down the Greasy Grass."

Braddock looked and this time what he saw made him catch his breath. Between two hills, fifteen miles away, he could see tepees that filled the land beyond the notch. He nodded and Young Buffalo signaled to Dull Knife to join them at the top of the hill. The Ree veteran rode forward and saw what Young Buffalo had seen and more.

"Ah, they are moving," he said. Not that he could see individual horses with travois. Many years of experience had enabled him to interpret patterns of motion as a village on the move. He rode down the hill at a rapid gallop, with Young Buffalo and Braddock following him. They tore past several other scouts and the advance skirmishers of the column before they found Custer, who was busy chewing out one of the privates for failing to pack a mule properly. The mule had lost its load the day before and nobody had noticed until nightfall. Nor had they told Custer, until now. A lost pack found by the enemy could tell them a lot more about Custer's battalions than mere tracks, and he was detailing for the young soldier his deficiencies in intelligence, family background, and industry. He stopped his tirade abruptly when he saw Dull Knife, Young Buffalo, and Braddock raising the dust down a grassy hill a quarter of a mile away.

He did not stand waiting, but galloped toward them, meeting them at the base of the grassy hill.

"Many Sioux. Too many to number," Young Buffalo explained through scout Mitch Bouyer.

Custer's eyes flashed. "These damned Crows are useless to me," he said, turning to his adjutant, Lieutenant Cooke. "Every Sioux looks like a hundred to them, that's how scared they are of them!" The adjutant shook his dark muttonchop whiskers. "Next time we'll just take the Rees," he responded.

Young Buffalo had heard some English in his life. Convinced that one of these days the Crow chief might hear something useful to him, Braddock had insisted on teaching him more. The Crow chief's right arm twitched, aching to flick its quirt and lay open the cheek of this arrogant man. Braddock gave him a quick look that said, What do¯ you expect of an idiot cavalry officer?

Custer was still speaking to Cooke. "Well, the Sioux know where we are, that's for sure." He turned to Dull Knife. "And what did you see?" he asked.

"Many Sioux," the Arikara answered. "Many Sioux. On the move."

Custer's brow creased in thought for just a moment. "Many Sioux?" he asked, almost talking to himself.

"Look like whole big village moving," said Dull Knife.

"Hah!" Custer slapped his gloves on his rawhide jacket and the dust flew. "They're running, by God. If we get after them, I mean really get after them, we'll put an end to them right here, right now! Cooke, I want Benteen and Reno up here on the double. We're gonna take the big bad Sioux and wrap 'em up, once and for all. No more Red Clouds. No more Spotted Tails telling us what to do. Next time I see them I want them on their knees!"

Captain Benteen and Major Reno had reined up by Custer. The crazy sonofabitch has made up his mind to do something and that's bad, Benteen was thinking as he looked beneath the brim of Custer's hat into the shadowed face. Reno stopped a few feet away. He didn't want Custer smelling his breath.

"Here's what we're gonna do," Custer said. "We got the Sioux running and we're gonna catch 'em. Benteen, you take your three companies over there to those ridges on the left and find some high ground where you can look for the damned Sioux. I don't want any of them gettin' behind us when we attack, you understand? I'll follow that valley right into the village. When you've made your reconnaissance you come down that valley and rejoin my command. Get going now. No delay. We're going in as fast as we can, before they get away."

Then he turned to Reno. "Your three companies ride with us. We've got a long, quick march and I don't want anybody lagging, you understand?"

Young Buffalo and Braddock were hurt and disgusted. They wanted no part of Custer, but they were ready to fight and they didn't want to go home. They weren't crazy about Reno, but they decided to ride with him and nobody came with any orders to the contrary. They rode well out on the right flank. Custer did not seem to be worried about flank security, but Young Buffalo knew the Sioux.

The big cavalry horses were tired, Young Buffalo could see that as they moved out. The day was warm, the pace was hard, and each one was carrying ninety pounds of ammunition and supplies in addition to its trooper. The soldiers themselves did not look in much better shape than their mounts. Their shirts were drenched with sweat and many of them drooped in their saddles. If Custer noticed, he didn't let on. He pushed his eight companies down the valley, which followed a small creek.

Braddock rode along a slope that ran parallel to the valley. His eyes were everywhere. He checked his rifle and his revolver, then checked them again. He wanted to fight, but he wanted to live. He hoped his two desires would not present a conflict.

The hours passed to the rattle and clank of canteens, the squeaking of leather, and the footfalls of four hundred horses. The horses clopped on; the men still drooped. If there was fear among them, it had been largely expunged by fatigue.

And then suddenly, they were there, forty warriors galloping down the creek toward where it drained into the

Greasy Grass. Cooke pointed to a ridge line on the right front. Dust clouds were rising over it. There was the fleeing village; of that, Custer was certain.

"Go after 'em, Reno!" Custer shouted, pointing to the fleeing warriors. "If you need help, we'll come after you."

No! The shout rose in Young Buffalo's throat, but stopped short of his lips. He knew the Sioux. He knew the Cheyenne. He knew their tricks. If they didn't want to be seen they would have vanished long before the column had arrived. Braddock was thinking the same. Damn fools!

And yet neither one was absolutely sure. Neither one was ready to peel away from a battle just before it started, without being certain that they were taking a sucker's bet. Amid the charge of the bugle and shouted commands and cheers from Custer's two battalions, Reno's battalion broke into a gallop and thus began the most famous battle in the history of American warfare.

Chapter 28

With the cheers of their cohorts ringing in their ears, Reno's battalion galloped down the valley, expecting that the fleeing warriors would lead them straight into a disorganized village desperately packing and running. It was an old cavalry plan that had worked before. The warriors were at their most vulnerable when they were forced to fight and protect their families at the same time.

Ahead was the Little Bighorn River—the Greasy Grass—and beyond a bend in the river was a stand of timber with thick dust blurring everything beyond it. Reno forded the river and raced for the timber—for the dust. He and his officers were slow to recognize what was about to happen to them. Out of the dust, like a huge herd of ghosts, flew hundreds of warriors, heading straight for the little battalion: screeching, angry, savage warriors, Sioux and Cheyenne, painted like the demons of a drunken dream.

Reno looked back up the hill behind him. No Custer. Arm upraised, he brought his horse to a sudden halt. Behind him the rest of his command followed suit, and obeyed his order to dismount. In admirable order, given the cataclysm that was descending on them, the cavalrymen followed their drill procedure, with one in three troopers grabbing the reins of the horses and leading them back from the fight. Dismounted, able to aim their carbines, the remaining men formed a line across the valley and began to fire at the attacking warriors.

It was a good tactic, for the moment. It's one thing to attack a group of cavalrymen trying to fire from the backs of shying, bucking horses, quite another to run your ponies down the steady sights of kneeling soldiers. But the carbines were short-range weapons, the Indians knew that, and they rode back and forth in the dust out of range, letting the bluecoats pop away at them. Through the brown, swirling dust more and more warriors were joining them. From their position on the timbered right flank, Young Buffalo and Braddock could see war-bonneted Sioux spilling around the left flank, trying to surround Reno's battalion. The two men galloped across the field in front of the horse handlers, intending to lend a hand to the men who would have to fight off the flanking movement. Reno saw the danger too, and led his men to the scrubby timber on the right flank.

Young Buffalo saw the men sprinting past them and decided to fight a rear-guard action. He and Braddock rode within a hundred yards of their pursuers, and with their repeating Henrys they poured accurate fire into the thick gaggle of pursuing Sioux, who were forced to slow up until they saw for certain that they were being delayed by a mere two mounted riflemen. Young Buffalo had triumphed over the Sioux many times. He had no special fear of them, and his coolness steadied his friend who wanted to fight but did not want to die. Several of the braver troopers stood with the two horsemen until they saw the Sioux slow down, then they turned and sprinted for the timber.

The two Crows backed their ponies toward the timber until their Sioux adversaries were numerous enough to charge them, then turned and raced for the cover of the woods, hoping that their friends the bluecoats would not panic and shoot them as they were coming in.

As soon as Young Buffalo and Braddock had ridden into the thicket they realized that Reno had made exactly the wrong move. They couldn't see the enemy but the enemy knew where they were. Buzzing bullets were splintering wood all around them, and occasionally finding flesh. The firing was getting closer. The Sioux were advancing and Reno could not even see where they were.

"Mount up!" he cried, or something to that effect; his men could hear his voice above the gunfire but not well enough to understand what he was shouting. Or maybe the stress was making him so shrill that the words sounded more like a screech than speech. So he led by example—or maybe he just rode hell-bent for safety hoping his men would see him. Enough of them did to give the appearance of a retreat back up the valley from where they had come.

There were plenty of mounted Sioux and Cheyenne to crowd them back and a surprising number had repeating rifles. In fact they were so many, and so well-armed, that if the two sides hadn't gotten so mixed up, the Sioux might have annihilated the soldiers with sheer firepower. Instead it was close, dangerous work, sometimes hand to hand as the Indians moved in and tried to pull the soldiers out of their saddles. Sometimes it was hatchets against carbine butts, and the hatchets were having a splendid time of it. Soldiers began to fall, and when enough of them fell, the rest turned and raced as fast as they could across the river. Fire from the banks of the river took down more of them. Young Buffalo and Braddock were a little lighter than most, less encumbered than any, with tough little Indian ponies under them instead of the jaded, overworked oatburners the soldiers were riding. Young Buffalo sensed a shallower crossing up the river, and they simply outran the soldiers in their flight from danger. Soldiers splashed into the river as Sioux bullets found them.

Across the river were some bluffs. Panicked as they were the soldiers knew enough to head for the high ground. Up they rode over a dusty, rocky trail, their horses struggling as if they'd rather die than make it to the top. Some of the troopers dismounted and pulled their animals up the trail to the top of the bluffs above the river. One of them caught a bullet between the shoulder blades. In his final agony he jerked hard on his horse's reins and the animal went bucking back down the trail toward the Indians.

Young Buffalo spotted a moving roil of dust in front of them as they gained the crest of the bluffs. Had the men not been done in from their frantic flight across the river they would have cheered Captain Benteen as he and his three companies arrived following their reconnaissance.

Benteen took over the organization of the defense, even though he was junior to Reno. He arranged the soldiers in a circle around the crest of the bluff. They may have had the high ground but it wasn't high enough, and they had very little cover. The warriors must have had a lot of ammunition, because throughout the late afternoon the soldiers were working desperately to avoid the appalling gunfire, using every bit of cover that they could find.

Young Buffalo found a subtle depression and quietly invited Braddock to share it with him. At first Braddock resisted. The thing was way too shallow, he was thinking. I want to be far away from here. Now. Damned officers. I have nothing better to do than die for the army after having left it three times in my life. But he wasn't going to run away in front of all these people, and besides, there was no place to run. The Sioux were pressing them on all sides. So Braddock lay down in the depression, behind some thin but effective brush concealment, and he found relief from the eternal *ffwwp!* of bullets whipping overhead. The perfect place. He could see them and they couldn't see him, at least until he fired his rifle. But Young Buffalo was not about to lie still and wait. His rifle was busy and effective. Lying beside a fighter, Braddock could not desist. Frightened he was, but he thumbed back the hammer of his Henry, pulled the trigger, absorbed the recoil and the noise, pulled the lever, chambered another round, and fired again. And the bullets began to whistle over their heads.

Reno was not a factor in this fight. Instead, cool as ice, Captain Benteen was walking from man to man, encouraging, not bothering to conceal himself from the gunfire below.

"Come on, son," he said to one wide-eyed private who was little more than a recruit. "If you don't cock it, it won't fire," he said. "And you want to kill some Sioux before a bullet finds you—there's the boy. You just make those shots count. If we kill enough of these devils by sundown they might go away." He went on to the next group of soldiers.

"You do want them to leave now, don't you?" he asked, and all the soldiers within hearing distance nodded without taking their eyes off the slope in front of them.

They could see, down the hill, more and more Sioux joining the enemy horde below. Where were they all coming from? And then Young Buffalo heard a new sound, a *zing* sound two feet above his head.

He squeezed the trigger and saw a rider jerk backward, head over heels over the back of his pony. Two more rounds passed over with the new *zing* sound, then another. Then more.

And he knew.

The heavy high-velocity rifle shells made a solid sound as they sped overhead. The lighter, ringing sound was the sound of the short round from the single-shot carbines the soldiers carried. There was no way the Sioux would have traded for such bad guns, but desperate warriors who had only bows would use them if they won them in battle or stole them.

They must have gotten them from horse soldiers, he thought, astonished. Horse soldiers meant Son Of The Morning Star. Could they have . . . ? Another round kicked up the dirt in front of him. This was no time to think. This was a time to shoot a lot of bullets at a lot of Sioux and hope to make it hot enough to let the bluecoats live one more miserable day.

Hazy clouds sailed overhead. The soldiers and warriors had settled down into a lengthy, heated exchange of gunfire. More and more Sioux were coming from somewhere to make heavier the blanket of gunfire they were spreading over the hill where the soldiers lay, desperate for water, desperate for hope.

Braddock realized that his rapid-fire Henry had consumed most of the ammunition he was carrying and there was no chance to get more, since the soldiers were using different bullets. He needed no further incentive to make himself flatten against the ground and wait for the firestorm to pass. The sun was a huge blood-red ball on the horizon now. Young Buffalo was busy thinking: was darkness better or worse? Better, because nobody could shoot at them with any accuracy. Worse, because the Sioux could creep up a lot closer and maybe, if it felt right, attack the army position just as the soldiers began to nod off. The sun was blood on the horizon, sinking, sinking, and with it sank the hopes of the troopers around him.

As the darkness took over, the gunfire ceased, and from the heights the soldiers could look down the river at hundreds of campfires in a village that seemed to stretch for miles along the Greasy Grass.

The drums pounded through much of the night and many sounds of emotion were emerging from the village. The soldiers could not know that the biggest of the fires were bonfires cremating dead Sioux warriors, and that much of the drumming and chanting was mourning for the dead. In their maddening thirst and fatigue, what the soldiers saw from the heights, brightly illuminated by flashes of lightning, were endless circles of shadows dancing like demons, seemingly *in* the fires.

In spite of the lightning there was little rain. The men were out of water, and those that got any sleep that night awoke with a raging thirst. With the morning the clouds faded and the sun beat down upon the suffering soldiers. Wounded men cried for water, offered money for water. Dead horses swelled up, and when hit by a stray bullet, exploded in a rain of putrid flesh. The tongues of the soldiers swelled up too, and their mouths were so dry they could not even eat a biscuit.

Young Buffalo and Braddock had preserved their water carefully, but by afternoon even their canteens were dry.

And the Sioux were not through yet. Maybe the soldiers were tired. Maybe their brains were addled by the heat. Whatever the reason, they did not spot braves moving through the long grass until suddenly there came a flash from just off to the right or left, and a body would slump with blood gushing from a head wound.

And there were long-range shooters too, warriors who had watched buffalo hunters use forked sticks to steady their rifles. From long distances they fired their rifles, and if they didn't hit many, they brought the soldiers to an even higher state of apprehension. While Major Reno sat passively watching the drama, Captain Benteen lay down beside him.

"Major, we've got to do something quick or we'll lose every man we have," he said. Reno looked at Benteen blankly, through bloodshot eyes.

"Major, we've got to charge them, got to drive them back. They won't expect it."

There was no response from Reno. The man might as well have been in Ohio.

Benteen sighed. "I'll lead the charge. I'll get 'em out of there. All right?"

Reno nodded weakly, as if the trauma of the battle had deprived him of speech and strength.

"All right, boys, who wants to go with me and get the hell out of here?" Benteen asked.

To his surprise he found more than a dozen volunteers. To Braddock's surprise, Braddock was one of them. Young Buffalo was another.

"Listen up, men," said Benteen. "You follow me and we're gonna clear out those Indians on the slope down there. If we move fast we'll surprise 'em. All ready now, men. It's your time. Give 'em hell. Hip hip. Here we go."

Benteen was smart. He didn't give them any time to regret volunteering. Hip hip, here we go, and he was off, down the hill, with more than a dozen screaming marauders following him. Released from their position as stationary targets, the men raced straight toward the warriors with savage fury. In their rage and desperation it seemed almost natural that the terrifying Sioux leaped to their feet and ran down the slope as fast as they could with the soldiers in hot pursuit. They could not go too far or other warriors might cut them off and make mincemeat out of them. Benteen brought them to a halt, but made sure that they returned to their line without haste. Not only had they cleared out the closest and most annoying of their besiegers, but he had shown his men that their enemy wasn't any more superhuman on this day than they had been on other days. Every soldier who saw the desperate charge was heartened. Braddock returned to his place more than a little amazed that an officer had actually thought his way to a proper conclusion, made his move, and possibly saved the entire command.

Late that afternoon more Sioux arrived, and some of them were wearing blue soldier uniforms with yellow cavalry trim. Braddock turned to Young Buffalo to ask him what he thought the uniforms meant. Young Buffalo knew the answer before Braddock asked.

"Son Of Morning Star dead, I think," was his comment, and once more Braddock felt a cold blob in the pit of his stomach. If Custer was dead, then there was no one to prevent the Sioux from finishing them off too. Benteen saw the uniforms too, and the looks on some of his men. He eyed Reno with disgust for a few moments, then took matters into his own hands. He rose to his feet and began to walk among his men.

"Better get down, Captain," said a sergeant, but Benteen laughed. "They won't get me," he said with confidence he made them believe. "We can make it out of here if we don't waste our ammunition, if we don't panic, if we remember who we are. This is a groundhog case. It's live or die. We have no choice but to fight it out. Come on, soldier. Point your carbine. Don't let your brothers down. That's it."

Those who had not known before of the steel in the man would remember him for the rest of their lives. He was the man who pulled them together just before they could come apart for good.

Among the Sioux down below there was a council going on and the men on the bluff could see it occurring. "Fought in a lot of fights and I never seen this before," Braddock told Young Buffalo. "Here we sit with our rifles watching them decide when and how they're finally gonna slaughter us."

Young Buffalo did not answer. He had pulled out his pipe, packed it, lit it, and was puffing away with pleasure as he watched.

"What's so funny?" Braddock asked him, for there was a smile curved around the pipe stem.

"They pull out soon, I think," said the Crow chief.

"I'll take your word for it," Braddock replied in sarcastic English that was lost on Young Buffalo. The council was breaking up. Decisions had been made. The men braced themselves for the next assault. The minutes went by and nothing happened. Still they waited. And very late in the afternoon, Young Buffalo thought he saw what he had expected to see, way off in the distance.

"Sioux leaving," he said quietly, to Braddock.

Braddock looked down the valley toward the village. He could see movement but he could not see what Young Buffalo saw. He looked around him and saw a sergeant lying prone, his carbine aimed and perfectly steady, but the hammer was not cocked. The man was too steady. His stillness was the stillness only seen in death.

He had a binocular strap around his neck. Braddock did not stand on ceremony. He crawled to his left, slid the strap past the sergeant's neck and head, and headed back to his position. He trained the binoculars on the village and focused them. There they were, pulling covers off their tepees and folding them. There was no doubt. The women there were busy packing and the men—

The warriors were gradually withdrawing from their positions around the soldiers. Many of the soldiers were too numb or mortified to notice at first. Some of the younger ones had found what they thought was a safe spot and had lain there, their bodies flat against the earth. They did not fire their rifles. They did not keep a wary eye out for stealthy Sioux scouts. They just lay flat and hoped for the best.

As he watched the warriors closest to them disappearing, Braddock felt his burden lighten. He could actually swallow again and he realized that at least some of the dryness in his mouth was due to two days under continuous fire from the deadly weapons of the hated Sioux.

He was still playing with the binoculars, trying to focus them better, when Young Buffalo tapped him on the shoulder and pointed down the valley. A dust cloud was being raised by figures too small to be seen with the naked eye, and a long gray cloud of smoke arose, as if the dried grass above the river bank had been set afire. Were there soldiers down there or were they merely a relief for the warriors who had given Reno's battalion two days in hell? He focused his lenses on the dust cloud and almost cried when he made out General Gibbon's horse soldiers.

He glanced at Captain Benteen, who was staring down

at the dust cloud through his binoculars. The old officer was registering no emotion. He looked completely worn out from his ordeal of command. His face was coated with sweat-streaked dust; his shirttails flapped in the breeze behind him. But he had stepped in for Major Reno and never lost his composure or his courage throughout the siege.

A faint cheer began among the liberated soldiers, faint perhaps because their mouths were stone dry, more likely because most of them still were not ready to believe that the Sioux were gone. But the officers continued to watch the other side of the river, where a huge caravan slowly, like a long train, was gathering motion and moving south in a huge dust cloud.

One captain from Reno's command raised his .50-caliber Springfield, took aim over the sights, and fired a shot through the windblown smoke in the direction of the caravan, an impossible shot, but one that infuriated Braddock. For just a moment he forgot himself. He grabbed the rifle and held it hard by the receiver. "Dammit, Captain, you wanna get those red bastards back on our necks?" he asked. The captain turned quickly, fire in his eyes, ready to dress down an impertinent private. When he saw a black-braided, war-painted Crow warrior addressing him in standard west Tennessee English, his mouth dropped open and he told himself that too much hot sun was making him hear impossible things. He turned and walked away.

"Must be General Crook," growled one of the dry-throated sergeants to nobody. Half the soldiers were rushing down to the creek for water.

Benteen shook his head. "Gibbon," he said. "And Terry."

"And Custer?" asked the sergeant. "He was heading that way last time we saw him."

Benteen studied the approaching column through his binoculars for a full minute but said nothing. The men around him went silent. If Custer was not with Gibbon and Terry, where was he?

Chapter 29

The white-hot sun beat down on them, as fierce as any Sioux war party. They rode slowly. Very slowly. A Crow warrior on a long campaign often took several ponies with him. These men had been forced to endure the long march and all the fighting with one pony apiece, and they had no desire to work their animals any harder than necessary.

Young Buffalo had been quietly weeping since Two Rivers had given him the full report. Two Rivers was part of a scout that had been sent out by Crook to find Custer and Terry. They found Custer all right, and much of his command, lying white naked in the still warm air, toes turned up and bodies mutilated in a hundred ways.

Many of the Crows were heartbroken by the death of Son Of The Morning Star and his men. Though it seemed obvious to them that he did not fully respect men like themselves, they felt that the white men were out there to fight for them.

"Here is what I do not understand," Young Buffalo was telling the wise old warrior. "When we fight the Sioux by ourselves we always whip them, is that not true?"

"That is how it has always been," Two Rivers replied.

Young Buffalo turned to Braddock. "And do we not keep good relations between ourselves and the white men because the white men are so powerful that they can whip anybody?"

Braddock nodded, and Young Buffalo turned back to Two Rivers.

"Then how is it that when you and all the other Absarokees were with the best of the American war chiefs, the Lakota attacked you and whipped you, and then they attacked and wiped out all the soldiers with Son Of The Morning Star, and then they almost whipped our bluecoats? If the white men are so powerful, why are the soldiers like women? No Absarokee warriors would behave like the soldiers behaved."

Two Rivers did not answer. He was taciturn by nature, but at this time it was his emotions that kept his mouth shut tight. On his way to join up with his cohorts he had passed over the ridge where Custer and his men had met disaster. He had seen first-hand the stripped and scalped bodies, the scores of dead, bloated horses, the red-tinted grass around the bodies.

And he had heard the silence. Two battalions of cavalry had been wiped out in less time than the sun takes to move the width of a thick stick through the sky. How could that have happened? That many Absarokee on a hill could have held off the entire Teton people all day, and if things had gotten too hot, they would have mounted their ponies, broken through, and run from their enemy to fight another day.

Braddock was not slow to express his opinions. "I know it seems queer," he said in fluent Crow dialect that was heavily accented with rhythms from his Southern childhood. "Our soldiers don't fight so good, not out here on the plains anyway, and our soldier chiefs all—" he wrinkled his nose so the other two understood perfectly. "Even Crook, the man you think is so good. He's a general, ain't he? And as for Custer. Huh! Don't surprise me one bit he got his whole command wiped out. If his brains was gunpowder there wouldn't be enough to blow his nose." He used Crow words but American idiom so they did not know his exact meaning, but they already knew he did not have a high regard for army officers, and in general they agreed with him.

They rode on in silence for a while. Two Rivers and Young Buffalo knew that Braddock had not answered the question that Young Buffalo had posed but they were too polite to insist, and anyway, they knew he wasn't finished. He spat into the dust and shifted on his McClellan saddle to get more comfortable.

"Now what we have that you don't have is lots of people. Have you noticed, when you're with the soldiers, how many of them speak English funny?"

Two Rivers and Young Buffalo thought all English sounded funny, so an Italian or German accent did not make much of a dent in their consciousness.

"Across the big water—not the big river but a much bigger water—" he swept his arm in a long horizontal arc— "the big *salt* water—there's lots of people who live hard lives and they want a better one so they leave their tribe and come to America."

"Ahh." Young Buffalo could understand. Crows sometimes left their village to go to live in another village for one reason or another, and he said so.

"But this is not one German or one Italian or one Irisher," Braddock continued. "Or one Crow. As many as the drops of water in that river," he said, pointing toward the Rosebud, which flowed along to their left. And they believed him because they had seen the wagons that flowed along the Bozeman Trail, and they had seen the railroad trains that puffed from horizon to horizon more quickly than they could smoke a pipeful of tobacco. Always different people, appearing on the sunrise horizon and vanishing on the sunset horizon and never coming back. They knew the trains west held many more folks than the trains that traveled east. They knew what to make of it all.

"These men who speak English funny, they join the army so they can have food to eat. They never learned how to fight when they were children, not like a warrior. They get into a fight like the other day and they die real easy because some lousy general . . ." Another idiom. The two Crows wondered why a general would be more likely to have lice than a private ". . . and then they die, but there's always many more to come out here and replace them."

"So what do you think will happen now?" Young Buffalo asked.

"I know what will happen," Braddock answered. "Sherman'll get mad, and then Grant—the Big Chief in Washington—he'll get mad and every soldier they got they'll send out here and sooner or later they'll burn every Teton village on the plains, in the mountains, wherever, until the few that's left go and live with Red Cloud or Spotted Tail. Then the soldiers'll probably go and burn down those agencies and the Sioux won't have anywhere to go.''

But that was in the future, not in the present. For now there was a party of about a dozen young Sioux warriors who were disgusted that Sitting Bull, Crazy Horse, and the other chiefs had decided to let the other soldiers live. Instead of finishing off Reno, Crook, Terry, Gibbon and all the other soldier chiefs who had chosen to attack the biggest Sioux assemblage ever with their puny little horse battalions, they had decided to pack up their villages and head south away from the troops.

A young would-be chief named Day Not Come was all afire from his first two kills, two privates from Miles Keough's battalion. When the battle had ended he had searched out his two kills and pushed away the women who were dismembering them because he had wanted the scalps for himself. Then he had returned to the metropolis along the Little Bighorn meaning to change ponies and join the warriors who were attacking Reno's battalions, only to find that the chiefs had ordered the women to start packing. He had ridden through his Oglalla tepee circle trying to round up enough young warriors to attack another battalion or two and wipe them out for the greater glory of Day Not Come.

But he did not suddenly go from a nobody to a chief just because he was walking around with somebody else's hair tucked in his breechclout. Most of the other young men laughed and flicked their fingers in derision at him, but about a dozen who either had missed some of the action or who wanted more agreed to go with him. Among them was a man in his twenties named, simply, Owl. Owl did not have a family left to worry about, so he was free to maraud as he wished. However, he did not have any desire to follow a wetbreeches like Day Not Come, so once they had left the village, he stopped them and announced in no uncertain terms that he would be leading the party.

Since Owl had a major reputation as a fighting man he received no objection from any of them. He explained quickly that because the soldiers were traveling in large groups it would be foolhardy to attack them. Why not, he suggested, go after the Crow or Ree scouts who would probably be heading for their villages in twos and threes after the fighting?

Now there was an idea! A Crow scalp on one's belt—that would be something to brag about in council. Why, the white men just rode into your valley with their scalps in their hands *begging* you to take their hair from them!

So off they had ridden toward the Rosebud, and there they had come upon Young Buffalo, Two Rivers, and Braddock, riding very slowly, their heads, and those of their ponies, drooping with discouragement.

"Ho, the mighty Crows!" Owl smirked, and the others laughed as they looked down at the three bedraggled campaigners, riding down the center of a wide valley. The Sioux might have followed them and waited until the valley narrowed, then found a position from which to set up an ambush, but they were cocky from the events of the past few days. Instead they simply rode down the hill into the valley and galloped after their prey, whooping their war cries as if they could terrify Crow warriors the same way they had terrified the white soldiers.

These faint battle challenges reached the ears of Young Buffalo first. He turned, saw the approaching train of dust, and alerted his comrades. He and Two Rivers immediately knew what they had to do, and Braddock had no choice but to go along. First they put their ponies into a tired-looking gallop to stoke the fires of overconfidence in their foes. The animals were tired, but not so tired that their spirit was quenched, so that when the whoops got loud enough, and the Sioux ponies close enough—less than a hundred yards—Young Buffalo turned and led a charge right into the center of the Sioux line.

The droop was gone now, replaced by a proud, loud Crow whoop. Young Buffalo blasted a warrior from his saddle immediately. Only half the young Sioux had rifles, and they were old rifles. Anyway, the boys had not enough ammunition to do a lot of firing from the back of a galloping war pony. Their shots went wide and then Two Rivers was going through them, with a lance thrust that pierced Day Not Come and put an immediate end to his ambitions. Down he went, belching blood.

The young Sioux were in shock. With a suddenness they could not have imagined, two of their lifelong friends had fallen before a foe they had thought toothless. They wanted to flee, but Owl rose to the occasion, rallying them. Young Buffalo and Two Rivers immediately sized up the situation and squeezed off rifle shots in his direction, but his medicine was strong and they missed. Braddock followed their lead, firing a well-aimed shot that clipped a feather from Owl's war bonnet but otherwise did no harm.

"Surround them," Owl shouted. "Shoot their ponies. Once they are on foot we can finish them off."

They obeyed, and now Young Buffalo knew he and his cohorts were in trouble. They dodged a shower of arrows and bullets, racing for the thinnest part of the circle and making it through, but now Owl had what he had wanted from the first—a long chase, his fresh ponies against their tired ones.

Young Buffalo had a trick up his sleeve. The ponies of the two slain Sioux were nearby. Young Buffalo and Two Rivers each caught one and switched mounts as they rode, holding on to their own ponies by the long leads. They picked up the pace and the two now-unmounted ponies were able to keep up with ease.

But Braddock still rode his jaded animal and he was having a tough time maintaining the pace of the others. The young Sioux took a few moments to get themselves collected and running in the right direction, about two hundred yards behind the Crows. Young Buffalo knew a narrow, shallow ford of the Rosebud, and he took it. This was Crow country. Their pursuers missed the ford and floundered in deeper water, giving their prey another hundred yards of distance. On the other side of the valley lay a treeless hill with good fields of fire all around and a long steep ledge that could not be climbed easily by horse or man. The three Crows rode around the ledge, dismounted, pulled and led their ponies to the top, and watched, waiting to see what the youngsters would do.

If Owl had not been around, the Sioux either would have given up and gone home, or made a foolish charge up the hill that would have cost them unnecessary casualties.

"What you'll do," Owl told them, "is stay out of range. I'll look around and see what kind of cover we can find on that hill. If we can get close enough we'll kill their horses and then they'll be ours."

When Owl moved out of a cottonwood thicket to the base of the hill, Young Buffalo and Two Rivers immediately knew what he was up to. They knew that their ponies, tethered in the open at the top of the hill, were unconcealable targets, and that they could not afford for the animals to be killed or wounded.

Among the three Crows the best marksman with the best rifle was Braddock, who was also the most cautious. But when Young Buffalo told him what he must do, Braddock agreed to do it. He leaped up from behind a bush, ran along the side of the hill, tripped, rolled, regained his feet and found cover behind a large flat rock. His journey had covered a hundred yards and put him within range of Owl, who sensed his exposure immediately and flattened himself in the grass at the base of the hill.

Young Buffalo had not become a chief simply because he was mighty in battle. He was able to size up men and guess their thoughts, and his guesses were often close to the mark. He knew that Owl would try to move around the hill, flank Braddock, and kill him. So he waited at the top until he saw which way Owl was moving, then he descended along the backslope and worked his way down and along the side of the hill until he found a place of concealment. He waited for about three minutes before Owl appeared, far off to his right, his eyes glued to the area where he would first catch a glimpse of Braddock as he made his way toward the white man's flank.

The range was not more than a hundred and fifty yards, about the maximum reliable for his rifle. He felt it was critical that he not miss and for a moment considered risking detection by moving closer. But once again, he thought he knew his man.

Young Buffalo fired and saw the bullet kick up dirt just behind Owl. He cranked the lever and fired again as Owl fled away from him and toward Braddock, as he knew Owl would. The last time the Lakota had looked at the top of the hill he still saw two men, and therefore he reacted as if somehow it was Braddock who had outflanked him.

A moment later Young Buffalo heard a shot from Braddock's Henry, heard a grunt when the bullet hit home, and saw Owl stumbling down the hill, clutching his shoulder. He had dropped his rifle, and the way he was hunched over, it was clear that Braddock's bullet had caught more than flesh. The Crow chief raised his rifle to take a shot, then lowered it. The Sioux warrior was struggling with his breathing, so severe was his pain, and Young Buffalo reasoned that while a dead Owl might inspire a quick revenge strike by the emotional young Sioux warriors, a wounded Owl meant someone the Sioux war party must care for, perhaps someone they needed to bring home.

So he let Owl go, and went back up the hill.

There was no further action throughout the afternoon. In fact they only saw one of their besiegers, an exhibitionistic youngster who walked to the foot of the hill, untied his breechclout and exposed his hind end to them. When that action inspired no reaction, he retied his breechclout and stood still, arms folded, legs apart, facing them, as if to say, "I dare you to put a bullet in my breast." He stood that way for ten minutes, during which time Young Buffalo surmised that some of his cohorts were hidden in a nearby thicket ready to attack if the Crows came down for a closer shot at the tempting target.

"Might be time for you to get some sleep," Young Buffalo said to Braddock, but he was too late. Braddock was lying on his back with his slouch hat over his face, his chest rising and falling slowly and evenly.

Chapter 30

Young Buffalo considered that their pursuers might attack them in the night. To that end he let Braddock sleep for three hours. Just before dark he awakened the white man and Young Buffalo slept for about two hours, then awoke and suggested that Two Rivers and Braddock both sleep for the rest of the night while he stood guard alone.

Keen as his eyes were, his ears were even keener. There was no way the young Sioux warriors would come anywhere near them without being heard. The stars were out, but the slender crescent moon did not provide great long-distance vision. So he did not bother to watch. He listened, and heard nothing. He stood his watch patiently, unmoving, until about two hours before dawn, when he thought he heard something.

He shifted his position, then lay motionless, not breathing, waiting. There it was again, this time from another direction. He awakened the other two and all three lay motionless, unbreathing, rifles at the ready.

The next sound was that of a plucked bowstring, followed by a half-dozen more of the same. They heard the arrows hit the rocky dirt in front of them, the closest landing more than fifty feet away. They were atop the sharp-sloping bluff, which was a good seventy feet from the top of the hill, where the ponies were tied. Quietly as they could they scrambled up and waited for the next volley of arrows.

When they came hissing through the air, still well short, Young Buffalo did something he hated to do: he stuck his knife about a half inch into the rear end of one of the ponies. The animal let out a pained whinny and continued to scream and plunge for a minute or so, before it quieted down.

Braddock was impressed. His chief had quickly realized that the Sioux were walking the arrows up the hill, hoping that they might somehow wound something and thereby find out the range. At the very least they could harass their enemy without much risk to themselves.

Young Buffalo's assumption again was correct. The Sioux fired seven more volleys. Twice more Young Buffalo stabbed the flank of the unfortunate weakest animal. Twice more it hollered its displeasure and thrashed around noisily.

And then the arrows stopped coming.

They waited, quietly, listening for a clue to the next act. But all they heard was silence and the wind whistling through the cottonwood thickets. They heard the hoot of an owl, a real owl. They heard a coyote that sounded real, then a coyote chorus that convinced them.

Braddock went back to sleep. He knew the other two would not sleep and his constitution had not stood up to the rigors of the last campaign as well as that of Young Buffalo or Two Rivers. Sleep took him quickly. He was so tired he did not care whether or not the Sioux came again that night.

He awakened suffocating in the blue-white dawn. He struggled to breathe, but his nose would not open up. He opened his mouth to scream, then opened his eyes and saw that Young Buffalo was holding his—Braddock's—nose and laughing. The Sioux must be gone.

They were, and they had given Young Buffalo two ponies and the lives of two warriors, maybe three, if Owl did not recover.

The three Crow warriors were dead tired. After the stress of a battle campaign under the leadership of feckless U.S. Army officers, it had almost been too much for them to have to withstand yet another siege, this time from a gaggle of advanced boy warriors.

They watered the ponies in the Rosebud below, then rode

eastward at a brisk pace. They never stopped looking around, expecting at any time to see the feathers of the Teton warriors again streaming in the breeze as they lurched for the collective throat of their Absarokee enemy. They were two more days getting home, and then home wasn't there. They followed the path of the village's ponies down the creek for yet another day, finally arriving at camp just before sunset.

When the people in the village learned of the great disaster that had befallen Custer on the Greasy Grass, a great cry of mourning went up within the village. Braddock was sad about the unnecessary loss of so many soldiers who hadn't the slightest idea of what Custer was getting them into, but he could not grieve for Custer.

Ambitious officers got themselves and their men killed with their bumbling efforts at brilliant tactics. Why was the death of these 200 soldiers more tragic than the death of thousands and thousands at Shiloh? he wondered. Was it worse because their killers wore feathers?

But he understood that his Crow cohorts were also mourning for their allies, fearful that the Lakota were rising up again, and when the Lakota rose up, that was always bad for the Crows. Not being one to stand idly by while powerful enemies rolled over him, Young Buffalo sent out messengers to neighboring villages and kept wolves busy scouting the area. But they saw no sign whatever of their Teton nemesis. This was surprising, because for many years they had been used to finding signs of the Sioux prowling on Crow lands, taking their game without permission, stealing their ponies, occasionally killing their people, and once in a while even waging serious war. Now, suddenly, after their greatest victory over the *Wasichus*, they seemed to have vanished from the northern plains.

Young Buffalo had an answer. "I think the Sioux are afraid," he said. "It is not a good idea to win too big a victory over the white soldiers. That just gets them mad. It is as you say, Long Kill. There are many Lakota, but there are many more white men."

Braddock smiled at Young Buffalo's use of his new

Crow name. Although he had never shown remarkable scouting skills, his shooting abilities had amazed both Young Buffalo and Two Rivers. Young Buffalo had started calling the Tennessean Long Kill, and Two Rivers followed suit because he liked the sound of the name. Braddock liked it too. It made him feel recognized, even though there had been no elaborate naming ceremony.

It wasn't long before army messengers were back knocking at the doors of the Absarokee, so to speak.

It'll be different this time, they said. We will have soldiers coming from all over, thousands of them, and the Sioux will have no rest. When we get through with them they will beg for the reservation, where at least there will be food for their children.

Young Buffalo was skeptical about a quick victory, but he did not doubt the final outcome. He was still young enough for another big fight, and announced that he would lead his wolves to Fort Lincoln himself. After the council was over he walked to the lodge of Long Kill Braddock to talk to him about the coming campaign. For all his years with the Crows, Braddock was still a white man, and if he was not a thoroughly reliable warrior, he knew how white men thought. Young Buffalo wanted Braddock with him on the long campaign with the unpredictable horse soldiers.

Young Buffalo sat by the fire and lit his pipe. "You will go with us?" he asked.

"I've had enough of following army officers," Braddock answered. "I want to go to the rising sun and live with my people again."

Young Buffalo was surprised. Who could understand the ways of a white man? To suddenly stop being an Absarokee and leave the finest, best land in all the world, to go where?

"You will take your wife and your children to the white man country?"

"I would not make my wife leave her people," Braddock said. "I have heard that when a woman is taken from her people she sickens and dies. But I would miss her and I hope she will go with me."

Wild Berry's eyes were shining as she heard her husband's words, but she said nothing as she stirred her kettle.

The savory mix of antelope meat, vegetables, and herbs normally stirred Braddock's appetite but on this night he was thinking about sweet potato pie and cornbread, white man cornbread. He was thinking that he had left Tennessee in despair, his roots and his confidence ripped from him by the events of the great war between the North and the South. His years among the Absarokee had restored in him a sense of himself. He wanted to return to the rolling farmlands west of the Tennessee River. The Crows derided farming as woman's work but Braddock had grown up with the soil, and he wanted to go back.

A week later Braddock and Young Buffalo stood outside the village, shaking hands, dealing with the likelihood that they might never again look upon each other's face. Young Buffalo looked at the three children mounted on their ponies, and at Wild Berry, strong and smiling on her own spirited mare. She who had once known the bed of Young Buffalo's childhood friend, Big Chin, would spend the rest of her life in a white man house made of wood or bricks, with glass windows and a bed that sits high off the wooden floors.

"My brother," said Braddock, anxious to be away lest his carefully concealed emotions began to stir. "You must keep well, and see to it that America keeps its treaty with the Absarokee. Your land is truly the most beautiful land in America."

Braddock had cut his braids, and removed his earrings. Instead of a breechcloth and leggings he wore soldier trousers and a plain, unbeaded buckskin shirt. For the first time since the day he had arrived at Young Buffalo's village he wore boots, not moccasins. An old army campaign hat he had retrieved from the Reno battlefield now crowned his head. In his pocket was thirty-two dollars he had saved from scout pay and from a raid on a Sioux village. His nine ponies were all in fine shape. He had a good rifle, a Colt .36 revolver, and a well-honed knife. From an Indian point of view, he was ready for the world.

But he was not an Indian. It was time for him to go.

He sat atop his best war pony and watched as Young

Buffalo and six of his wolves rode across the Rosebud and vanished into a grove of cottonwoods. Cottonwoods, cotton: the two could not be further apart in his life. Cotton was the stuff once picked by slaves. Cottonwoods were the tough old trees that grew along the river banks on the plains where the horse tribes rode free as the wind.

He was certain that he could find a way to make a life out of the soil with what little he had. He had spoken with Wild Berry and found to his surprise that once he had explained that across the big river families did not have to fear midnight attacks from the dreaded Lakota, she was willing to leave her heritage behind. She was a wife and a mother first and an Absarokee second, she had said.

But he needed money. He had heard that to the east, in the Black Hills, gold was plentiful and horses were scarce. If he could sell some of his ponies, he might have enough money to buy some land when he got home, maybe even buy back some of the old home place.

He could understand now why the Sioux had fought so hard for their beloved Black Hills. Even with the gritty mining camps and the acres of cleared forest he could see that there were deer to be hunted, beaver to be trapped, fish to be netted in clear fresh water, and most of all, cool shady forests to comfort a man on a hot summer day—compared to the miles and miles of treeless plains where a summer sun could bake a man's brain.

He found that as he rode he was talking to himself, speaking English, trying to erase the Indian from him. How strange, after years of being as Indian as possible, especially around soldiers he was afraid might spot a deserter, that now he must be as white as possible. Miners and other whites gave the Indians no rights, and the law seemed to back them up. To protect his wife and children they always camped far away from the towns and mining camps. When he had to leave Wild Berry and the children to do business in a camp, he hid them in a hollow that could not be detected from any road or trail. He was careful with his horse-selling, riding one pony and leading another, planning to sell only one at a time, and not selling unless he got his price.

And so far he had only sold one, this morning in a mining camp. The price was two hundred dollars, not in gold dust that might be diluted with sand, but in cash. He was very pleased by his business deal, and almost careless as his pony picked its way down a scanty forest trail, into a dry stream bed, slowly approaching the cave where he had left his family.

There was a stream that ran by the cave, tumbling over rocks in tones that suggested a splashy melody. For a moment he thought he could even hear the soft soprano voice of Wild Berry in the falling stream. The pony climbed over a rock shelf and rounded a bend in the stream and suddenly it became clear to him that he was hearing his wife's voice, not in melody but in terror, a wild scream meant to warn, meant to protect, meant to make an attacker think again before he continued his attack.

He quirted his pony and galloped along the bank of the stream, then up a steep slope that led to a clearing, and the scream grew in volume.

"Hold out! Fight just a little longer!" he muttered to himself, pulling his Colt and cocking it. He saw them then, a bearded, bear-like creature with dark hair swirling around his head like a squirrel's nest, with a red longjohn shirt spouting from a pair of ragged, faded blue overalls.

Her teeth were sunk in his wrist, which held a big bowie knife, and both of her hands were clamped around his arm, leaving his other hand free to beat her with hammerlike blows to her head. She was moving her head as much as she could, given it was attached to his strong right arm, but she could not dodge all the blows, and even as he approached he could see that her strength would not last much longer.

He was afraid to shoot, for fear of hitting Wild Berry, so he simply rode his pony into the melee, sending Wild Berry and her attacker tumbling in separate directions. The impact jarred the revolver from Braddock's hand but he pulled his knife even as he leaped from his horse.

The bear-man was stunned and slow to get up, blood flowing from his right wrist, but the right hand still held a big butcher knife. He staggered to his feet and attempted to charge Braddock, but Braddock was not going to give him a chance. Quick as a wildcat he ducked beneath the man's flailing arm, plunged his knife deep into the man's abdomen, and ripped it open with a downward tug on the handle.

The man stared for one amazed moment at his entrails as they slithered to the ground, then fell to his knees, his mouth open, and pitched forward, dead before his head hit the ground.

Braddock did not think then. Quickly and naturally as if he had been born to it, he placed his knee behind the man's neck and wrapped the man's hair around his fingers. He sliced into the skin above the man's forehead and made an incision as far around the man's head as the knife would easily go, then inserted his fingers into the incision and with a mighty effort jerked the man's hair off his head. Far from being revulsed, Wild Berry gave a triumphant whoop. Braddock, who had fought so well for his Crow brothers, had never counted coup in battle. Today was his first.

Wild Berry was bruised and sore but otherwise unhurt. The three children were too young to have helped her in the fight, but they had seen it all. Wild Berry felt the need to calm them down and reassure them that the big man was dead, and would remain that way. Meanwhile Braddock rifled the dead man's pockets and came up with a few coins, a few pieces of paper, a comb, of all things, and a pocket knife. He looked quickly at the paper, which turned out to be mining claims and maps. He had no desire to start a mining career, so he threw the papers into the little fire Wild Berry had built at the mouth of the cave.

The cave itself was a deep one, with a drop-off inside. It would not do to leave the body around to be found, so the two of them began to drag the dead miner toward the cave mouth. On the way it occurred to Braddock that a surly, hostile, violent man like this was probably suspicious—probably hid his money somewhere, like in his boots. So he pulled off the boots, reached his hand inside one, then the other, and each time came up with a twenty-dollar gold piece stuffed under the inner sole. This man was proving to be a valuable kill.

He tossed the scalp to Wild Berry, a token of his esteem,

and dragged the body the rest of the way into the cave. Fifty feet in he found the drop-off and shoved the dead man off it. A couple of seconds later he heard a loud splash.

While he was in the cave Wild Berry heard an irritated bray and walked upstream about two hundred yards, where she found a mule so large that it had to belong to the dead man. She spoke a few soft words to the animal, untied the rope from the tree that held it captive, and led it downstream to the camp.

It was a strong mule but dreadfully overworked and badly cared for—this Braddock could see immediately as he emerged from the cave. Quietly he petted and soothed it and noted that beside a saddle it carried three large leather bags. Braddock lifted the bags—heavy, at least ten pounds apiece. He didn't have to look inside to know what the bags contained. Either this man had been a successful prospector or a successful thief. But then, why had he been prowling around their camp? Wild Berry supplied the answer. From the interior of the cave she had heard a commotion outside and seen the miner trying to steal one of the ponies. Ah! So good ponies were so scarce that even a successful miner might steal a horse, because to buy one cost too much. He had had his hands on Braddock's biggest pony when Wild Berry came out and tried to shoo him away. The miner had grabbed hold of Wild Berry's face, Wild Berry had opened her mouth and chomped down on the man's wrist with all her strength, and that was how Braddock had found them.

Chapter 31

They crossed the Mississippi on a ferry that left them at the mud flats of Memphis. They had four poor-looking ponies, a mule, three strong young children, and enough gold and money to make them rich in a West Tennessee county still poverty-stricken from a war more than ten years gone. Their clothes were ragged and worn, not so unusual in the Absarokee villages, but very odd on the streets of Memphis. People stared at them as they made their way from the mud flats to the dirt streets. The children simply stared back through their large brown eyes.

In Memphis Braddock found a way to convert his gold dust into coin and they made their cautious way east, then north until they crossed the South Fork for the last time and set up a tepee on the old homestead. There were two hours of daylight left when he started his walk around the three hundred acres that had constituted the family farm before the bank had taken it.

The house foundation was still there, and that was about all there was—that and a few chicken coops. He had expected to find the farm in the hands of old friends who would give him space on which to camp until he could buy a place. He had not expected to find such fine bottomland deserted.

But deserted it was. The fields had already started reverting back to woodland, with the beginnings of scrubby

cedars and piss-elms all over. The hundreds of yards of slave
walls that surrounded the south field were in drastic disre-
pair. But the well near the house had plenty of water in it
and the old stone springhouse had somehow managed to
hold together—give or take a few sheets of slate on the roof.

He took a walk down the old road that ran by the house.
Tall grass grew down the middle. There was just enough of
a wagon trail to indicate that one or two families down the
road still survived. As he walked, his spirits sank. One of
the neighboring houses had fallen in on itself and another
had been partially burned and completely destroyed. At last
he came to a house that looked occupied. The fields around
it were overgrown except for one, which looked as if it were
being worked. But when he walked up the path to the door
he was greeted by a black man he had never seen before.
The man rose from a ladder-backed chair on the porch and
received him a good thirty yards from the house. Tall, dark,
angular, and bald, the man eyed Braddock suspiciously.

So this was a free black. This was going to take some
getting used to, Braddock thought. He wondered how things
had gone here since the end of the war. Had most of the
blacks hung around or had they all headed north? Where
had this one come from? Did the whites around here try to
treat the free blacks like slaves, and how did the blacks
accept their treatment? Even as a soldier he hadn't heard
much news about Tennessee, and once he had gone to the
Crows he had never heard any.

"Who are you?" asked the black man in soft but unfriendly tones.

"Name's Braddock. My family owned the farm mile
back on the right."

"Nobody with that name live around here," the black
man said dubiously.

"There is now," Braddock replied with an edge to his
voice.

The man sensed the hostility and drew back. "What can
I do for you?" he asked, like a man who did not wish to
be polite but had decided he'd better for his own good.

Braddock was silent for a moment. Silent and angry because the man was a stranger. An unfriendly stranger. An

unfriendly black stranger. "Anybody you know of own that land?" he asked.

"Don't know of nobody," said the black man.

"What about the bank?"

"What bank?" asked the black man. "Don't know of no bank. Nobody 'round here I know of got money. What for need a bank?"

"Yeah," Braddock replied. "What for need a bank? Is there a store in town? A sawmill?"

"Uh-huh." The man had decided that Braddock had asked enough questions. He turned suddenly and walked back to the porch, where he had been whetting the blade of an ax.

Braddock turned and headed back to the farm. Winter was coming on. He needed to get a start on rebuilding the house. His skills did not run much toward homebuilding. He'd have to hire a man who knew about building a house if he was going to get it done. He didn't fear winter. He'd been living under buffalo hides for six years and he knew there would be plenty of wood along the creek for the fire. He had bought a little coffee, tobacco, bacon, and a sack of cornmeal at a trading store east of Memphis. He had been amazed at how much a little five-dollar gold piece bought. There had been a shortage of change, so he had picked up an old saw and other assorted tools, almost as a favor, before he and Wild Berry had ridden the final leg of their journey.

That night, after they'd seen to it that the boys were sleeping, he sat by the fire smoking, watching Wild Berry trying to create a pair of breeches for one of the boys. She had never sewn breeches before and he was tickled by the grotesque shape they were taking. But soon his mind wandered far away from the tepee, across the big river, up the South Platte, then north to the Little Bighorn and the Rosebud. He found himself in a wake-dream about Young Buffalo.

Braddock knew he would never see his like again, and the thought saddened him. Young Buffalo was the man most boys he had grown up with would have liked to become—brave, heroic and honest—but none of the boys came close to reaching these chivalric ideals.

He looked across the fire at Wild Berry. Wild Berry caught his glance and told him what was on her mind.

"You better stay well," she said, without smiling. "This place strange place for Crow lady to be and I don't know how to get back home from here."

Young Buffalo knew it was all over. In the months following the battle, every Teton village of any size had Crow wolves stuck on their trails, and behind the wolves were armies led by officers sworn to do the job they were given. The glory hunters were gone now, and the methodical Indian fighters remained.

One by one the Sioux bands were flushed from their camps, stampeded into the hills, leaving their lodges, their pony herds, their winter meat supplies—and their glorious past. One by one, surrounded, starving, wanting to fight to their deaths but not to the deaths of their families, they surrendered and moved onto the despised reservation. The day Crazy Horse brought his people in, he led them in what looked more like a victory procession than a caravan of surrender and defeat. But Crazy Horse's days were numbered, and the days of the free-roaming Teton people were gone, though they did not know it.

The young braves especially did not know it. Some of them slipped out once in a while, and a few of them refused to come in at all. Some had no families they needed to protect, and others had young wives who could keep up with them as they continued loose, living off the remnants of the northern buffalo herds. One of these young men was called Falling Hawk, who had promised his mother that he would come to Spotted Tail's reservation in the fall. He was determined to have one more summer of freedom on the plains.

He also made a promise to his gnarled, crippled, arthritic old father: that when he returned in the season of the falling leaves, he would have in his pouch the scalp of at least one Crow warrior. It was the Crows, they all agreed, who had betrayed them to the *Wasichus*. Without the eyes of the Crow to guide them, there was no way the white men would ever have been able to find the Sioux villages.

And so Falling Hawk and three young companions were roaming the valleys of the Little Bighorn and the Rosebud, looking for a village, looking for a lone Crow rider, looking for a kill.

They found Young Buffalo and Two Rivers on their way home from the last successful campaign against the Sioux. The fighting was over for the two great warriors, and they had no doubt that they had done the right thing. For the first time in the memory of their people there would be no ambitious Lakota man-killers preying on them, stealing their horses in the middle of the night and killing their people.

Neither would there be any Sioux villages out there for Crows to attack. The young men of the long-beaked bird would have to be content hunting deer on the reservation, because they were all alone now. Young Buffalo asked himself how he felt about that, and a part of him had to admit that life had felt fuller when there was an enemy to hate.

Young Buffalo was normally careful when riding through a narrow valley, but he had not considered the possibility that with the surrender of all the main Teton chiefs, there would be any Sioux warriors left roaming the lands of the Crows.

And then came the volley from a nearby riverbank that killed Two Rivers' pony and broke the old warrior's shoulder.

Two Rivers was a man of many wounds and many scars, but Young Buffalo had never seen him this badly hurt. The old warrior reached up with his left hand and Young Buffalo pulled him up behind him on his pony. The four young Sioux were whooping in triumph, knowing their swift ponies would quickly overtake the double-riding Crows. Young Buffalo could feel Two Rivers grip his shoulder with his good left hand, but then the veteran slipped off the pony, rolling in the dust, regaining his feet with a .38 Colt in his left hand.

The four Sioux swooped in for the kill. To the Sioux, a dismounted warrior was a dead warrior, and now they came riding hard, competing for the opportunity to count first coup. His blood-covered body must have seemed easy pickings to them, because they rode hard and straight at him.

He raised his pistol and fired three quick shots. Two Sioux tumbled from their ponies, bounced in the dust, and lay still. The third warrior counted coup with his quirt on Two Rivers' broken shoulder. The fourth warrior came on hard, reined up suddenly, cocked his rifle, and sent a bullet through the old warrior's neck. Two Rivers fell in the short buffalo grass and lay still. Coldly the shooter reached down with his gun barrel and took a second coup on Two Rivers.

Now it was Young Buffalo against the two Sioux who had just celebrated a victory over the last of the great old-time Crow warriors. Screaming his tremolo war cry, Young Buffalo urged his pony into a steady gallop at the warriors, who sat in their saddles two hundred yards away. They met the challenge by kicking their ponies forward in a dead run, and the gap between them closed quickly. At eighty yards Young Buffalo fired a bullet into the chest of the closest Sioux pony. The pony stumbled and then fell, pitching its rider head over heels toward Young Buffalo. The remaining rider fired at Young Buffalo and missed. Young Buffalo chambered a new round, cocked the hammer and at fifty yards pulled the trigger. The rifle did not fire, so he simply rammed his big pony into the Sioux pony. The impact stunned the Sioux, making it easy for Young Buffalo to knock him to the ground with a sharp butt stroke of his rifle.

Now he had two warriors on the ground, shaking off the impact and reaching for weapons. Young Buffalo dropped his rifle, reached for his bow, notched an arrow and sent a shaft into the center of the nearest Sioux, who stood no more than ten yards away. The other one fired at Young Buffalo and missed, but hit his pony. The animal bucked and Young Buffalo left the saddle, landing on his feet ten feet away from the shooter. Young Buffalo lost the bow, but he had a second arrow in his hand. He took two steps toward the Sioux, who fired too quickly and missed again. Young Buffalo had but one more chance before the enemy could cock his revolver. He took two running steps at the warrior and with his right hand sank the shaft between his ribs. The Sioux staggered but did not fall. Young Buffalo pulled two more arrows from his quiver. The Sioux was trying to take aim with his pistol but his wound was causing his right arm to wave wildly. Young Buffalo ducked under the gun hand and tried to push a shaft into the Sioux's abdomen but he struck too high. The arrow hit a rib and its shaft broke. He took a strong grip on the other arrow, ducked under a wild swing by the warrior and sank the arrow deep into the warrior's belly. The man screamed from the sudden pain and tried to cock his rifle, but he had no strength. Holding his belly with both hands, he sank to his knees, then fell forward, pushing the arrow in up to its feathers.

Young Buffalo had no time to enjoy his double victory. Quickly he rode to where he had left his friend and was surprised to find the old man sitting up. The bullet through his neck had somehow missed everything vital. The bleeding in his shoulder had slowed to a trickle.

"Come on," Young Buffalo said, and pulled the old warrior up behind him. "You must live to see our freedom," he added. They had a two-mile ride to the village. At first Two Rivers wrapped his arms around Young Buffalo and hung on strongly, but as the time passed Young Buffalo could feel his friend's grip begin to loosen. The chief could not bear to lose the old warrior. He took a rope and wound it around Two Rivers and himself, and brought Two Rivers home. By the time they arrived at the village Two Rivers was barely conscious, slipping way. Young Buffalo brought his friend to the tepee of Dark Eagle, the new village medicine healer. When Two Rivers had been made comfortable inside the lodge, Young Buffalo rode off to the pony herd and returned with two sturdy buffalo ponies as a token that Dark Eagle must do all in his power to save Two Rivers.

Dark Eagle had only recently risen to his post after the death of his mentor Comes From Nothing. Young Buffalo had little faith in the abilities of the new healer, but when Dark Eagle told Young Buffalo to return to his family, that he would send for the chief when the time was right, Young Buffalo did as he was told.

White Hot Smoke received the news of the battle calmly. Her husband had simply stated the facts, and made no big deal of his part in the fight. His concern for Two Rivers was deep, yet she sensed that his mind was somewhere else.

"What is it?" she asked.

"It is over," he replied, and because she was wise, she understood what he meant by that short phrase. It meant that everything of the old was over. It meant that the life-and-death struggle with the Sioux was over. It meant that the years of following the buffalo herds were over. It meant that the struggle for the land was over. Young Buffalo had told her before of the treaties which would leave them with many of their old hunting grounds, but with less to hunt.

She spooned out stew for him. He offered up the food to the Creator, then he ate without appetite. Before he had finished, a boy was at the door flap, telling him that Dark Eagle wished for him to attend him at his lodge. He walked hurriedly to the tepee of the healer. Outside were more than a dozen people, standing patiently, waiting for news of Two Rivers' state of health. They let Young Buffalo through, and when he ducked into the warm, smoky lodge, he saw Two Rivers stretched out, unconscious, breathing softly.

The young healer had done no public ceremonial chanting, done few of the things Crows had come to expect healers to do when they were calling upon the aid of Great Spirit to help save a life. But he spoke with confidence.

"He will live," he said. "But he is no longer a young man. He will not be as he was. His force has been spent in battle."

"So it is for the children of the long-beaked bird," Young Buffalo replied, looking down at the old warrior with a sadness that tore at his heart. "We are an old people. Our force has been spent in many battles with those who would wipe us from the face of the earth. But we have survived and we are free. It is up to us to preserve what we have so our children will have their land to make them strong again, some day."

TERRY C. JOHNSTON

THE PLAINSMEN

THE BOLD WESTERN SERIES FROM
ST. MARTIN'S PAPERBACKS

COLLECT THE ENTIRE SERIES!

SIOUX DAWN
92732-0 _____$5.99 U.S. _____$7.99 CAN.

RED CLOUD'S REVENGE
92733-9 _____$5.99 U.S. _____$6.99 CAN.

THE STALKERS
92963-3 _____$5.99 U.S. _____$7.99 CAN.

BLACK SUN
92465-8 _____$5.99 U.S. _____$6.99 CAN.

DEVIL'S BACKBONE
92574-3 _____$5.99 U.S. _____$6.99 CAN.

SHADOW RIDERS
92597-2 _____$5.99 U.S. _____$6.99 CAN.

DYING THUNDER
92834-3 _____$5.99 U.S. _____$6.99 CAN.

BLOOD SONG
92921-8 _____$5.99 U.S. _____$7.99 CAN.

ASHES OF HEAVEN
96511-7 _____$6.50 U.S. _____$8.50 CAN.

CAMERON JUDD
THE NEW VOICE OF THE OLD WEST

*"Judd is a keen observer of the human heart
as well as a fine action writer."*
—*Publishers Weekly*

THE GLORY RIVER
Raised by a French-born Indian trader among the
Cherokees and Creeks, Bushrod Underhill left the dark
mountains of the American Southeast for the promise of
the open frontier. But across the mighty Mississippi, a
storm of violence awaited young Bushrod—and it would
put his survival skills to the ultimate test...
0-312-96499-4___$5.99 U.S.___$7.99 Can.

SNOW SKY
Tudor Cochran has come to Snow Sky to find some
answers about the suspicious young mining town. And
what he finds is a gathering of enemies, strangers and
conspirators who have all come together around one
man's violent past—and deadly future.
0-312-96647-4___$5.99 U.S.___$7.99 Can.

CORRIGAN
He was young and green when he rode out from his family's Wyoming ranch, a boy sent to bring his wayward
brother home to a dying father. Now, Tucker Corrigan was
entering a range war. A beleaguered family, a powerful
landowner, and Tucker's brother, Jack—a man seven years
on the run—were all at the center of a deadly storm.
0-312-96615-6___$4.99 U.S.___$6.50 Can.